By The Same Author
Grand Openings Can Be Murder[1]
70% Dark Intentions[2]
Out of Temper[3]
A Shot in the 80 Percent Dark[4]
A Study in Chocolate[5]
Something Borrowed, Something 90% Dark[6]
A Chocolate is Announced[7]
Free Chocolate[8]
Pure Chocolate[9]
Fake Chocolate[10]
Story Like a Journalist[11]
There Are Herbs in My Chocolate[12]

---

1. *https://amzn.to/3PLlcZd*
2. *https://amzn.to/3BWjvSN*
3. *https://amzn.to/3jdm9gv*
4. *https://amzn.to/3PLYBvs*
5. *https://amzn.to/3NyQi5r*
6. *https://amzn.to/3UKrrQS*
7. https://amzn.to/4jJUEWE
8. *https://amzn.to/3VnxCaG*
9. *https://amzn.to/3hPCvM3*
10. *https://amzn.to/3PPgJV7*
11. *https://amzn.to/3BVLBOg*
12. *https://amzn.to/3FPxpHN*

AMBER ROYER

VANISHING INTO THE 100% DARK

GOLDEN TIP PRESS

GOLDEN TIP PRESS

A Golden Tip Press paperback original 2025

Copyright © Amber Royer 2025

Cover by Jon Bravo

Distributed in the United States by Ingram, Tennessee

All rights reserved. Amber Royer asserts the moral right to be identified as the author of this work.

This novel is entirely a work of fiction. Names, characters, places, and incidents are the products of the author's imagination or are used fictitiously. Any resemblance to actual events, locales, organizations, or persons, living or dead, is entirely coincidental.

Sale of this book without a front cover may be unauthorized. If this book is coverless, it may have been reported as "unsold and destroyed" and neither the author nor the publisher may have received payment for it.

ISBN 978-1-952854-25-5

Ebook ISBN 978-1-952854-26-2

Printed in the United States of America

To Jake, who is at my side for all my travels.

Chapter One
Monday

If someone told me five years ago that I would be a chocolate maker on the way to give a class at a world-class festival in Japan, I would have said it's impossible. Of course, I would have said the same thing about all the murders.

But here we are. After losing my husband a couple years ago, I'd moved from Seattle back home to Galveston to reconnect with family. I'd completely changed careers. And at the grand opening of my chocolate shop, I'd stumbled awkwardly into the role of amateur sleuth. Now, I've just arrived in Tokyo, hoping to get a little distance from all that, and spend time with my friends and my new fiancé, half way around the world. Nobody knows me here. I don't come with any associated baggage. And the food here is supposed to be divine. Priorities, am I right?

Stepping out of the gangway from the airplane, it doesn't yet feel like I'm in a foreign country. Just like at any other airport, there are smiling people in uniforms, whose eyes are telling me in no uncertain terms that I need to keep moving, clear the gangway, make way for the next set of passengers. Most of the staff here look tired. I'm tired too, after such a long flight.

But even more than that, I'm excited. I've traveled solo before, meeting farmers and testing beans for the chocolate I make, with multiple trips to South America. But this trip is different. I'm here with a whole group of friends. They're going down the hallway ahead of me, laughing and joking with each other. Some of these folks wouldn't even know each other, if not for me introducing them, and now they feel comfortable enough to fly thirteen hours together just to support me at a chocolate festival. Well, that, and I suppose they all wanted an excuse to travel to Japan.

Still. It makes cheesy levels of emotion well up in my chest. Before I moved home to Galveston, I didn't have many friends left. Between my own personal withdrawal after the death of my husband, and the awkwardness of our couple friends not knowing what to say to someone newly single, I'd realized I hadn't worked hard to make deep friendships, or be a good friend.

From behind me, my fiancé Logan says, "I love travel, but it's a lot more fun when you're flying the plane." He stretches his tall, well-built frame.

Now that he's not confined by the narrow aisle between seats, Logan steps up next to me and takes my hand. He gives it a light squeeze. I look up at him, and a little fission of happiness goes through me. Logan. My fiancé. Not everybody gets a second chance at love. Especially not with a tall, green-eyed, chisel-jawed ex-bodyguard.

Without stopping, I lean in towards him and say, "Ask the cabin crew on the way home. Maybe they'll give you a turn."

Logan laughs, a deep sound that bounces up that frisson. Logan is a puddle jump pilot now. I'm sure he could have gotten a job for a commercial airline, but he values his independence and loves small planes. "Can't you just picture it."

I can, actually. Logan used to be in law enforcement, and he still has some connections in high places – which has come in handy more than once when we've gotten involved in solving mysteries. If he wanted to fly us home, he could probably call in a favor. He looks the part, in his pilot's jacket and jeans.

"Careful you two," Ash Diaz says, looking back over his shoulder at our linked hands. "Japan isn't big on PDA."

I notice that Ash and his own fiancé are walking very close to each other, but his hands are occupied carrying both of their bags. Ash and I haven't always been friends. I used to find his lightly stubbled face, with his square hipster glasses and his skinny ties vaguely annoying. But given the fact that he's helped save my life – twice – I can overlook the rocky start between us.

Logan's sister Dawn, who is walking just ahead of Ash, turns enough to say, "Don't worry, Diaz. They're always discreet, don't ya know."

By which she means that even though Logan and I are engaged, we're still taking things slow.

Dawn's husband is busy looking at a map he has pulled up on his phone, debating with Dawn which way it is to the baggage check. All I can see is the back of his head, with his short spiky dreadlocks, above his hunter green hoodie. Dawn is wearing a cream-colored sweater knit in a complex textured design that emphasizes the green in her eyes.

Arlo – my ex, who I had almost rekindled a romance with – is here with his girlfriend Patsy. They look more focused on each other than on figuring out the way out of here, especially once we start hitting moving sidewalks, which we are pausing on because Chloe, the teenaged social media influencer I'd agreed to chaperone on this trip, keeps stopping at the front of our little line, trying to compose the perfect video clip. Out of all of us, Chloe is the most likely to get into trouble here. Not only is she young, but she's stubborn and I am already second-guessing my decision to bring her to a foreign country.

"Okay, Chloe," I say. "Let's try to be a bit more discreet about taking pics."

Chloe pouts. She has her bleach-blonde hair up in a messy bun, and she's wearing pink sneakers, pink and black leggings and a white Hello Kitty sweatshirt, with an outline of the character, and pink writing. She says, "I'm surprised you're not taking pics, Mrs. K. You need them for your Instagram."

I say, "I will, once we're not blocking traffic."

She says, "You never know when a little video could come in handy. I've even seen documentaries where they've solved crimes."

Logan says, "You are not bringing that kind of talk into our workation. The only thing I want to investigate is whether wagyu beef is worth the hype."

Still, Chloe snaps a couple of photos of the airport.

Eventually, the slidewalks end. We make it through customs, and after carefully tucking my passport away, I pull out my phone to let the couple who got us the invite to the chocolate festival know we have arrived. The minute I turn my phone on, my carrier charges me $12 just for being in a foreign country. Right. I'm supposed to set up a new temporary SIM card to avoid that. But whatever. I'm nervous about getting a big group of people lost somewhere where I don't know the language. So if it costs $12 to contact our de facto guides, so be it.

I'm still texting back and forth with them when Logan turns away. He's moved to the baggage carousel. And he's already pulled one of our bags – the big one with extra stuff for our event table.

"Excuse me," a deep English-accented voice says. I look up and there's a tall blonde guy standing unreasonably close to me. He's mid-twenties, built like an athlete, and wearing a tee and jeans. We make eye contact, and he grins, showing a full mouth of sparkling white teeth. I'm a little bit fluttery from how attractive he is. He asks, "Do you know which exit will take me to the train?"

I don't have a clue. I glance around for signage that might help, and I start to say, "I'm sorr-" but before I can finish the words, the guy snatches my phone, and grabs at my backpack, which is mostly full of chocolate bars. The backpack rips and chocolate goes everywhere but before I can react, the guy is sprinting away with my phone.

"Hey!" I shout, but of course he doesn't look back. I grip onto my purse, like he's going to come back and take that too. Which is ridiculous, but I'm not thinking clearly.

Logan spots the commotion and almost instantly figures out what is happening. He sprints past me, following the pickpocket, but the guy must be a marathoner or something, because he easily outpaces my ultra-fit fiancé. Within seconds, he's out the doors, leaving the airport with my currently unlocked cell phone.

I let out a squeak of dismay. I was going to use translation apps and virtual cash. Now what am I supposed to do? And where exactly did Hudson intend for us to meet up? He was in the process of sending me a map. Now, I just have to hope someone else has his phone number.

Logan chases the guy outside, leaving me standing there surrounded by chocolate bars. Dawn sees what's going on and chases after Logan, and Arlo says something about going to find someone I can give a theft report to. The rest of my friends just stare gobsmacked in the direction the pickpocket had gone.

Chloe finally says, "Man, that guy was hot. Shame he's a thief."

That breaks the bubble of tension surrounding us. Patsy starts helping me pick up the chocolate bars, which prompts the rest of the group to help. Only the backpack is badly damaged, so I wind up just holding it awkwardly in front of me like it's a bowl full of bars.

"Excuse me," a petite Asian woman says. She speaks with an American Midwestern accent. "I have an extra bag."

Like Chloe, her long hair is done up in a messy bun, and she's wearing sweats, but the styling looks expensive, and her nails have a classic French manicure with one nail adorned with a tiny heart. She is holding out a reusable nylon grocery bag done in a floral print.

"Really?" I say. I take the bag. "Arigatou!"

"Iie." She waves a dismissive hand, like *no problem*.

I say, "I can pay you for it."

She laughs. "It wasn't expensive."

I pour the chocolate from the ruined backpack into the bag. Then I pluck out a single bar of our Madagascar chocolate. It is one of my favorites, with bright fruity notes that make me think of chocolate covered cherries, even though it is a two-ingredient bar, nothing but cacao and sugar. We're just able to coax that much flavor out of the beans. I hold out the bar, but she hesitates to take it. I tell her, "I became a chocolate maker because I wanted to make people happy. And your kindness has made me happy, so let me at least thank you."

Her eyes soften with gentle emotion as she takes the bar. "You grew up wanting to be Willy Wonka?"

"Not hardly," I say. "I was a physical therapist until a couple of years ago. Then – things changed and I couldn't handle dealing with so much pain. So I moved back to Texas and opened a chocolate shop."

That's a vast oversimplification of what happened, but it is enough to satisfy this woman. She says, "It sounds like you've been though a lot." She flaps a hand in the direction the thief had gone. "And on top of that, you get your phone stolen. Right at the start of your vacation. I mean – I'm assuming you don't live in Japan."

"We're here for the big chocolate festival. So it's half work trip – but half vacation, too."

She smiles. "Good for you. Maybe I can help. . ." Her words trail off as she notices Logan and Dawn walking back towards us.

"Did you catch him?" Chloe calls.

Dawn shakes her head and scrunches up her nose. "Yeah, no." I can barely hear her add, "He sure does know his way around here."

The woman who gave me the bag says, "Logan? What are you doing here?"

I blink in surprise. How could this woman possibly know Logan? I mean, Logan is from Minnesota, so given her accent, it is possible that they could have grown up in the same area. I'm no expert on the regional differences in the Midwest. And the way she's looking at him – could she be one of Logan's ex-girlfriends? I know he's dated but picturing him with someone this sophisticated – not to mention kind – puts me on the defensive. Which is unfair to Logan, I know. He's nothing if not loyal.

Logan says, "I'm here on a business trip. You?"

She says, "I'm visiting my grandparents. They still live in the countryside."

"That sounds lovely," I say, not about to be left completely out of the conversation.

Logan says, "Emi, I can see you've met my fiancé. Fee, this is Emi Rodriguez."

Emi must be able to read the nonplussed expression on my face, because she laughs and says, "I'm not Logan's ex-girlfriend or anything. I'm a former client. Logan was my bodyguard when I was bringing testimony against my employers. I was a whistleblower, and there had been an attempt on my life. Of course, they're in jail now, so they have bigger concerns than following me."

She says this easily, like it doesn't bother her at all. Or maybe that's just a façade. Maybe she, too, had to reinvent herself after a brush with death.

I say, "That must have been traumatic."

Emi giggles and says, "When I saw Logan, for a split second, I thought he was here to warn me that I was in danger." It feels like her giggle is meant to cover a sense of nervousness.

But otherwise, she hadn't reacted at all. I wish I was that good at keeping a calm façade. I practically wet my pants every time I'm faced with physical danger. I mean, I bluff that I'm brave, but I doubt it's that convincing.

"Is there anything else I can do for you guys?" Emi asks. "I have a rental car. I'm not sure all of you would fit, but I could drop a few of you off and come back."

Once we assure her that we have a ride coming, Emi waves and trundles off with her suitcase.

A guy in a grey suit, also heading for the exit, soon obscures our view of her. It's a busy airport, and people are moving around us, like we're a rock in a river.

Dawn gestures after Emi and says, "That sure was a sweet girl."

"Yeah," Logan says absently.

And I can't help but wonder – did he have a crush on Emi, once upon a time? It wouldn't be unreasonable if he did. She seems like a good person. I'm not insecure enough to worry about him running after her, but the thought makes me feel plain. Not that I don't think my long brown hair, brown eyes and pale skin with just a sprinkling of freckles on my nose aren't attractive.

It's just – been a weird day. I chalk it up to one more thing that fits a new piece into the puzzle that is Logan. I love him, and he cares about making me happy. So there, universe. I'm not going to fall apart just because I've lost my phone and a cute girl from Logan's past said hi.

I look around the group and ask, "Does anyone else have Hudson's number?"

I get a number of head shakes and feel a moment of panic, up until Chloe says, "Duh! He's all over social media. Just DM him."

Which makes sense. Hudson is a Youtuber, like Chloe. They're online on a whole different level.

She pulls out her phone and does a quick search. Moments later, she has the map that Hudson was trying to send me. He's parked outside a 7-Eleven, in a lot about a ten-minute walk from the airport. Of course, I still have to report the stolen phone – and cancel everything associated with it – so we tell him to wait for us, and we will walk to him. I have no illusions about the police finding the device, but I do have travel insurance, so I need the paper trail.

We finally get out of the airport terminal, onto the narrow sidewalk, and I have an urge to take pics – of the group of us, of the huge hotel, and interesting bits of architecture. Only, unlike Chloe, who is recording all of those things, I have no phone. It makes my hands itch, not being able to do any of the things I habitually do. I try to focus on being in the moment. I'm in a nice place, with friends, and we're going to a really cool event. So what if I can't share it on Instagram? Even without pics, it is still happening. And I can get a new phone tonight, after we leave the festival.

I love traveling, seeing new geography, trying new foods. Some of the most interesting conversations I've had have been with people I only met for a day, somewhere I'd never been before. So despite everything, I'm still excited to be walking down this random street.

When we finally get to the spot where our ride is meeting us, Hudson is leaning against a black van, which he said he was going to borrow from a friend, since it has enough seats for all of us. Hudson is presumably live-streaming from the way he is talking to his phone. He waves us over and invites us to be on camera.

Hudson is a lot to take in. He has purple hair, and is wearing a black hoodie over a tee-shirt with Japanese text on it. The guy has a thick, uneven scar running down the right side of his face. And I can't see it now, but there's a tattoo at the base of his neck that looks like a snake.

But underneath all that, he's a sweetheart.

He hands us each a small gift bag, saying, "These are courtesy of the sponsor of today's stream, Ready Mic. They're sets of earpieces and microphones for content creation on the go."

Chloe squeals and rushes to hug him. I don't try to stop her. She doesn't mean anything by it. And they had both been through a lot at the hotel. He returns the hug awkwardly. He is, after all, a newlywed and Chloe is a force to be reckoned with.

Ash opens his bag and shows it to the camera. "This is great! It makes me feel like a spy."

Ash's fiancé, Imogen, says, "That's only if they self-destruct in the next nine seconds."

I figure this gift isn't going to help me much, since I mainly Instagram, and I currently don't have a phone. Still, I say, "Thank you. It's very generous."

Hudson introduces us to his fans, and then cuts the stream, saying he will pick it up at the chocolate festival.

He is oddly respectful of our time and presence for a YouTuber, especially since he is a huge fan of Ash's podcast, and I know he'd like to share a lot more of Ash and me to his followers. But before the botched surgery that left his face scarred, he had been a child actor, trying to find his breakout role as an adult. The scars had ended his career. What he'd been through had probably made him more aware of people's privacy than most.

Hudson opens a sliding door for us to climb into seats in the back. Then he gets into the van. It's weird to see him sitting in what looks like the front passenger seat. I have to remind myself that people drive on the other side of the road here.

And I find myself gripping onto the seat in front of me every time Hudson makes a left turn, because the traffic pattern here makes no sense to my brain, which keeps insisting we are going to die.

The hotel we're staying in is in Shinjuku, an area of Tokyo a bit away from the airport. Hudson booked us into a place with a giant Godzilla head looming over the roofline. We see it several times as Hudson circles the area looking for a place to park. He finally finds a spot, and then he walks with us to help translate once we can get checked in.

When we're in optimal view of the giant Godzilla head looming over the building, Hudson nudges Logan's shoulder. "What do you think of the place?"

"It's pretty cool," Logan says. "I love monster movies."

"Right?" Hudson looks pleased with himself. "I thought you seemed like the type."

"I love monster movies too," Fisher says.

"Now that I did not see coming," Hudson admits.

Fisher is more of a nature guy. He's a landscape architect who often wears tees that declare his love of plants. Right now he has on one that says, *Plants are My Love Language,* above a stylized image of a terrace garden, with plant tones that match his dark green hoodie. Fisher says, "When I was a kid, I watched a lot of classic movies with my grandfather. He had a soft spot for misunderstood monsters."

Only half-listening to Fisher, I glance over at Logan, hoping he doesn't see the uncertainty in my face. I had no idea he liked Godzilla movies. Does that make me a bad fiancé, the way in the past I've been a bad friend? We are engaged, but I keep uncovering things I don't know about him. There's been two things just today. Or is that normal, as two people grow into a relationship?

Large parts of Logan's past are complete blanks to me because they are painful for him to talk about. I do know some of it. Logan used to be a cop, but he made a mistake that got people killed, so he got fired. Then he became a bodyguard and lost a client. But those are just the big, sharp pains in his life. I've helped him heal some of the edges, and he's helped me climb out of the depths of a widow's grief. It's part of why we're good together. But we don't often sit around and talk about the good times in our pasts. We probably should.

I want us to have the strongest foundation possible for our future together. But how do you ask questions when you don't even know what you want to know?

I ask Logan, "So what do you like better? Monster movies or baseball?"

Logan grins. "Baseball, no question. But that may be because it's something that me and my dad both like – but my sister doesn't. It was kind of our thing, when I was growing up."

"Aww," I say. "I didn't know that. Now that he's moved to Texas, we'll have to take him to an Astros game."

Logan looks pleased at the idea. He's come a long way in rebuilding his relationship with his father. "That would be fantastic."

I feel pleased that I said the right thing. Maybe I am a good fiancé, after all.

Arlo says, "I hate monster movies. There are enough dangers in real life without having to invent new ones."

I'm surprised by this. Arlo has always seemed something of a romantic soul. It's hard to think he wouldn't see something poetic in misunderstood monsters. But he's a homicide detective. Maybe he's had enough jump scares in real life to seek more relaxing escapes in his fictions. He's Cuban, with warm brown skin and generous lips, and I can still see in him my first love, from when we were in high school. Whatever he's been through hasn't hardened his face.

Patsy takes his arm and says, "I'll take you to all the rom-coms and musicals you want."

Arlo breaks into a grin. "Promise, babe?"

She gives him a quick kiss on the cheek. "Promise."

I've gotten far enough from having potentially re-kindled my romance with Arlo that this doesn't bother me. It's actually kind of sweet how perfectly dorky they can be together. And I've gotten to the point where I think it is funny how much Patsy and I look alike. She is like a more polished version of me, with long brown hair and pale skin – but also more makeup.

Hudson says, "They're actually filming a movie across the street from your chocolate event. And guess who has a bit part?"

Chloe says hopefully, "Me?"

Hudson laughs. "Sorry, Chloe. They only invited a handful of Youtubers with channels about Japan. I just get to get stomped by the monster midway through the first act, which motivates my girlfriend to hunt it for revenge."

"Lucky," Chloe says sullenly, crossing her arms over her chest and pushing her bottom lip out.

Hudson goes with us as far as the elevator, then he promises to meet me and Logan at the chocolate festival after he runs a few errands. He says, "Shinjuku is more touristy than a lot of Tokyo, so that means you may run across scammers. And some of the districts in this ward don't have the best reputation, so if you're going out at night, maybe ask me or Savannah if it's the kind of place where you should feel comfortable. And if anyone tries to beckon you into a bar, don't go. You could wind up getting stuck with an outrageously inflated bill – or worse."

"We're not exactly bar kind of people," Logan points out.

"I didn't really think you were," Hudson says. "I just thought I'd warn you, because sometimes when people travel, they step outside their comfort zones. Japan offers many positive ways to do that, from mountain climbing to high-end shopping. I'm happy to give recs for whatever you need. Whatever it is, I've probably made a video about it, or am friends with someone who has."

I say, "I heard Japan has a reputation for being safe."

Hudson says, "It does. It has one of the lowest crime rates in the world. It's also one of the cleanest places in the world – even though in many places, you are expected to carry trash home with you. People just cooperate. It makes sense to stay here, close to your festival. And this is a good hotel. Just – you will want to leave the ward if you want to see some of the best that Tokyo has to offer."

"Fair enough." I hope the room lives up to that hype. As soon as Hudson gets on the elevator, I turn to check it out.

I'm sharing a room with three beds with Chloe and Patsy, the better for me and Patsy to keep an eye on Chloe. She's a bit too independent for a seventeen-year-old, and I promised her mother I'd chaperone her this entire trip.

Chloe hops into one of the beds. "Y'all go enjoy the day. I'll just sleep it away."

Patsy and I exchange a skeptical look.

"Yeah right," Patsy says. "You've been watching too many teen movies if you think you're going to ditch your chaperones that easily. If you really want to take a nap, I'll stay here and take one too. But I warn you, I'm a light sleeper and I'm hanging a bunch of keys and bangle bracelets on the doorknob."

Chloe laughs. "It was worth a try. I just wanted to see if I could sneak onto that movie set and see if they'd let me be an extra."

Patsy says, "After our nap, we can go check it out. But you will ask if you can go on the set. There will be no sneaking involved."

Chloe grins. "You're the best, Aunt Pat."

Chloe has never called me Aunt. If she does, I better be careful, because whatever she wants is going to be something big.

Patsy says, "You're a good kid."

Chloe asks, "Can I ask you something personal?"

Patsy says, "Shoot."

Chloe sits up in bed. "Ash is engaged, and Felicity's engaged. You and Arlo have been together longer. So why hasn't Arlo proposed yet?"

Patsy leans back against the wall. She runs a hand across her face, then says, "He did. I told him to ask me again in six months."

I find this startling. And there's heat at the base of my neck, because I hope I'm not the reason for their troubles. They had been broken up when Arlo and I had almost gotten back together.

"Why?" Chloe asks.

Patsy says, "We were apart for a while, and I'm not the only one he's been in love with. I want to make sure he still feels the same way then as he does now. And if he does, and he asks me again, I'll say yes." Patsy doesn't bring up the role I'd had to play in all of that. Because she's actually my friend now.

And I really do hope Arlo asks her again.

I freshen up a bit and change out of my slouchy airplane clothes and into a crisp purple blouse and black slacks. I add the teardrop earrings Logan recently gave me, for a touch of understated elegance. They're opals, one of my favorites.

I yawn and dab an extra layer of concealer under my eyes. I'd slept on and off on the flight, but it would be great to have a more solid rest now, even though it's morning. Of course, there isn't time for that. Technically, we're already late. The venue is a seven-story department store, and the week-long festival started this morning. We're getting a late set-up, but it was the only way for us to have gotten flights we could afford. We sent our stock of chocolate ahead, so the boxes should be waiting for us at our spot. We've just brought some last-minute additions.

By the time I get out of the bathroom, Patsy has indeed produced a dozen bangle bracelets and a set of keys that clank together when I try to move them off the lever to open the door. Patsy lifts her head and opens one eye. Once she has verified that it's me, she goes back to sleep.

Chapter Two
Monday

Leaving the others at the hotel, Logan and I head to the festival. Given all our supplies, public transportation seems out of the question. But it's easy to get a taxi. On our way in to the festival venue, I make it a point to check out the movie set too. If it doesn't look respectable, I'm going to call Patsy and tell her not to let Chloe go. I let out a frustrated huff. Rather, I'm going to have Logan call Patsy, as I have yet to remedy my phoneless situation.

We get our taxi driver to drop us off near the spot where Hudson had said the filming is taking place. It turns out to be a three-story, modern, white building. I think it is an annex to the shopping center we're going to for the festival. I stop and peer through the door.

"Pardon me, love," a woman's voice says from behind me.

I turn and there's a blonde British woman with gobs of curly hair. She's holding a tray with four cups of coffee. It looks like she's trying to get in the door – only I'm blocking her way.

"Oh, I'm sorry," I say, moving off to one side, where Logan has our case.

She studies me critically. "You have a movie to pitch? You know Kudo only works in Japanese. Are you fluent?"

"Oh no, absolutely not," I say, flustered. "I'm conversational in Spanish, but that's about it. And I don't write movies. I'm here for the chocolate festival, and my niece was hoping she could be an extra. She's a Youtuber, and one of her friends said he was going to be in it."

"Really? What's her channel?"

"I don't know what it's called now, but it used to be about Mr. Tunaface. Until he became the reformed Mr. Tunaface. She's also doing a pet collab with some other YouTubers while she is here."

"Really? I used to love that jerky cat." She points with her coffee tray. "I'll have a word with the director and see what I can do. I'm just the protagonist's stunt double, but you never know." She notices Logan glancing down at her coffees and says, "I like to get out and walk when there's nothing for me to do on set. I can't handle just sitting. So I'm the first person to volunteer for coffee runs. We have catered coffee." She makes a disgusted face. "But I know the shop where the good stuff is."

"Really?" Logan holds up his phone. "May I?" Logan takes a picture of her cup logo. After all, he also appreciates a good cup of coffee.

We thank her, then move down to the crosswalk so we can finally get to the building that is the reason that we are here.

Once we are out of earshot, Logan looks at me and says, "Niece?"

I shrug. "It was less complicated than explaining how we happen to be here with Chloe."

Logan seems satisfied with that answer. Out of the blue, he says, "We're going to be in a really cool department store. Maybe they do a wedding gift registry."

And that squee of excitement is back, missing phone or no. We're getting married. In three months. Everything is finally coming together. Logan's sister finally likes me, his parents moved closer to us to run the hotel we are living in, we have couple friends together. Logan has excellent taste, so I'm sure that our wedding is going to be just as beautiful as my first wedding. There's pain in that thought, and I realize it's the source of my unease. Marrying Logan will mean letting go of Kevin and my memories of my first marriage on a whole different level. I'm excited – but also sad. Kevin and I had done our gift registry at Target. Logan wants to do something on a totally different scale.

Which is understandable – we both have all the basics in our respective suites. So why not ask for cool décor and a fancy rice cooker? Assuming we can figure out the shipping.

I give him a warm smile. "We should check later. I'm sure one of our friends would watch the booth."

The entire sixth floor is an exhibit hall dedicated to the event. There's a big sign declaring, "Fête du Chocolat," and behind it rows of booths and dessert cases, where bonbons shine like shimmering jewels. A woman walks by wearing stiletto heels and a brown and cream dress with tiered lace that makes her look like a dessert topper. The tutu attached to her skirt looks like it is made of chocolate curls. She's carrying a tray of chocolate samples.

I suck in a breath, trying to steady myself. This is one of the biggest chocolate festivals in the world. Famous chocolatiers from Paris will be here, along with top innovators in Japan. What business do I, a bean to bar chocolate maker from Galveston, Texas – not to mention someone who is relatively new to the craft – have being here? Seeing the sheer scale of the space, I feel an urge to turn and run.

Logan looks encouragingly down at me. "You got this."

I shake my head. "Nope. I am definitely underdressed, and I'm not going to be able to talk to anybody. Let alone give a class."

Hudson's wife Savannah had gotten me a spot on the roster to do a demo on the basics of bean to bar chocolate making.

Logan says in a reasonable tone, "You look lovely, and there are people here from all over the place. Some of them are bound to speak English. And Hudson will be here soon to help translate."

I pull up the map for our booth. As we make our way through the crowd, I realize that most people are dressed more reasonably, in business casual or with company tees or in chef coats or cute aprons.

I still feel overwhelmed, but people are smiling at me, and I get a few friendly nods. One older guy waves. I've studied a few phrases before coming here, so I manage to stammer out a good morning. "Ohayo gozaimus."

The guy responds, echoing my phrase, then starts to talk to me like I'm fluent. Panic rises in my chest. I have no idea how to respond.

I say, "I'm sorry."

He grins good naturedly and shrugs. He says, "You enjoy today."

Then he walks off into the crowd. Maybe that was the extent of his English, and he was afraid I was going to talk English back to him. I get exactly how he feels.

We find our booth, and there's Ash, unloading a box into the display case. Which is really sweet. Everyone had promised to help me and Logan out over the course of the week, but Ash had gone straight to his room once we'd arrived at the hotel, so I had assumed he was planning to sleep after the long flight. But he must have slept on the plane, because he looks alert and put-together, with a blazer over his usual dress shirt and skinny tie.

He says, "Imogen is scouting the festival for wedding ideas. She said with our two weddings being so close, she didn't want it to look like we were copying each other."

I understand that. I say, "You know I'd love to do chocolates for your party favors, and Carmen and Enrique want to cater. But if you decide to do something else, I'm sure none of us will be offended."

At least I'm sure Carmen won't be. She's the pastry chef at Greetings and Felicitations – and now one of my close friends. She's in charge of the shop this week, while Logan and I are gone. Enrique is a little more temperamental. He's a pop-up chef I first met when he was a suspect in a murder I was trying to solve. I've never actually sought out crimes to get involved with. It just keeps happening that I'm in a position to uncover information – partly because several of the cases happened at my shop, or the hotel. And I've discovered I'm good at uncovering obscure clues.

On the counter next to the box Ash is unpacking, there is a stack of books. I start to feel a vague sense of unease, down in the pit of my stomach.

"What's that?"

Ash bites his bottom lip to try and hold back a grin. He looks like he's trying to respect the fact that I'm probably going to freak out, while at the same time trying to hide that he's excited. He says, "They've been coming all morning. Apparently, one of the local universities has a detective fiction club."

I can already see where this is going, and I don't like it. I find I'm hugging myself, with arms crossed over my chest. Every time a vintage book falls into my life, there happens to be a murder that follows, and I get sucked into investigating. Ordinarily, I'm not a superstitious person. But this has happened to me seven times. Count it. Seven times I've found a book, or had one handed to me, and the books in some way connected to seven cases I've helped solve. I get that the universe is trying to tell me something.

I scowl at Ash. "Don't look so excited. How will you feel if someone really does die?"

"Horrified, obviously," Ash says. "But it's cool to know that you have international fans. And that by extension, I have international fans."

Ash has a true crime podcast. So far, it has only featured cases I've been involved in. I've appeared on the show – begrudgingly. But Ash is right. It's startling to know that people are listening to what Ash has to say about me this far around the world. Instead of coming here for Pierre Herme or, more locally Palet d'Or and Caramel et Cacao, there are a few people here specifically hoping to meet me. Of course, I wish it was for the renown of my chocolate, rather than my status as an amateur detective.

Ash adds, "The club members have given me some great sound bites for the podcast. There's actually been some interest from a movie studio on doing a docudrama about Emma Turner. I've been meaning to talk to you about that."

I still feel sad when I think about Emma. She had been one of the first people I had hired at Greetings and Felicitations, right when I had opened my bean to bar chocolate business. She had been murdered at the grand opening party. I wish I had been able to get to know the real her, to reach out somehow to help her, before it had been too late. I tell Ash, "If you can get her family's permission, I'm okay with it. Although, I'll probably come off looking like an idiot, since I had never investigated anything before, and I had no idea what I was doing."

"I didn't make you sound like an idiot on the podcast," Ash protests. "And if I'm being honest, you did better than a lot of people would have. You faced off against Emma's killer and survived."

That is true. It had been a big turning point in my life, a wake-up call that I needed to reclaim my future after having lost everything.

I'd been living my entire life in the memory of someone who wasn't there anymore. Kevin and I used to love to travel. I even have a collection of maps I keep in a special box, of all the places I've been. We had dreamed of traveling together to buy cacao beans and make our own chocolate once he retired, but his accident meant that never happened. So I'd made it my dream, and slowly I'd shared that dream with Logan, making him a partner in my business – and now in my life.

I've come so far since that day when I thought I was going to die that it's hard to remember how it had felt. And how it had felt to be so lost.

I gesture vaguely at the books. "Do something with those. I haven't touched them, so it doesn't count."

Of course, I don't know that. I can't even prove that the books have anything to do with me getting involved in crime. It could, in theory, be one huge cosmically improbable coincidence. But I have to believe that I have at least some small element of choice here.

"All of them?" Ash protests. He glances down. I let my gaze follow and there, on a chair behind him, is another stack of books.

A girl steps up to the booth and leans a small pink teddy bear against the books, then gives me a deep nod. She then brings her hands up to her mouth and giggles as she moves away. I realize there are already a few small trinkets beside the books, making it look like some kind of memorial. There's a magnifying glass, and under it a hand-written sign that says, "Thank you for loving mystery books as much as we do."

Clearly, something has been lost in translation. It is true that I have a number of mystery books on display at my shop. And it is true that I love to read, voraciously, in many genres. But at least half of the books I've picked up that have gotten me involved in crimes have been mysteries. Honestly, I'm afraid of them.

A woman wearing a business suit approaches the booth. She's maybe thirty, with shoulder length hair and bangs that almost touch her eyes. Her features are sharp, with thin lips painted with deep red lipstick. She is carrying multiple small shopping bags, so I guess she has really been enjoying the festival.

"Koerberu Sensei," the woman says.

I get that she's trying to say my last name, Koerber, but isn't sensei a word for teacher or coach? I tell her, "Yes, I'm Felicity Koerber." I gesture at my booth, "I own Greetings and Felicitations."

In heavily accented English she says, "I wanted to share this with you." She reaches into her purse and, before I can think to stop her, deposits a book into my hands.

It's an old book, written in Japanese. Part of me wants to drop it and head immediately back to the airport, but I try to be polite. My hands are shaking as I try to give her the book back. "I'm sorry. I don't read Japanese."

She makes an "x" with her hands, a clear symbol for no. "I heard you collect first editions. This is the first book by one of our most famous mystery authors, Yokomizo Seishi. It's technically not a first edition. *The Honjin Murders* was serialized in a magazine in the 1940s, before being published in this edition in the 1970s."

My heart is beating fast, and I take a deep breath to steady myself. A first edition. This book might as well be radioactive. "What's it about?" I ask, sure I don't want to know.

"It's a meta take on the mystery genre, with mechanical tricks and a character who collects both Japanese and Western mystery literature. The narrator admits in an epilogue that he owes a particular debt to Agatha Christie. It is a good example of the play of ideas, back and forth between our cultures. As is mystery fiction in general, with so many influences we borrow from each other." She gestures at the book. "I can find you an English translation, if that is good."

Logan steps up to the woman and says, "I'm Logan Hanlon, co-owner with Felicity of the chocolate shop. And you are?"

"I'm Suzuki Nao. I am the faculty sponsor of the detective fiction club that has been bringing you all their favorite books."

I think Nao is her given name, since Japanese names are traditionally presented with the family name first.

Logan says, "Thank you for your generosity. Have you been enjoying the chocolate festival?"

He side-tracks her into looking at our bars of chocolate.

I sigh. I already have a book in my hands. I might as well look at the rest of them. I step around the counter, inside the booth space and peruse the titles. Some are in Japanese, some are clearly translations of work by Japanese authors. *The Devotion of Suspect X* by Keigo Higashino. *The Decagon House Murders* by Yukito Ayatsuji. *Inspector Imanishi Investigates* by Seichō Matsumoto. It's a window into a whole field of literature I never realized existed. I'm intrigued by the covers, and in less ominous circumstances, I might be excited to read them. There are a few works here that were always in English, by Christie and Doyle and Dorothy Sayers. I guess this group really likes the classics.

I look up to ask Nao why she brought all this to me, or to warn her that she might be in danger, since now there's a connection between her and the book, but she's already gone. Which feels like a huge disconnect. How could she give me a potential murder book and then disappear?

Logan says gently, "You can call her later, if you want. She gave me her card."

"I think I need some air," I say. "I'm pretty sure the map said this place has a rooftop garden."

"I'll come with you," Logan says. He arches an eyebrow at Ash. "You can handle the booth, right?"

Ash laughs. "I might as well become an honorary employee. I've spent enough time researching your business practices."

Mostly that means coming to the shop and talking Carmen into giving him free pastries.

Logan looks at me and says, "Are you sure we should leave him alone with the samples?"

Chapter Three
Monday

The rooftop garden is lovely. There's a wall of vertically planted succulents, with a sleek water feature cascading down the middle. On the opposite side, there's a long stretch of glass panels forming a tall railing, offering a glimpse out onto the city. We're so high up that even from the middle of the deck, it's got a great view.

There are even a couple of full-sized maple trees in planters built into the decking up here, and tables where people are sitting drinking coffee or eating onigiri, a triangular rice ball, and other snacks. I immediately feel the tension in my shoulders start to relax.

After all, nothing terrible has actually happened yet. And how can the universe hold me responsible for a book I can't even read? And I only know maybe six people in this whole country. Maybe – just maybe – everything is going to be okay. I've certainly got enough issues going on trying to deal with the festival.

My best friend, Autumn, couldn't come on this trip because she's pregnant and unable to fly. In solidarity for my trip, she's taking care of my bunny, Knightley. She and Drake are staying in a suite in the hotel I live in, to be close to Knightley, and to have a mini-vacation. It's a credit to them both that they feel comfortable staying there after the incident that happened a few months ago, where a murderer was threatening anyone who attempted to leave the building. Autumn had gone missing for a while. I think I had been more frightened by the whole situation than she had been.

Before I left for Japan, Autumn had strictly instructed me to video call her the first chance I got, despite the time difference. The time change has left me jetlagged, but I'm pretty sure that this morning in Tokyo is somehow last night in Galveston. I don't think it is terribly late there yet, so I gesture Logan over beside me and ask to borrow his phone. We face the succulent wall, so the amazing city view will be in the background.

Logan grins, obviously thinking we're taking a selfie. Which isn't a bad idea, honestly, so I snap a couple of pics. Logan squeezes my shoulder gently. He says, "If anything happens, we'll figure it out. We always do."

"I know," I say, leaning my cheek against his hand. So what if we don't know everything about each other yet? Logan has been there for me on some of the worst days of my life, no questions asked. He's saved my life more than once – and I've saved his. When I think about how close he came to being electrocuted because I'd misread a clue and taken a long time to get to him –I shudder. I just can't imagine life without him.

I'm still holding his phone up. Logan gestures at it and says, "You want a silly pose or something?"

"Actually," I say, "I figure we should check in with Autumn."

"Makes sense," Logan says. "Didn't she say she's going to set her next book in Japan? She's going to be counting on you to give her all the little details she could have gotten if she'd been able to come with us."

Autumn is a mystery writer, and her comeback as an author has made her even more successful than the original height of her career.

I make the call, and when Autumn answers, she waves enthusiastically. She's wearing a fuzzy terrycloth headband with a giant bow pushing back the front part of her afro, and her face is covered with a cracking mint green mask. Glancing off camera, she says, "Hey, guys, it's Felicity."

There's excited chatter, and someone says, "Turn the camera over here."

Autumn turns, and there on the sofa, in similar masked states of self-spa-night, are my aunt, my shop's pastry chef, and Marilyn Midge, one of my favorite mystery authors. I only recognize Marilyn because of her distinctive ombré red hair – and the thick-rimmed cat eye glasses she's wearing over the goop on her skin. Autumn knows a lot of people in the literary world. I feel a brief flash of jealousy that I'm not there having a girl's night along with them.

But then I remember – Autumn was totally jealous of me getting to go to Japan. It's all a matter of perspective.

My Aunt Naomi reaches down to the floor and picks up my white, lop-eared rabbit. "Here's Knightley," she says, trying unsuccessfully to get the bunny to wave a paw at the camera. Knightley wriggles like he would very much like to get down. But Naomi says, "Say hi to your mommy, little bun."

"Hi, little guy!" I wave. I've been through a lot in the past couple of years, and Knightley has been one of the few constants in my life the whole time. Just seeing him safe and happy takes away a lot of my unease about the mystery books.

Marilyn says, "That's a spectacular space behind you. Where are you?"

I tell her, "It's a rooftop garden, above a shopping mall in Tokyo."

Autumn takes a sip out of something in a wine glass – which has to be her low sugar grape juice. Then she splutters. "What's that about?"

Logan and I glance at each other. "What's what about?"

She points at the camera, and I get the idea that she's actually pointing at something behind me. I turn to see two people standing by one of the tables, having an argument. Without meaning to, I let out the word, "No."

Because seriously? The two people are Nao, the faculty sponsor of the detective club, and the blond guy who snatched my phone. For all I know, he might still have it. It's an improbable coincidence, him even being here. Tokyo is a huge, sprawling city. I'm not about to miss what will probably be my only chance to get my phone back.

"Hey you," I shout, shoving Logan's phone back into his hands as I turn to stalk towards the thief.

The blond guy's eyes go wide, and I can see he recognizes me. He has a phone in his hand, and while he's distracted, Nao snatches it. Clearly, he'd just pulled the same act on her that he'd pulled on me at the train station. Only – why try for a snatch and grab up here, in a closed in space where there's no easy exit? He's a fast runner, so maybe he'd been counting on sprinting down the escalators inside the mall, but it seems like there would be easier plans.

The guy takes off running past me but sees Logan ready to block his way back inside the mall, so he doubles back, heading for the railing. I grab at him and he basically drags me the rest of the way to the glass panels. I've never been the most athletic person, having suffered from asthma most of my life. My symptoms usually only appear now under the most extreme circumstances. Right now, I can feel myself breathing heavy, but I'm all right.

The guy reaches inside his jacket pocket and throws a phone at me, but I ignore it. Because, A, it isn't my phone and B, he seems intent to jump off this building. Adrenaline is racing through me, and my nerves are on end from the sudden shock. The moment feels outside of reality. There's no way this guy is going to kill himself, just because I'd confronted him. Right? That makes even less sense than trying to purse snatch from way up here.

"Noel," Nao shouts. "Don't!"

I dimly register that it's odd that Nao knows this guy. But I'm too busy trying to keep hold of his jacket while he slap-fights at me to let go. He finally shrugs out of the jacket, leaving it crumpled in my hands as he vaults up onto the railing. I drop the jacket and jump for the top of the railing to try to pull him back by the belt loops on his trousers, but he has too much momentum, and there's a sickening off-balance feeling as I feel myself tipping over, my finger caught in the loop.

A scream escapes my lips as I start to fall. And my stomach feels like it's flipping inside out. It's seven floors down. There's no way either Noel or I will survive this. But Noel isn't screaming. He seems perfectly calm as he extracts my hand from his belt loop.

It can't end this way. I'd gotten a murder book, hadn't I? Actually, more like forty murder books. What was the point of all that if I wouldn't even be around to solve the case? Yet, cold prickles all over me with the certainty that this is the end.

Time feels gooed out. It had taken a split second to think all that, and I'm still falling. I close my eyes, not wanting the sidewalk to be the last thing I see. I'm waiting for my life to start flashing in front of my eyes. It will be full of awkward moments and grief, but still, it has been a good life. With my chocolate shop as a hub in the community, I've brought people together, and even found love again. Poor Logan, though. He's suffered just as much grief as I have – and losing me in such a stupid way is going to set him back emotionally in a way he might not recover from.

Noel pushes me away from him, and then there's impact. Which feels weirdly springy. Still, it hurts, knocking the breath fully out of me, and that's it. My shattered lungs won't be able to draw in another breath. Only – I do.

And I realize that while the landing had stung like belly flopping into a pool, and something rough has scratched at my face and arms, I'm on a huge air mat.

"How is this here?" I wonder, my voice scratchy and tearstained.

"It's for a stunt for the movie," Noel replies. His voice is pinched, like he's in pain. Yet, he's climbing off the mat and hobbling away from me.

I try to follow, but pain radiates through every part of my body. I test my fingers and toes, but it doesn't feel like anything is broken. Finally, I manage to crawl towards the edge of the mat and climb down off of it.

Noel is gone, but from what he said – he has to be connected to the film studio across the street. I carefully cross at the signal – Hudson told us that jaywalking is a lot more serious in Japan than it is in the States – and approach the door we'd seen the stunt performer go in earlier. Now, though, the room beyond the door is dark. I try the handle, but it's locked.

I start to turn away, but then I notice a drop of red liquid – clearly blood – on the pavement. There are two or three more dots heading back around the building, and when I look back, there's a dot in the crosswalk, showing the trail started around the other side. Small hairs prickle at the back of my neck, and a shiver runs through me, noticeable despite my aching body. I glance up at the roof I'd just fallen off of, and I feel a bit faint thinking about how it had felt to fly helplessly through the air. But I had survived, more or less unharmed, and part of me is marveling in triumph. I. Am. Alive.

Which is a total dopamine rush.

There's a gate leading into the backlot, where someone has mocked up one side of a street lined with shops, their façades slightly off scale. Could Noel have disappeared that direction? The gate is open, so there's a good chance he came this way. The idea of stepping through that gate still gives me pause. Pursuing Noel could be dangerous, though so far, he's seemed more likely to run than to attack anyone. Maybe I can make it clear to him that I don't want to turn him in to the authorities. I just want my phone back.

Besides, he's clearly injured. What if he needs help?

Of course, that's probably just me trying to reason myself into doing this. If he needed help, surely he would have stayed where he was. Unless he was afraid of getting into trouble.

I push the gate farther open with my elbow and make my way onto the deserted mock street. "Noel?" I call. "You okay? I just want to talk."

There is no response. I can hear a couple passing on the sidewalk behind me, conversing in loud Japanese. Somehow, that gives me the confidence to move forward. This is just a movie set, not a ghost town. And the real world is only a few steps away. "Noel? You looked hurt. I have medical training."

There are doors into the cityscape façade. I open one, and it's just part of a plywood floor, with patchy grass behind it, and then a white wood fence. No sign of Noel. I close the door and turn back around.

"I'm not even mad about the phone anymore," I say. "Nearly dying puts things in perspective."

There's still no answer.

I see a calico cat near the back door of the building, sniffing at something on the ground. I step over to the cat and bend down, letting it sniff my hand. "What you got, little bit?"

The cat's tail is vertical, the end twitching just a little bit. Which, according to one of Chloe's videos, means it feels comfortable around me, may even find my presence reassuring.

But I'm not reassured, because near where the cat is standing, I can see drops of a dark liquid spattering a leaf. More blood.

Which means Noel probably went inside the building. And I've been talking to no one.

I try the knob, and this time the door opens. The cat zooms around me, going inside and dashing down a hall. I halfheartedly call, "Hey, come back." But I know the cat probably isn't going to listen.

I follow it, trying to coax it back outside. It's embarrassing. Not only is it breaking and entering to come in here without permission – well, entering anyway, since I haven't actually broken anything – but I've let a stray animal into someone's property.

The cat disappears. But there's a spot of blood in the hallway, right in front of a door with a paper sign that says, *Quiet, please! We are filming!* in English, along with Japanese text that probably says the same thing. Could Noel have gone inside? If he's part of this movie, the crew would expect to see him. But how would he explain the fact that he's suddenly bleeding? If he's in there, I need to talk to him.

I put my ear up against the door, but I don't hear anything going on on the other side. They're probably taking a break. I take a deep breath and square my shoulders. I'm going in. I haven't come this far just to give up without talking to Noel. My whole life is on that phone, and I may even have some leverage in getting it back if he thinks I'm going to tell his co-workers that he's a pickpocket.

As quietly as I can, I open the door. My senses are assaulted by the smell of a strong cleaner or air freshener. It's like marzipan, or a bakery selling almond cake. It's so strong, I gag on it, and I can feel my lungs trying to close into an asthma attack. I fumble for the rescue inhaler in my pocket, disappointed at having to use it. It's been so long without an attack. But the inhaler helps.

From the hallway, I take in the immense space. Half of this room has been built into a waist-high cityscape of Tokyo, complete with Sky Tree Tower. I start to back away, but then I notice a pair of sneakers and part of a pair of jeans poking out from the scenery.

Without thinking I rush into the room. It's Noel. He's lying on the floor, unmoving. He had clearly opened the front of one of the buildings, which is on a hinge like a doll house, to stash something inside. There are already half a dozen purses and at least one cell phone. Which isn't mine.

I'm embarrassed that I took the time to note that before focusing on the injured guy on the floor. He's facing away from me, not talking. Maybe he didn't hear me come in – or maybe he doesn't want my help.

"Noel," I say leaning down to him. "You probably didn't hear me when I said I have medical training. I want to help. We can worry about what happened at the airport later."

He doesn't respond, even when I touch his shoulder. My heart leaps in panic. He didn't shrug me away, and he isn't moving. I knew he was hurt, but it didn't look like he'd lost enough blood to be unconscious. "Noel," I say again in a higher pitched voice. I roll him over, and his head lolls.

I suck in a gasp. He's clearly dead.

"Noel," I repeat, more softly now. "What happened?" There was no reason to say it out loud. Noel clearly can't hear me, let alone respond. I put two fingers to his neck, but there's no pulse. I check him for an obvious injury, but all I find is a gash on his elbow where he must have landed on the bunch of keys attached to his belt. Given that he's a thief, I can't help but wonder if they're even his keys.

He'd been so vibrant just a few minutes ago, snatching Nao's phone, running away from me. Maybe this is shock from the impact, if he landed worse than I did. But honestly – that seems unlikely.

Whatever the cause, the responsible thing is to at least try resuscitation techniques. Kneeling down beside him, I start to get cold, probably shock setting in. Way too much has happened in the last few minutes for my body and mind to process. I do chest compressions on the guy for a couple of minutes, but there's no response. It isn't until I'm doing it that I realize my lungs are doing fine, after the hit from the inhaler. I think I'm getting used to the smell, too. Or else it is dissipating.

There's nothing else I can do to try to help Noel. I need to call an ambulance, and the police. Though by the time they arrive, it will be too late to try other techniques. Out of habit, I reach for my phone – which I obviously do not have. I move around the body on the floor and grab the phone out of Noel's secret stash. Thankfully, it lights up, but I don't get a signal.

I take the phone outside. My heart is still beating fast from the shock of discovering a dead guy, and my fingers are jittery as I operate the phone, which thankfully unlocks to a code of 111111. The screen has a picture of two little kids – a boy and a girl – as the wallpaper. I try calling 911, but that's clearly not the emergency number in Japan. I take a steadying breath and try to figure out who I need to call. I've typed *Emergency number in Ja-* when I hear the gate crash open.

Chapter Four
Monday

"Fee," Logan shouts, rushing over to me and crushing me in his arms.

"Ouch," I say. "I just fell off a seven-story building. Everything hurts."

He releases me. "Sorry." His eyes are wild with panic, and he's out of breath, and he grasps my shoulders gently, like he needs to touch me to believe I'm really okay. "I'm sorry it took me so long to get here. I sprinted down the escalators, but by the time I got there, there was an ambulance leaving the parking lot, and I thought you were in it, so I chased it a couple of blocks, until they stopped at a red light. Then I had to backtrack, and I followed the blood trail." He starts glancing at various parts of my body. "Where are you hurt?"

"It's not me," I say. I gesture inside the building. "Noel. The phone thief. He's dead."

Logan frowns. He heaves a shuddery breath. "If I have to be honest, I'd much rather it be him than you. I don't care if you think I'm horrible for thinking that. I just couldn't – I thought you were gone – when you went up over that railing I tried to catch you, but my hand just brushed your hair." His hands, still on my shoulders, are trembling. As a bodyguard, he'd lost a client he'd fallen in love with, and he's always felt guilty for failing to protect her. Thinking he'd lost me must have triggered memories. And then when he'd gotten to the sidewalk, I had disappeared. I can't even imagine what he must be going through right now. He musters up a weak smile. "You're going to have to call Autumn back. I think she saw the whole thing before I hung up on her."

Yet he's shaking too much to hand me his phone.

I move my hands up and take his hands in mine, steadying them as best I can. "I'm still here. We just need to call the police. And it's not 911."

He manages a weak laugh, though his eyes look like he might cry. "I'll take care of it." He gestures with his chin at the phone still in my hand, pressed now between our palms. "Where'd you get that?"

"Long story," I say. "Let's just go back inside, see if there's any resuscitation technique I might have missed."

"That seems unlikely," Logan says, but he follows me back into the building and down the hallway. When we get to the room, Logan scrunches up his nose. "It smells like almonds in here. But not bitter almonds."

"No," I agree, trying to sound detached, even though I'm still shaken by Noel's death. "It's not arsenic. We wouldn't smell that across the room anyway."

"You okay, Fee?" Logan asks.

I guess the expression on my face makes it clear how not okay I am. I've seen a dead body before, obviously, but I feel like I've failed Noel somehow. And I don't want to look at his face, knowing that.

Logan squeezes my hand and says, "Wait here."

He heads into the room.

I say, "I can't help but feel responsible. If I hadn't chased Noel, then he wouldn't have jumped and whatever happened to him wouldn't have happened. He'd be alive."

"Fee," Logan says. "Maybe this guy is alive. I'm not seeing a body."

"What?" I exclaim, moving back into the room. There where Noel was just lying, the floor is clean. Even the blood smears from his injured elbow are gone. I rush over to the toy-sized building where his hidden cache of snatched purses and phones is hidden. I swing open the door, and it is empty. "This is impossible," I tell Logan.

"This was full of stuff he had stolen. I was only outside for a couple of minutes. And he was dead, I'm sure of it."

Logan looks at me, concern in his eyes. "Fee, you're probably in shock, from falling off a roof. Is it possible you just thought the guy was dead?"

"You don't believe me?" I ask incredulously. Logan has always supported me before, no matter how unlikely my theories have been. Even when I've been wrong. I slide the phone I'd found into my pocket as an act of resilience. After all, it is proof that what I'm saying is true. Where else would I have gotten this phone?

"It's not that," Logan says. "I believe that you believe the guy was dead. But you're so shaky. Maybe he had a weak pulse and you just didn't feel it."

I think about the chest compressions, and how hard that would have been on his body had he been alive. I say, "But you at least believe that he was here. That this prop building was full of purses."

"Of course I do," Logan says. "You're one of the most level-headed people I know. Fee, we'll figure this out."

"Okay," I say. "Noel may still be in this building."

"How do you know his name, anyway?" Logan asks. He kneels to peer into the hiding space.

I say, "Nao called him that. Just before he started running."

"I must not have noticed," Logan says. "I was too busy trying to outthink the guy, since I obviously can't outrun him. I never imagined he'd jump off the roof, though. He was nuts."

I tell Logan, "He knew the air mat was there. He wasn't in any danger until he had to worry about me landing on top of him. He's part of the movie's cast or crew."

"Possibly another stunt performer," Logan speculates.

"We should talk to Nao," I suggest. "She probably knows something."

"And after that, we should find a discreet way to talk to people on this production."

I look around the room, realizing that we're still trespassing. This space is cluttered with equipment and props, some of them parts of kaiju monsters, for close-ups. One is clearly supposed to be a spaceship. The cavernous size of this space, and the emptiness, makes it feel creepy. I shudder.

The police are on their way, and they're going to find out that we came in without the permission of anyone involved with the movie – and there's no body to justify it. Not to mention the cat who is now somewhere hidden in the building.

"Where is everybody?" I ask.

Logan shrugs. "We're not even sure someone is supposed to be here. Maybe they're not filming today."

There's a vague thudding coming from the other side of the room. Logan and I look at each other, and his hand goes to his jacket. Of course, the gun he carries isn't there, because he couldn't bring it on the plane, or have it in his possession in this country. Very few people are allowed to have guns here. Despite that, we cross the room. I pick up a plastic dinosaur leg the size of a log, ready to smack whoever is on the other side of the door. I move to the side of the door jamb, while Logan moves in to open the door. It's locked so he uses a credit card to pop open the door.

As it opens, he gets a puzzled expression on his face. "What are you doing in there?"

Chloe says, "Oh thank goodness! The movie staff took lunch. They told me to wait in here for the director to come back, so I could talk to him, and it wasn't until I heard someone talking out there that I realized the door was locked.

I peek around the door jamb. Chloe is sitting in a conference room in a fancy leather chair, petting a calico cat. It looks like the same one I had let in.

"Oh, good," I say. "You found the cat. But how did you let her in if you were locked in the room?"

Chloe blinks. "I didn't let her in. She must have been hanging out in here the whole time. She jumped up out of a chair just a little bit ago and climbed into my lap. I've always been good with cats, so I was happy for the company. Did you know almost all calico cats are girls? And they're super affectionate."

Chloe got started as a YouTuber with a channel featuring her jerky unruly cat, who only got trained to be civilized after someone else inadvertently walked off with him. So her saying she's good with cats might be a bit of an overstatement.

Still, this cat seems perfectly content draped across her lap.

I say, "I could swear that's the same cat I let into this building. But it has to be a different one."

"There are lots of calico cats in Japan," Chloe points out. "If there's a cat mentioned in Japanese folklore, it's usually a calico."

I guess she must have studied up before coming on this trip. And honestly, I'm not super surprised she's here. It's difficult to say no to Chloe, or to stop her once she has an idea in her head. I don't even want to ask where Patsy is.

Chloe looks at me and says, "Dude. What happened to your face."

I tell her, "I dove face first off a seven-story roof and landed on an air mat."

Chloe laughs, but her grin fades as she realizes I'm serious. "You know. It's not that bad. Just a few scratches here. And here." She points at the side of her own eye, and then her chin.

Great. I'm going to have to be at my booth at the festival, and teach a class, looking like I have road rash. It does say something to the state of shock I've been in, and the pain from impacting the mat, that I'm just now starting to feel the sting of these more minor injuries.

Chloe hurries to say, "I have some foundation that can help minimize it. But why on Earth would you jump off a roof?"

"It wasn't exactly my idea," I say. "You didn't see anything, did you? Maybe involving that guy who stole my phone."

Chloe looks grim. "Look. Mrs. Koerber. I'm sorry I acted like I didn't know him. We only met the one time, when I visited California. I snuck into that party, and he handed me a drink, but when he found out I'm a minor, he backed off fast. He even sent an apology gift basket to my house. Which was super hard to explain to my mom."

"Wait," I say. "You know Noel?"

Chloe's expression goes flustered as she realizes she's given us more information than we expected. Then she smiles, shaking it off. "Yeah. Noel Bell. He's a stuntman, worked on a lot of big movies five years ago. He fell out of favor for a while. But he keeps trying to restart his career, probably for the sake of his wife. She's a stunt performer too."

So Noel was married, but he had tried to flirt with a kid? Maybe Chloe had misunderstood his intent, and his apology had been sincere. Or maybe Noel is – or was – a huge jerk.

"But why would a stunt man turn to being a pickpocket? Especially if he's working on a movie."

"He's working on *Kaiju's Day Out*?" Chloe asks, sounding surprised. "When he took your phone, I assumed he'd fallen on hard times and couldn't get work right now."

"We assume he's working on the movie," Logan says, "inferring from some things he said."

Logan moves closer to Chloe to have a look at the cat. He sniffs loudly. "Chloe, why do you smell like almonds?"

"Do you like it?" Chloe asks, as she lifts the cat so Logan can take it. "It's called Marzipan at Midnight, with almonds and musk.

It's merch from one of the Japan Youtubers I'm trying to collab with. She's a baker and all her perfumes smell like cake."

"It's fine," Logan says. "It's just a bit of a weird coincidence is all."

Chloe gives him a questioning look.

I tell Logan, "I'd like to have a look around the rest of the building before the police get here. Noel's body has to be somewhere."

"Body?" Chloe asks uncertainly.

"We're not sure," Logan says. "Either way, it's nothing you need to worry about."

"If anyone asks, I'll say I need to find the other cat," I say, turning to walk back towards the hall. "And hopefully I can talk to whoever might have seen something. Surely someone is in this building, if they just left you in here."

"You have to tell me about the body. Was it in here? While I was?" Chloe's nonchalant façade has cracked and she actually looks upset.

Logan says, "We think it might have been over there."

Chloe gets a determined look on her face. "I caused this problem, I want to help." She must be remembering the documentary, because she takes out her phone and starts filming the set, not only the part where I had found Noel's body, but the table full of props, the cameras and other equipment. There's even a crane mounted to the floor with a giant dinosaur-like head suspended from it. I get the unsettling feeling that it is watching us. Distracted, Chloe says, "I think they forgot about me. I'm pretty sure it was the janitor who locked the door."

I start to ask her why she believes it was the janitor. Maybe someone came by with Noel's body in a trash barrel or something.

But I hear police sirens in the distance, so I head in the direction where the janitor's closet is likely to be, to try and get a peek before the police kick me out.

Logan tells Chloe, "Whatever happened to Noel, it is not your fault. Understand?"

Chloe says, "Okay. Still . . . I should help collect evidence."

That girl. At least she doesn't seem to be traumatized by this situation.

There's a long hallway leading from the set to the front of the building. Using my long sleeve to cover my hand so I don't leave fingerprints everywhere, I open a couple of doors leading into offices. They're mostly bland spaces with desks overflowing with manila folders and computer monitors. I don't see any signs of Noel's body, and the desks aren't solid enough to hide anything behind them. Finally, there's a bigger office with a shelf lined with movie awards and posters hung neatly on two walls. There's a door off that office, which turns out to be a bathroom complete with a shower and a sink set into the top of the toilet, so the drain water can top off the toilet tank. Interesting, but hardly relevant. I turn back into the hall and keep looking. Logan and Chloe join me. He's still holding the cat, who looks half asleep in his arms. I've never seen such a friendly, agreeable feline.

One door on the other side of the hall leads into a lab full of random electronics and half-finished monster prosthetics. We've obviously found the special effects department.

Anything could be hidden in all this mess, but there isn't an obvious disturbance as of someone hiding a body. There isn't time to look more deeply.

Chloe says, "That's all so cool. I'd love the chance to dig around in there." She's holding up her phone, still taking video.

Logan says, "No time. We need to head for the front door, so we can meet the police."

Reluctantly, we turn back into the hall and close the door. I say, "I never did find the janitor's closet. These doors are labeled, but I can't read them."

Chloe does something to her phone, then hands it to me. "Here. Google Lens is part of Google Translate. You point it at something, and it translates the text. It's not perfect, but it is really helpful."

A few doors down, I finally find the janitor's closet.

Chloe takes her phone back, so she can take video as I open the door. There's a mop bucket in here, but no barrel trash can. More importantly, there are no almond scented cleaning supplies. So what was the overwhelming almond scent on the set?

There's a loud knocking sound on the front door. The sound echoes through the building, making me jump. Clearly, I'm still freaked out from the surreal nature of everything that has happened since I went up onto that roof garden. It can't have been more than twenty minutes ago.

Chloe closes the closet door, and we turn to see two Japanese policemen looking in at us through the glass front door. We move into the front lobby, and Logan lets them in.

One asks, "You speak Japanese?"

Logan shakes his head. "You understand English?"

The cop shakes his head. "Sorry. Sorry." He takes out his phone and talks into it in rapid Japanese. He holds up the phone, which says, "Who of you reported a murder?"

He holds the phone out. Logan speaks into it. "I did. But the body seems to have disappeared."

The phone translates, then the cop blinks at Logan, like he assumes the phone mistranslated.

Logan holds up a finger in a gesture to wait. He calls Hudson, who agrees to be our translator. Logan quickly summarizes the situation, and Hudson conveys the key points over speakerphone.

The cops have a lot of questions about Noel, and why we think he's dead. They keep coming back to the fact that I'm the only one who saw the body, and that neither Logan nor Chloe saw the same thing even though they had been in the same space. And they can't seem to wrap their brains around how I knew Noel.

"I made a police report about my stolen phone at the airport. This was the same guy." I look over at my fiancé. "You saw him, right, Logan? Up on the roof?"

Logan looks a bit sheepish. "I never saw the pickpocket from the front. The guy Fee chased could have been the same guy. But I couldn't verify that or pick him out of a lineup."

I know Logan has to tell the truth here, but it still stings that he can't be more supportive.

As Hudson explains all of this, the younger of the two cops sucks in a breath, and they start talking to each other. They seem to be disagreeing about something. But after a few more exchanges, they both nod, and the older one says something into the phone.

Hudson translates back, "Mrs. Koerber, he says if you're the lady who got pulled off the building, you're going to have to come to the station for questioning. And the other guy seems to think you might have been trying to push someone off the roof. He says you're the one everyone's been looking for."

Logan and I exchange a concerned look. The cat Logan's still holding lets out a soft meow.

Logan tells me, "I'll make some calls." By which he means he's not going to let me wind up in jail. Then he tells Hudson, "Tell them we need to get Fee checked out by a doctor."

I groan. It's going to be a long day. I'm probably not going to make it back to the chocolate festival before it closes. I tell Logan, "Somebody needs to let Ash know he's going to be manning the booth longer than he thought."

Through Hudson, the police communicate that they would like us to wait outside the building while they search it. We agree to wait on the bench near the outdoor movie set.

Hudson says, "The police here are nothing if not thorough. The conviction rate is high, because they don't make an arrest unless they are reasonably sure they will be able to win the case in court. If there's something to be found in there, they will find it."

Chapter Five
Monday

Before long, a group of people enter through the gate, laughing and bantering in multiple languages. There's over a dozen people, mostly Japanese, though two in the middle of the group look Latino. The British stunt woman we'd talked to earlier is at the edge of the group. She notices me and waves.

There are two Japanese guys next to her, speaking to her in English. One is tall and exceptionally good-looking. He has thick hair and equally thick eyebrows that give him an imposing look. The other guy has thinning salt and pepper hair and hesitant watery eyes. His round face has a good-natured smile, though, and I find myself smiling back.

"Who are you?" The guy with the eyebrows asks, obviously surprised that we're inside his gate. But his eyes are on the cat Logan has.

My guess is he's the movie director, or whoever owns the studio. How are we supposed to explain everything?

Logan, still cradling the cat in one arm, points at Chloe. "We're with her."

Right. Chloe may have snuck out of the hotel, but she is actually supposed to be here.

Eyebrows guy still looks confused. If he's the director, he never did get to meet Chloe.

Connie the stuntwoman breaks in a broad smile. "So you're the chocolate maker's niece." She turns to eyebrows guy. "This is the YouTuber I was telling you about, Director Kudo. She is a huge fan of cats."

"Speaking of cats," Kudo says. He holds his hands out for the calico. "I see you found Honda. She got out and has been missing for days. I don't know how to thank you."

He's probably not going to thank us once he realizes we're the reason the police are searching his building. Before that happens, I try to solidify his good will. I ask, "How can you tell one calico cat from another? I mean, how do you know that this is Honda? Her easygoing personality?"

Director Kudo takes the cat and settles her in his arms. He turns so I can see the back of the calico's head. "Calicos have distinctive spots to their fur. See the little brown heart behind her ear? I say that's how I know she was always meant to be a sweetheart."

"It is true," Watery Eyes says. "He talks about his cat always."

"Not always, Taniguchi San," Kudo says. "Sometimes I talk about movies."

I try to remember the markings on the cat I had let into the building. Did it have a heart behind her ear? Honestly. I had been too scared and hyped up to look that closely.

The others in the group are giving us curious looks, and one woman comes over to pet the cat. She coos at it and says, "Hisasshiburi, Honda Chan." *Long time no see.* Chan used this way is an affectionate addition to the cat's name.

The door to the building opens and the two cops come outside. They look visibly relieved to see Japanese speakers standing with us. Gesturing at Logan, but speaking to Kudo, the older cop says something, and then makes that crossed hands *no* gesture.

Looking very confused, Director Kudo says, "Officer Fukuhara wants me to tell you they found no signs of a dead body in the building. Or any crime."

Logan says, "About that. It's a long story."

I start to explain about being up on the roof at the mall, and how Noel had dragged me over the edge with him, onto the air mat. And how Noel had known the mat would be there – which led me to following him into the building.

Connie nods along as I speak. "That's right. We have the permits for the shoot tomorrow morning. The character I double for is fighting the bad guy for the serum that will shrink the kaiju, and he goes off the roof. It's the climax of the film."

"I think you're going to need a new stunt man for the project," I say, trying – and failing – to come up with a delicate way to segue into my bad news. "When I found him inside the building, Noel was dead."

"That's preposterous," Kudo says.

Taniguchi sucks in a startled breath. "You saw this yourself?"

I nod gravely. "I tried to resuscitate him, but he was gone. And then his body disappeared."

Connie lets out a soft sound of distress. She faints, collapsing towards the stone path leading towards the set. Director Kudo catches her before she hits. The calico lets out a meow of protest at having been plopped unceremoniously on the ground.

At first, I'm not sure why she's taking the death of a co-worker this hard. After all, she's trained to leap from burning buildings and crash cars without losing her nerve. And yet this news caused her to faint.

But then I remember what Chloe said. I turn to her, and she gives me a subtle nod. She says softly, "Connie is Noel's wife."

Sympathy courses through me, prickling at my nerves. I hadn't fainted when I'd learned about Kevin's accident – but I hadn't been particularly functional either.

I'm frozen, hit with a wave of emotion I'd thought I'd gotten past. Grief, raw and simple, like I'd lost Kevin yesterday. It's been a long time since I'd been hit with something like that. I take a few deep breaths, trying to keep my composure.

In that moment, I look down at Connie, still in Kudo's arms. He smooths back a lock of her hair and his hand touches her cheek in a way that feels loving. His expression is tender in a way that doesn't seem completely appropriate for a film director to his employee. Is something going on here? Something that could have led to murder? Because even though I couldn't tell you how Noel had died, I am very certain it wasn't natural causes. You don't hide the body and make the evidence disappear when it is natural causes.

I sigh. Like it or not, I'm getting caught up in the case. And I'm looking at my two main suspects.

Especially because the police, not having found a body, aren't entirely convinced there's been a murder. Plus, they're asking questions of the other people standing in the group, so clearly, they missed the moment I'd just witnessed. I wish I knew what the police are asking, because it would be helpful to know who was where and when. I keep hearing *lunchi*, which sounds like a Japanese pronunciation for lunch, and *ramen*. So clearly, they've all taken a lunch break. But what else happened?

I notice Chloe subtly videoing the group. She can probably throw some translated subtitles on it later, and then we can figure out what was being said.

The phone in my pocket buzzes, and by habit I take it out and peer at the screen. Right. I have a phone that isn't mine. That's going to be awkward to explain to the police if they ask to see my phone once we get to the station. I'm trying to decide if I should ditch it or turn it over right now. A notification flashes up on the screen.

You're in danger if . . .

Okay. Is that a threat? Or a warning? Whoever this phone belongs to clearly needs to know. For a second I think it might be Noel's phone. But his wallpaper isn't likely to be a picture of two Asian kids.

I unlock the phone, using the same code I used before, and read the rest of the text. *You're in danger if you don't hand over the file tonight. I've arranged a meeting at a bar in Shibuya. It's quiet and discreet. Say you're meeting Nichijo.*

I feel my eyes go wide in alarm. Whoever sent this text doesn't know that this phone has been stolen. It hasn't been deactivated, so presumably the victim of the theft hasn't gotten a new device. Which means that person has no way of knowing they are in danger.

But whose phone is it? There are several social media apps. I pop open the Instagram – since I am partial to it – and flip to the profile page. I blink in surprise, because there, smiling out at me, is Emi.

I flip back to the text. The person desperate to meet with her is in the phone as Wataru T. This is the only text from him in the phone.

I flip back over to her Instagram. The last pic she posted is her outside the airport, being all chatty about how she just landed in Japan and desperately needs a latte. I can only imagine her typing up the post, less aware of her surroundings than she should have been, getting her phone taken out of her hands just as she hit post. Or perhaps Noel, polite thief that he was, posted it for her.

We need to find Emi and let her know she's in danger. But how are we supposed to do that, since we have her phone?

I slip the phone into Logan's hand since, even if I do get detained by the police, he's the one who's most likely to be able to figure out where she went.

The gate creaks and Arlo steps through it. It looks like he was able to find me without a phone. I guess anything is possible.

But it turns out, Arlo isn't looking for me. He's here for Chloe. I can tell by the steely eye contact he makes with her, and the way she breaks the eye contact to look down at her lap. What exactly did Chloe do to Patsy that Arlo is here instead of her?

He gives a nod to the cops as he walks over to her, slowing down from his brisk pace as he takes in the scene. The two officers are still questioning the group who work in the building. They seem to be having some trouble communicating with the two Spanish speakers. Arlo may be Cuban, but he only speaks about a dozen words in Spanish. Still, it's pretty obvious what's going on.

He looks at me and says, "It's happened again, hasn't it?"

"Unfortunately," I say. My voice sounds a lot steadier than I feel.

"And this time I don't even rate a phone call?" Arlo honestly sounds hurt. He's actually played a role in investigating the other cases I've gotten involved with, so I can see how he'd feel slighted.

"Sorry," I say. "No phone. And I was a bit distracted from falling off a roof."

"That was you?" Arlo's eyes go wide in concern. "You're all over the news."

Great. That's bound to get back to people in the States. I tell Logan, "You better text Carmen. As soon as the news outlets release my identity, she needs to be prepared for the next wave of true crime aficionados descending on the shop."

Logan says, "Don't you think that is a bit premature? We can't even prove there's been a murder yet. The news won't be reporting on anything other than a bizarre stunt."

Connie accepts Kudo's offered hand as she stands back up. She says, "Well, I'd like to report Noel as a missing person." She takes her phone from her pocket and tries to make a call. "Right. He's not answering his phone, and he disappeared under mysterious circumstances to say the least."

Logan says, "A person has to be missing for a while before it can be reported. When was the last time you saw him?"

"Yesterday," Connie says. "We'd had a row, and he said he'd just stay at one of them capsule hotels. So he's been gone almost a full day."

Logan says, "Felicity saw him on the roof within the last couple of hours. And if it made the news, there must be other people who saw it too."

"About half a million of them," Chloe reports. "Some tourist was taking video from the street." She flips her phone around so I can see the clip. I look like a doll, falling through air, my arms flapping awkwardly as though I believe I can fly.

While Arlo, Connie and I are watching the clip, Logan finally looks at the phone I've handed him. He makes a startled noise, then walks away to make a phone call using his own phone.

The clip ends with me struggling to make my way off the mat and heading for the crosswalk. My hair is disheveled and my blouse came untucked somewhere along the way. You can't even see my face.

I groan. "I look like a crazy person there."

"I wouldn't say that," Arlo says. "Determined maybe. Angry, possibly. But not crazy."

Connie says, "You look really good for a first-time. I can give you some pointers if you'd like."

I start to tell her no, but then I realize it would be a great excuse to talk to her and find out more about Noel. Instead, I say, "I'd love to get your phone number – only my phone got stolen." I study her response, trying to find out if she knows Noel was a thief. Maybe she'll flinch.

But she overtly says, "It wasn't Noel, was it?" She drops her voice and cuts a glance over at the cops. "That's what we'd had the row about. We've had some money troubles lately, and Kudo has hit a delay in paying us. Noel always used to nick things when we needed to make ends meet, and he found out there's a black market in Japan for foreign phones. Apparently, with Japanese phones, you can't take a picture without it making a camera shutter noise. It's supposed to stop unwanted photos of girls on public transportation. But I digress."

"So you wanted Noel to stop stealing phones?" Arlo asks. I can tell he's still trying to catch up in the conversation but has probably figured out that Noel is the murder victim.

"Well, yeah." Connie studies Arlo for a moment. "Excuse me, but who did you say you are?"

"Arlo Romero," Arlo introduces himself and holds a hand out to shake. "I'm a police detective from Texas, in town with these three."

Connie shakes his hand. "Good to know. But since you're way out of your jurisdiction, I'll tell you. Just don't tell those blokes over there."

"I won't," Arlo says. "I promise."

"I didn't think phone snatching was worth it. Too visible, and too much chance of getting caught. If Noel has one more scandal, his career is down the tubes. If we couldn't get the money we need to keep the house legally, I thought we should pull a heist. One and done."

"Bell San!" Kudo says in a scandalized tone.

Connie shrugs and gives him an apologetic look. That potential scandal, and keeping her current stunt gig, are probably low on her priority list right now.

"And that fight is why he decided to stay at a hotel?" Arlo asks, the cop in him really showing, his jurisdiction or not. It wouldn't be the first time we'd investigated where he wasn't officially on the case. His body language is stiffer and more formal, his expression intimidating.

Connie gives him a wistful smile. "It was part of it. We've had other problems for a long time now. You won't have to look very deep to find out Noel is – or was – a bit of a flirt. He's also an adrenaline junky. The more stress there is in our relationship, the more likely he is to go bungee jumping or rock climbing. I'd accused him of paying a little too much attention to one of the actresses a day or two ago. I shouldn't have been so harsh. It's not like he ever goes past flirting. And she was only playing a bit part."

Suddenly, she looks like she might cry.

Arlo asks, "Do you know the name of this actress?"

Connie waves a hand in Chloe's direction – but she can't mean Chloe, since we weren't even in the country yesterday. Connie says,

"It was one of them YouTubers. I don't know her name, but she makes cakes and throws glitter."

"Annabelle Clarendale," Chloe says. "The one who makes the perfumes."

"That's the one," Connie says. "She had the audacity to feed my husband cake cubes."

"To be fair," Chloe replies, "he probably didn't try to stop her. And he knows he's really hot."

"He said I was overreacting," Connie says. She points a finger at Arlo. "Don't you ever tell a woman she's overreacting."

Arlo grins, but she gives him a sharp look, so he forces his face into a somber expression. "I'll try to remember that."

Connie says, "I threw a shoe at him, and he told me to calm down." She points at Arlo.

Before she can chide him, he says, "I'll remember not to tell my girlfriend that either." He turns to Chloe, and says, "Speaking of which."

Chloe says, "I only left Patsy at that tea shop because I thought I would look like a kid if I showed up at the movie studio with an adult in tow."

"You are a kid," I point out. "Besides, I thought you were napping."

"I'm very persuasive," Chloe says. "And the tea shop had a boring tea museum. But Patsy was loving it."

Arlo says, "I'm sure she was until you took off with her wallet. She's too embarrassed to leave without paying. Which I'm sure was your intent."

Chloe says, "I didn't mean to leave her there so long. I'll apologize to her when we get back."

"She's still at the tea shop, you know." Arlo gestures wildly in the direction of the supposed shop. "She was more worried about you than herself and told me to find you before coming to pay her bill."

"Sorry," Chloe says. She is now the most subdued I've ever seen her. "I'll pay for it when we get there."

Connie says, "I knew I liked this kid."

Kudo says, "I am beginning to wonder if having YouTubers do cameos in my movie is worth the happiness the audience will get out of it."

"It will be," Arlo assures him. "Chloe isn't a bad kid. She's just too excited about being in a new country.

Logan pulls me off to the side and hands me Emi's phone. He drops his voice soft to say, "Do you realize what this means?"

I nod. "We have to find her. But she's gone to the countryside. Do you know where that refers to?"

Logan sighs. "When I was protecting her, she mentioned that her grandparents live in Japan, but she didn't say where. Aside from Tokyo and Kyoto, most of this country could be considered countryside."

I say, "But here's the big question. Why hasn't she deactivated this phone?"

The cops turn back to us and apologize profusely to Kudo for having entered his building without his permission. Then they turn back to me. I guess it is time to head for the station.

Logan restates that I still need medical care. Taniguchi relays this to the cops, who agree to take us to the hospital and question me there, as long as we can arrange a translator. Logan works it out with Hudson. Arlo and Chloe head off to rescue Patsy from embarrassment – and from being alone in a country where she doesn't speak the language. The movie crew start to head back into the building to get on with their workday.

Connie gives Logan my number so he can pass it along to me when I get a phone. She promises that if Chloe comes back tomorrow, she will manage to get her a part as an extra in the movie.

I tell Logan, "I really need to thank whoever talked me into getting travel insurance for this trip."

"It was me," Logan says, sounding pleased with himself as we get into the back seat of the Japanese police car. It's a sedan, and the seat is rather comfortable. I let myself sink into it.

As I'm buckling my seatbelt, a call comes in on Emi's phone, from someone named Ricky. But the officers are getting into the car too, so I send the call to voicemail. It doesn't look like the caller leaves a message.

This is the first time I've gotten to sit down since our taxi ride to the chocolate festival, and I'm beyond jet lagged. I start to fall asleep in the back of the car, but Logan jostles me awake. "No sleeping until the docs check you out, Fee."

I grumble, but there's no stopping a worried Logan.

Chapter Six
Monday

When Hudson meets us at the hospital, he sucks air through his teeth looking at the scratches on my face. "Careful, Mrs. Koerber, or you're going to wind up looking like me." His hand goes to his scars.

I say, "I'm glad you are in a good enough place that you can joke about that."

Hudson hands me an unlocked cell phone. He says, "It's hard to buy a phone in Japan, but one of my friends had an old one. I loaded a temporary digital SIM card in there that's good for two weeks."

Logan asks, "How can we pay you for the SIM card?"

Hudson waves a dismissive hand. "After the day you two have had? It's the least I can do."

The sense of relief I feel just having a phone in my hands is overwhelming. It may not have all my data, but I can access the apps that will help me get around. And I can at least try to contact Emi.

We're in a screened off area, where I'm sitting on a hospital bed, waiting for a doctor to come back with the results of my tests. My wounds sting where the nurse disinfected the scratches on my face and arms. The two officers are sitting in uncomfortable looking chairs at the side of the bed.

They start talking to Hudson. Meanwhile, I start following Emi's social media accounts and DM-ing her on all of them, in case she checks them on a computer. I try not to think about how ominous it is that she hasn't deactivated the phone. Could she be in too much trouble to do so? I hope not. Surely there is a logical explanation that doesn't involve her having been abducted – or worse.

And now I find there's a lot I've missed with my own social media, including a couple of legit questions about my chocolate. I've answered one of them when Hudson finishes talking to the cops and turns towards me.

I tell him, "You're a lifesaver."

He cracks a grin. "I wouldn't go that far. I'm not even sure if I can keep you out of jail."

He then proceeds to translate my statement in real time to the cops. But as Hudson explains and re-explains to Officer Fukuhara that the only way I know Noel is because he stole my phone, and that I'm the only one who believes he is dead, I can start to see them deciding that maybe this is more than the paperwork is worth. They let me off with a stern warning, after collecting my passport information, the name of the hotel where we are staying, and contact information for all three of us. It seems to help that Hudson has a local address and phone number. Maybe it makes us less of a flight risk.

The doctor who sees me confirms that I am more or less okay. He cleans the scratches and prescribes painkillers, since he predicts I will be too sore to move tomorrow. He's wrong, of course. The chocolate festival is too important for me to just sit another day out, no matter how much my body protests. And, more urgently, we have to find Emi.

Hudson still has the van, so he offers to drive us back to the chocolate festival.

I look at the clock on the phone and realize we actually do have time to get back before it closes. Not long before it closes, but still, I'd like to check in on Ash and make sure everything is stocked and ready for tomorrow.

There's a game on the radio, so Hudson and Logan start talking about baseball. I find myself tuning it out. When I fall asleep in the van, Logan lets me sleep.

It feels like seconds later when he gently shakes my shoulder. "We're here."

I force my eyes open, force my hand to unbuckle my seatbelt. I can do this. And then in a few hours, I can pass out at the hotel.

Hudson comes inside with us. When we get up the escalators and across the festival floor to our booth, both Ash and Imogen are sitting behind it. Imogen has her head against Ash's shoulder, and she is fast asleep. The crowd has died down, so I'm guessing we're not getting many more customers.

"Thanks," I whisper to Ash. "How'd it go?"

He whispers back, "There were a lot of people disappointed that they didn't get to meet you. But we sold a lot of chocolate."

A lot of people is probably relative. But the booth does look even more crowded with books and trinkets. I find an empty box and start putting the trinkets in it.

Dawn and Fisher come up the aisle towards the booth.

Dawn is easily in the lead. Loudly she says, "Oh, thank goodness Felicity, you're finally back."

Imogen jolts awake. "No more taffeta," she says, as though coming out of a dream. I can only imagine. She is after all a first-time-bride-to-be, and if her mother is anything like she is, there's bound to be conflict.

I laugh. Then I ask Dawn, "Is everything okay?"

"Not exactly," Dawn says. "There's a woman here who is not happy with you. Fisher and I were working at your booth when she came by. Holy buckets was she loud."

Before she can say much else, a petite American woman approaches the booth from the opposite direction. Her wavy brown hair is layered around her heart-shaped face, and she is wearing a polka dotted pink apron. She should look sweet – but her heavily lined eyes are fierce.

Fisher takes a few steps back, practically hiding behind Dawn. Dawn crosses her arms across her chest, nonplussed. Since Dawn is a police detective, she's probably seen much worse than what this tiny person has to offer.

An official from the festival is trailing the woman. He's a middle-aged Japanese guy holding a tablet. He doesn't look at all happy to be here.

The woman looks back at the official and says, "There she is. This is the woman I want disqualified."

Disqualified from what? She has to be talking about the awards competition associated with the festival. I try to react calmly, but all that comes out of my mouth is, "Why?"

She holds up one of my chocolate bars. The logo is a silhouette of Knightley. It is only fitting that the bunny who helped me through some of my toughest days should be the symbol of my new business venture. Which makes the way she shakes the bar in my face extra distasteful. She says, "This bar tastes exactly like a chocolate produced by a specific premium brand that sells to bakeries and hotels. I don't think you're making your own chocolate. I think you're purchasing commercial chocolate, melting it down and re-tempering it. It's a scandal that has happened in our industry before. But I never thought someone would think they could get away with submitting it for an award."

"That's preposterous," I splutter. I'm trying to keep my calm, but my heart starts hammering in my chest at the word *scandal*. "Everyone at Greetings and Felicitations works hard to produce the finest bean to bar chocolate our skill and resources allow. It's flattering that you find it of such high quality, but these are single origin bars with beans I've selected myself."

"With a bit of help from me," Logan says. "I'm learning Felicity's process, and we have a part of our micro factory with a glassed-in area where I conduct chocolate making demos."

"Hocky pucky," the woman says.

I take a deep breath. This feels a lot like when I'd first opened my chocolate shop and a fellow business owner had stormed in accusing me of poaching employees. I could have handled that situation better through a little empathy. In fact, that business owner and I are friends now. Maybe I can use what I've learned from that experience about being a more empathetic person and better friend here to see the other perspective here and try to avoid a fight. This woman is simply mistaken. I say, "I'd be happy to offer you tasting samples of my different bars so you can see how the different flavors stand out."

She turns to the festival official. "See? I told you she'd try to weasel out of this."

"Sumimasen," the official says. *Excuse me. I'm sorry.* It's unclear who he is apologizing to or what exactly he plans to do about the situation.

I nod acknowledgement, then I turn back to the woman. I'm still upset, and my voice sounds wooden as I try to keep it neutral. "I'm sorry if someone at Greetings and Felicitations has done something to upset you, but these are baseless accusations."

The woman crosses her arms over her chest, mirroring Dawn's posture. She snaps, "You know what you did."

But I've never met this woman before. So, obviously, no, I don't.

"I'm sorry, but I think-"

She snaps, "Stop acting sorry. It's far too late for that." She turns to the official and says, "You know what? I also want to petition that Felicity Koerber be removed from the festival altogether. She was on the news taking a swan dive off the roof. I find her irresponsible, and I'm afraid to be around her."

I say, "I didn't think they had released my name on the news."

The woman hesitates. She must have seen what happened herself. Which means that she knows I didn't jump off the roof on purpose. But then she grins and points at me again, telling the official, "See? She just admitted it."

"Sumimasen," the official says again. "We will look into it." He bows slightly – barely more than a nod – then turns and walks away. The woman follows, still trying to get his attention.

"What was that about?" Dawn asks.

"I have no idea. Everyone I've met in the craft chocolate industry has been kind and helpful. I got a lot of good advice when I was trying to decide on equipment, or figuring out why certain chocolate techniques were not working. Okay, there's a few folks who have been more lukewarm about someone new opening a chocolate shop, but they were at least polite. I've never seen anyone be downright hostile before."

"Whatever her motive is for getting hysterical at you," Dawn says, "I plan to find out."

Fisher takes Dawn's hand and says, "You can take the detective out of her jurisdiction, but you can't take the need to detect out of the girl."

Dawn says, "Fish, honey, you're going to help me."

Fisher asks, "So I'm not going to the medicinal botanical garden tomorrow?"

"Maybe after," Dawn says.

"Okay." Fisher says, "But I get to pick where we go for lunch."

Logan's phone buzzes with a text. He takes out his phone and frowns.

"What is it, babe?" I ask. I've been trying out this pet name for him, and he seems okay with it.

He says, "I had a friend of a friend of a friend look into traffic cams and CCTV. Emi rented a car, but there's no record of that car leaving Tokyo. I think she's still here."

I say, "I don't think we're going to find her before her meeting tonight. Do you think I ought to go in her place?"

"No," Logan says. He tilts his head, considering. "It would be obvious that you aren't Emi, even to someone who has only seen a photograph. But I think I should go, see if I can make contact with whoever she is supposed to be meeting. If I can't explain the situation, maybe I can at least get the meet rescheduled, so we have more time to look for her."

I take out Emi's phone and pull up the Instagram page again. She looks so happy in that last post. What could she be hiding behind that smile? Is Logan putting himself in real danger by trying to protect her again? I get why he feels the need to. He's generally protective of everyone, and Emi was his past client. But there's a big difference between giving someone a phone back and warning them of potential danger and trying to intercede with potential bad guys.

I regret bringing it up. Although Logan probably would have made the same plan anyway.

All I want right now is to sleep, but will I be able to do that until he returns safely to the hotel? I doubt it.

But being anxious for Logan's safety isn't going to get me anywhere. I should at least try to work on putting clues together about the murder. Now that I have a phone, I reach out to Nao. She knew Noel's name. There's a connection there we need to explore. But I don't want to be that blunt about it. I get the card from Logan and then text Nao. *Hey! This is Felicity. I'm on a temp phone. Can we meet up?* And then, when I don't get an immediate response, I add, *Did you see what happened to Noel's jacket?*

After a few minutes, there's still no response. Nao had been nice when she'd met me as the subject of a true crime podcast, and a fellow lover of detective fiction. Who knows if she will even talk to me now.

My stomach grumbles. The whole group who traveled with me plan to meet up for dinner at a curry restaurant near the hotel, and that seems to be the signal for us to head over there. Hudson made us a reservation in advance, since we are such a large party. I've never eaten Japanese style curry before, but the moment Logan opens the door and we all step inside, the delicious smell lets me know we're in for a treat. I order my curry with a fried chicken cutlet, which comes out sliced into crispy-edged pieces that are easy to pick up with chopsticks, though the curry and rice are typically eaten with a spoon. I spoon up a big chunk of carrot out of the gravy. It's pleasantly spicy, but sweeter than other curry-style dishes I've had before.

Most of us are obviously tired, with the exception of Dawn and Fisher who had the good sense to get a nap in before going to the chocolate festival. Chloe seems particularly subdued. I'm guessing she realizes how much she hurt Patsy's feelings by ditching her.

I watch another couple make their way into the restaurant, hand in hand. He's a short muscular white guy with graying hair and a polo shirt, she's a slightly plump Japanese woman wearing a matching polo shirt, with no makeup and long hair gone completely gray. They somehow look made for each other. The two start to follow the waitress over to a small table, but the guy spots my group and waves. I've never seen him before, but Arlo waves back.

Arlo stands up and the guy walks over to us. The two men hug, then Arlo sits back down.

"Rob, man, what are you doing here?" Arlo says.

Rob says, "I'm working as a special consultant with the Tokyo Metro Police."

"How do you two know each other?" Patsy asks, looking from Arlo to Rob and back again. She looks politely interested in a past acquaintance of her boyfriend.

Arlo says, "Back in New Mexico Rob was one of the toughest instructors my police academy ever had."

Logan says, "It's unusual for a foreigner to work with the police in Japan."

"That it is," Rob acknowledges. But he doesn't clarify how he has ended up in such a position.

Logan doesn't push.

Dawn says, "Does that mean you can score us a tour of the local station? I'm a police detective myself, in Minnesota."

"More likely I can get you a tour of the morgue," Rob says. Which further clouds up things. What exactly is he *doing* for the police?

Dawn scrunches up her nose. "Yeah, no. I can see more than enough of that at home, don't ya know."

Usually, I don't really think about that side of police work. It has to take a toll. But somehow, the three cops at the table are some of the most determinedly upbeat people I know.

"Suit yourself," Rob says. He turns back to Arlo. "When we're all done eating our respective dinners, want to go get a few drinks and catch up? We live close, so my wife won't mind."

Arlo looks over at Patsy, who says, "Fine with me. I have someone to keep an eye on tonight."

Chloe rolls her eyes. "I'm not going anywhere. I promised, didn't I?"

Patsy gives her a skeptical look.

I'm glad I'm not the only one chaperoning this headstrong teenager. It was my idea to bring Chloe. Okay, honestly, it was Chloe's idea. But I agreed. So after this, I owe Patsy.

Our check comes, and once he's paid for me and himself, Logan stands up and stretches. He says, "I need to head out."

"Wait," I say, unable to let him walk out that door and into danger alone. "Let me go with you."

"Fee," he says, and I can tell he's going to say something about not putting me in unnecessary danger.

"I'll wait in the cab," I say. I gesture with my new phone. "I have plenty of things I need to load on here. I won't get bored."

"Okay," he says. And some of the tension goes out of his jaw. Maybe he didn't really want to go alone, either.

We wave at the others and give head nods to the staff and then head out the door – only to find Dawn and Fisher right behind us.

Dawn says, "It would be irresponsible to go into this situation without backup. You should know that better than most."

Logan flinches at this oblique reference to his past mistake. He protests, "Look. There's no way this many people are all going to fit in a cab."

Fisher takes out a set of keys from his hoodie and jangles them in his hand. "Then it's a good thing I rented a car."

Dawn says, "Four people aren't that many in a cab anyway. As long as you don't mind scrunching."

I ask Fisher, "Do you have a license to drive in Japan?"

Fisher says, "I got it when I was doing some work over here designing landscaping for a big shopping complex. When I had time off, I wanted to see gardens and landscapes away from the city, and that's hard to do without a car."

I say, "You didn't mention anything about that the whole time we were planning this trip."

Fisher gestures around us. "There's so much here to see. I wanted to take the trip you planned."

"Still." I feel a bit left miffed he hadn't told me he'd been here before.

Fisher says, "I've never seen Shinjuku before. It's been a lot of fun."

Dawn puts a hand on his arm. "Aside from Felicity falling off a roof."

Fisher pats her hand. "Of course. Aside from that. But we slept through that, and when we heard about it, she was okay."

"True," Dawn says. "Nothing good ever comes from getting up early."

Logan asks Fisher, "Have you ever been to Shibuya?"

He takes out Emi's phone and shows Fisher the location map for the bar.

Fisher bounces his keys again. "The main problem in that area is going to be finding parking. We should go now."

It's a long walk to the garage where Fisher left his rental car, and a twenty-minute drive to get to Shibuya, during the course of which Dawn uses the mics and earpieces Hudson gave us to rig up two-way communication between Fisher's phone, since he and I will be staying in the car, and Dawn and Logan, who will be going into the bar.

Dawn says, "Should we call Hudson and ask if this bar we're heading to is in a decent part of town?"

"Ha ha," Logan says. "I doubt there would be a clandestine meet in a scam bar or a red-light joint."

"You never know," Dawn says.

As Fisher predicted, there isn't easy parking near the building. It's in a shopping district that's a mix of swanky stores and touristy restaurants. After circling the block, Fisher finally just lets Dawn and Logan out at the front door. As Fisher prepares to get back into traffic, I watch Logan and his sister climb the outside staircase to a second floor of shops.

Through his mic, Logan asks, "Can you still hear me?"

Fisher says, "Loud and clear." He pulls away, heading for a parking garage he's seen on his map.

We hear the two go into the bar, and Logan mutters, "This place is worse than seedy – it's trendy."

Dawn whispers, "I kid you not, there's a photo frame to hold up so that when you Instagram, it has a QR code in it."

Fisher laughs. He tells me, "Dawn would rather eat anchovies than make an Instagram page."

Which tells me two things I didn't already know about Dawn.

Over the makeshift coms, we hear Logan and Dawn approach someone, and Dawn says, "I need to deliver a message to Nichijo."

Fisher snorts a laugh.

"What?" I ask.

"Nichijo isn't a name. It means everyday life, or something common or ordinary."

But a masculine voice with an Australian accent says, "Nichijo hasn't arrived yet. I can write down the message."

"We'll wait," Logan says.

"It could be a long time. Perhaps you would order a drink at the bar."

It doesn't sound like a friendly suggestion.

I'm hoping that they will just leave, but the next thing I hear is footsteps, followed by Logan and Dawn ordering drinks. I knew Logan was a beer guy, but who knew Dawn went for whiskey shots, neat?

Fisher mutes our end of the connection. He says, "Dawn and I love going to alcohol tastings. She's been excited to try out Japanese whiskey since we decided to come on this trip. And here she is, getting started without me."

"Sorry about that," I say, stifling a yawn.

We sit in silence for a few minutes, then Fisher asks, "Do you worry about Logan when he flies?"

Logan takes a lot of flights between Houston and Galveston, and sometimes does longer runs. I think about him when he's in the air. But do I worry? I tell Fisher, "I guess I do, a little. But no more than if he was traveling on a road trip. He's a safe pilot, and I trust he will make good decisions."

Fisher says, "Yeah," like he totally gets it. After a while, he says, "I worry about Dawn every day when she's at work. It comes with the territory. I'm worried about her now, but it's about the same."

"What are you trying to say?" I ask, leaning forward in the back seat to try and see his face.

Fisher says, "It's not your fault – or Logan's – that we're sitting here. But I know you. You're going to think it is because you're here that these things are happening. But people like Logan and Dawn – they'll find some way to fight against the darkness, no matter what. Even if it puts them in danger. You're no different. If Dawn hadn't gone with Logan, you'd have talked your way into going in there with him."

I admit, "Sitting here, waiting and not knowing what's going on is driving me crazy."

Fisher says, "You need a hobby that doesn't involve your work, and doesn't involve crime. Take me. I play racquetball, and I get a lot of frustrations out that way. Or when I have a problem I can't solve, I knit. There's something about moving my hands that often gets my mind unstuck."

"What do you knit?" I ask, trying to imagine Fisher shoving a wad of yarn and needles into his desk when a client walks in at work.

"That sweater Dawn was wearing on the plane, for one."

"Impressive," I say. I would never have guessed that particular sweater was home-made. "I would never have the patience to do anything that intricate. But I have a friend who has a yarn shop. And one of my employees knits, with his mom. You should check out the yarn circle next time you are in town." I yawn again. "I like to read. Mainly ebooks, these days. They just feel safer. Speaking of which, I should get started on the book Nao gave me. But I need to find a copy in English." It only takes a few minutes to order an English copy of *The Honjin Murders* to read on my phone.

From the front seat, Fisher asks, "Do you like chess?"

That seems like such a random question. "I've never been particularly good at it. My mom likes to play. She says it promotes logic. But I think I'm better at thinking outside the box." I can see that Fisher has a chess app open on his tablet. I realize he was asking me to play. "But if you want, I'll give it a go. I guarantee you I'll lose."

"It's okay," Fisher says. "I can just play the computer."

I suppose we each need something to do to break the monotony of listening to Logan and Dawn making meaningless conversation with the bar noise in the background.

I might as well get started reading the ebook. I scroll past the cover image – a sword hilt sticking up out of a white circle – and the first page is a list of characters, most of which belong to one of two families. After that the narrator starts talking about old houses and locked room murders. I'd actually solved one of those, not so long ago. It had involved an inventive use of technology. In the book, the narrator starts listing off other locked room mysteries and debating which is the closest to the case at hand.

Two car doors bang, one after another, jolting me from sleep. There are the dusty remnants of a dream, where I was standing on a mountain, looking down at men – or maybe chess pieces?

Logan relaxes back into the seat next to me and rolls his neck. Dawn is giving Fisher a quick kiss in the front.

I put a hand on Logan's arm and ask, "How'd it go?" I'm embarrassed that I fell asleep when I should have been listening.

He takes his other hand and cups my face. "I wish I could have had a nap, too. It would have been just as productive. I think we spooked the contact. Nichijo never showed up. We gave it two hours past the meet time, then I gave the bar guy a message to pass on. I told him we have the phone and that Emi didn't miss the meet on purpose. Only, I didn't use her name."

"Of course," I say. "It was the best you could do, given the circumstances."

Logan says, "I just feel so powerless. Emi's in danger, and not only can I not protect her – I can't even find her. Being in this country has put me out of my element. I don't have many resources for information here. So short of just randomly calling hotels, I'm not sure what else to do."

That look of frozen dejection is not the Logan I know. He's always got an idea, or a plan, or a resource. Not having any of that must be his worst nightmare. He's already had to give up his gun, and face almost losing me. I turn his face down towards mine and lean my forehead against his. "I guess we just have to wait. And sometimes that's harder than rushing into danger."

From the front seat, Dawn says, "I felt in danger tonight. There was someone watching us the whole time we were in that bar."

"Don't scare Felicity, Hon," Fisher says. But it sounds like he is the one who has caught Dawn's anxiety.

I pick up my new phone. I tell Logan, "I can't believe I was asleep for two whole hours."

I notice that I have a missed message from Nao. I click on it, and she's surprisingly chatty, agreeing to let us meet at her apartment late tomorrow morning. The address is in Shinjuku, which is convenient, since we need to spend time at the chocolate festival first. I respond with a quick, *We'll be there.* And add a couple of smiley face emojis for good measure.

There's a buzz, but it isn't my phone.

Logan takes Emi's phone from his pocket. There's a text message from an anonymous number, offering a substantial reward for the return of the phone.

I say, "That has to be from Emi. She must be using a temporary phone, just like I am."

"Then why did she block the number?" Logan asks.

I say, "Maybe she's not sure who has the phone. Maybe she already knew something was off when she came to Japan and she's afraid someone took her phone and is pretending to be us to lure her somewhere."

Logan gives a bitter laugh. "Let's clear this up."

He calls and leaves a voicemail. "This is Logan. If this is the owner of the phone, you are in danger. Meet us so I can protect you."

Logan and I stare at the phone for the whole ride back to the hotel. But a watched phone doesn't always ring, and Emi doesn't reply.

Chapter Seven
Tuesday

I feel a lot more alert the next morning. Even if my body clock is totally off and I'm up at 4 a.m. Patsy and Chloe are both crashed out, so as quietly as I can, I get dressed for the day and do my makeup. I smooth foundation over the cuts, even though it stings. I look at least presentable. Only . . . now what? Nothing is open at this point.

And the doctor was partly right – my body aches all over. SI don't really feel like going for a walk. But it's not as bad as he said it might be. I do a little gentle stretching and figure, yeah, I can make it through the day.

I might as well get a bit further in *The Honjin Murders*. It's a slow read, mainly because I have to keep looking up specific words. I learn that a honjin is an inn primarily for government officials, which may originally have also been someone's home. Then I spend twenty minutes watching – on very low volume – a video of a woman playing a koto, a long horizontal stringed instrument played with picks that attach to the first three fingers on one hand, because I just can't picture it from the book's descriptions.

I'm a couple of chapters in when there's a soft knock on the door. I go to answer it, and there's Logan, looking rumpled and half asleep. And sexy.

I look back at my two roommates, who haven't stirred, so I grab my room key and go out into the hall to talk to him. There's a sign on the wall that forms a little ledge, and a jumbled brown square pattern on the carpet, but all I can focus on is my fiancé.

Logan hands me a can of coffee. He has a plastic bag in his hand with *Lawson's* written on it. He holds it up, saying, "I found out convenience stores here are open 24 hours. The clerk said this was the good brand."

I eye the can. I own a chocolate shop with a full coffee bar. Shelf stable coffee isn't exactly my style. But I'm going to need coffee to make it through the long day ahead, so I pop it open and take a sip. It's a little on the sweet side, and milky, but not half bad. I expected worse.

Logan takes my hand and pulls me closer so he can kiss me, coffee breath and all. It's the first time we've really been alone this trip, without dealing with a crisis. I lean into him and feel warm and happy as Logan's arms circle my waist and he deepens the kiss. I want to just lose myself here, in this moment, the warmth of him this close to me, a can of coffee crushed between us, our love overshadowing the chaos of the day before. But eventually the kiss ends, and we break apart, a little breathless. The look Logan gives me sends fizzy energy all the way down to my toes.

He says, "Maybe Hudson and Savannah had it right. Maybe we should just elope, right here, right now, ditch the chocolate festival and head for the nearest ryokan with a private onsen."

Heat comes into my cheeks. Am I embarrassed? Or intrigued by the idea? Probably a little of both. I say, "We can't. Autumn would kill me if she doesn't get to be matron of honor. And I still want that night to be special. But we could come back here for a honeymoon."

Because a private hot spring at a traditional Japanese inn with like a forty-course breakfast sounds amazing.

"You're right," Logan says. "My mother would die if I got married and she wasn't there."

"True," I say. Logan's mom had been the one to remind me that, while this is going to be my second wedding, it will be Logan's first. He deserves to be surrounded by family, for all the glory and embarrassment.

Though there are aspects of the wedding I'm still nervous about. We have friends in common, but I don't know of anyone else he keeps in touch with, so I haven't even broached the topic of what friends from his past he might want to invite. Or whether I should invite any of Kevin's relatives. Would Logan feel slighted, like I've not really let go of the past?

"Fine," Logan says. "We can't elope. But how about another kiss?"

"I really am going to spill this coffee."

Logan takes the can from me and sets it on the ledge. He draws my hands up to his freshly shaven face. I lean up to kiss him again, feel his hands sliding around my back, the sheer touch fantastic. I really had better marry this guy, soon.

"Get a room guys," Ash says, coming out of his own room.

Logan kisses me for a few more seconds, before he pulls away. Still with one arm loosely around my waist, he asks Ash, "Where are you headed at this hour?"

Ash points with the travel mug in his hand. "I'm heading out to scout some locations for interviews for the podcast. The guys I've been talking to about doing a true crime movie say I need to have a video presence."

"Interviews with who?" I ask skeptically. I retrieve my can of coffee, because at this point, I think I'm going to need it. Ash's podcast has barely wrapped up talking about the first case I was involved in. So he wouldn't be interviewing people who know Noel.

"Dawn and Fisher have already agreed to talk about what they thought of you when they first met you. I'm probably going to have to sweet-talk Patsy, but you know how she feels about crystal figurines. I bought one of a butterfly at the mall yesterday that will probably change her mind."

"Crystal figurines?" Logan says, sounding puzzled.

At least I'm not the only one who has no idea what Ash is talking about. I sigh dramatically. "When I agreed to cooperate with you podcasting about me, you agreed not to pester all my friends." I add quickly, "Or family."

Ash says, "I have to have those perspectives, if we're going to do the movie. Otherwise, who knows what the screenwriter is going to fill in. Especially about the inherent conflict between you and Patsy. Love triangles tend to get ugly in dramatization."

I stare at Ash, but he doesn't flinch. Or blink. I should have said no to the idea of a movie immediately, but it had been a slippery slope, from hating his blog about me, to appearing on his podcast about me in an attempt to help find a missing goat, to saying he could do the movie if he got permission. It had just seemed wrong to shoot down his potential success. I hadn't fully considered how much more invasive to my life that success might be. "Fine," I say. "But only because we're friends."

Logan says, "That makes it easier to ask you to help us staff the booth today. You did promise to help out this week."

Ash protests, "But I was going to go by the movie set today and see if they'll let me try on one of the kaiju suits."

Logan says, "You can do that in the afternoon, once Dawn wakes up. She and Fisher want to be at the fest to figure out what that unhinged lady wants with Felicity."

With Emi in danger and Noel dead, I had done my best to forget about the chocolatier trying to get me thrown out of the competition. I still haven't been able to remember any reason she might have a grudge against me. I say, "It sounds like she's just being petty. I'm sure the officials aren't really going to take her seriously."

"You can't count on that," Ash says. "Chocolate making is a small world. If something like this ruins your reputation, it could be hard to be taken seriously on this scale ever again."

As if I needed that idea in my head right now. Even if it is true.

I say, "I'll try talking to her as soon as I get to the festival. What was her name? Maybe I can look her up."

Ash says, "Meryl McAdams from Butterfly Chocolates."

I look up the business. If I think I'm outclassed by being here among so many respected chocolate makers from France, Japan and far-flung parts of the world, I can't imagine what Butterfly Chocolates is even doing here. They're a tiny company that doesn't even have a storefront. If you haven't been invited specially to be part of the program, it costs over $5,000 to exhibit here. So what made it worth that kind of investment for Meryl? And why try to have me disqualified? She doesn't even make bean to bar chocolate. It would make some sense if we were competing in the same category. But I'm baffled.

Ash says, "Maybe she has you confused with someone else."

"I hope so," I tell him. "And I hope she realizes it soon."

Logan's phone buzzes with a text. He looks at it, and his brow furrows. He says, "My friend with the CCTV said face recognition found a match for Emi entering a Family Mart in Shibuya. So why come here, but not answer that voicemail we left on her new phone?"

Ash says, "Maybe she is she trying to figure out if you and Felicity are really safe to confide in. She's never met Felicity, and she hasn't seen you in years. For all she knows, you could be the reason she's in danger."

"Maybe," I agree. But how would I have even gotten her phone? "But that would mean I would have to have been working with Noel. Who would believe that?"

"In theory, the theft from you could have been staged," Logan says. "The company she whistleblew on had deep pockets. If they're holding a grudge, they could have anyone looking for her."

"Here's the part I don't get," I say. "Didn't this happen years ago? So why is she in danger now? It doesn't sound like revenge, if it has to do with a file."

I'm still trying to figure out what kind of file. Maybe new information about the company, which makes what they did even worse?

I keep thinking of the file folders on the desk at the movie studio office, but those would have more to do with Noel than Emi.

"Bad people aren't always logical," Logan says. "And sometimes when somebody pops back up on the radar, it triggers old feelings. You have to think about the individuals who lost money and power as a result of what she did. Those are two of the things that make people the angriest."

Ash says, "Maybe the file is a threatening letter."

"Let's see Emi's phone," I say.

Logan hands it to me. I don't find any files on it that seem like threats. There are, however, several more calls throughout the night from Ricky, the same guy who called when I was getting into the cop car, but he still hasn't left a message. And at some point, the calls just stop.

I say, "I don't know who this Ricky is, but should we call him back? He might know something about what's going on."

Ash says, "That could be dicey. What if he's the reason Emi is in danger?"

I hand Logan back the phone, saying, "But what if Ricky had been trying to warn Emi that whatever meet she had been about to walk into at the bar had been a trap? Since you know Emi the best, Logan, what do you want to do?"

"I *don't* want to do anything hasty," Logan says, putting the phone back in his jacket pocket. He turns to Ash. "Want some company for your scenery scouting?"

"Sure," Ash says. He turns to me, "You in?"

"I don't know," I say. "I'm still a bit sore from yesterday." Which is a staggering understatement.

"That reminds me." Logan takes a tube with a cap on it from the Lawson's bag. "I figured you wouldn't want to take the muscle relaxers the doctor gave you, so I picked up some painkillers that won't knock you out all day."

I tell Logan, "Did I mention you are incredibly thoughtful, as well as sexy?"

Ash says, "Still standing right here. Just so you know."

Logan shakes two pills out of the bottle, and I wash them down with sips of the canned coffee.

I say, "Okay. I'll at least try to keep up with you too. But if I ask for a taxi ten blocks from here, you're getting me one."

Ash says, "If you needed painkillers, you should have asked Imogen. She is the most organized person I know. She had an Excel sheet packing list for each of us, and an itinerary for exploring on our own. Since we got here, she decided a ryokan might be a good honeymoon spot, and she started making a master list of ones with views of Mount Fuji."

"No fair," I say. "Logan and I were talking about doing a ryokan."

Ash says, "It's not like we'd wind up at the same one at the same time, you know. I don't think it would be like copying the same wedding theme, or the same wedding dress. That would only be tacky because a lot of the same people will be at both weddings, but we're each on our own for the honeymoon."

My mouth gapes open. "I hadn't even thought about the dress."

I've decided I'm wearing off-white, but I haven't chosen the style. It would be awful to wind up wearing one that is close to Imogen's. She's ten years younger than me, and bound to carry it off with a lot more style.

I add, "I'm going to have to talk to her, soon, to make sure our design plans aren't overlapping."

Ash says, "She's heading for an onsen in a couple of hours. You should join her. The baths are supposed to work wonders for aches and joint pain."

"I'm not sure I'm ready for that." A private hot spring is one thing. But I've read that the public baths don't exactly allow swimsuits. "Besides, I don't have time. We need to be at the chocolate festival before it opens to the public." I start walking determinedly towards the elevator.

"You may change your mind by the end of the day," Ash predicts. He takes a sip from his travel mug. "Remind me again, what time is sunrise?"

"About now," Logan says. "Spring in Japan is when the sunrise starts getting earlier. By summer, it will be around four in the morning."

Logan takes my hand, and we follow Ash through the lobby and out onto the early morning street. People are already up, heading for work in skirts and suits. And there are a few tourists that I suspect are just staggering back to their hotels.

"You have to see this," Ash says. He takes us around the block, and points in the direction of the train station. "It's supposed to be just outside the station."

As we walk, I actually feel some of the stiffness going out of my body. I roll my shoulders. It feels good to move a bit. But after a bit, I start to have the unnerving sensation that someone is watching us. I whirl around, but there's no one particularly suspicious on the street. A woman walking a small dog looks at me curiously, then crosses the street. I try not to take offense. I must look paranoid.

But I'm sure there's someone there.

Ash takes us all the way down to the crosswalk leading into the train station. The intersection is already starting to get busy, with commuters heading for the train. But there are also twenty or so people standing with their cameras pointed right at us. It's not hard to see what they are photographing. There's a giant 3-D cat on a billboard directly above us.

When we cross the intersection and turn around for a better view of the cat, I relax a little. If someone had indeed been following us, they are surely across the intersection from us now. Unless they crossed the street along with us. Which is possible.

I pretend to be caught up in the whimsey of the billboard, where a giant calico is edging a paperclip holder towards the boundary of the 3-D frame. It feels so realistic that I flinch when the object topples, even though it can't actually fall onto the people passing below. Part of my reaction is because I am on edge. I'm trying to surreptitiously scan the small crowd of people around me, trying to find someone who looks familiar – or someone who feels dangerous. I'd reported a murder that no one was supposed to know happened. Maybe the murderer thought I had seen what happened. Maybe even that I know the murderer's identity. That could make me a threat, at least in the killer's mind. But surely they wouldn't attack me on the street, with all these potential witnesses, right?

I tell Ash, "This is a horrible spot for an interview."

"I know," Ash says. "I just wanted to see the cat. I thought you'd think it was cute, since you liked that artist's cat. Though, I also have a cat, and you have never once asked to meet her."

"It's never occurred to me that you would want me to."

"We are friends, after all. You should be following my cat on Instagram." Like anyone even knows his cat has an Insta account. Ash points out a tree with a sign attached to it. It features a picture of an elephant throwing trash on the ground, with a big not symbol around it. "No elephants allowed," he jokes.

But there's movement, someone ducking behind the tree just as I turn that way. My skin prickles and I want to flinch away.

Instead, I force myself to rush forward, determined to figure out who it is. I find Emi, flinching back away from me. She hesitates, then takes off running into the train station.

"We're trying to help you," I call after her retreating form. "Please. Let's talk this out."

Logan moves toward the entrance to the station, but Emi, with her neutral-colored jacket, is already disappearing into the crowd, while Logan is getting startled looks as people move out of his way. I'm not surprised when he returns a few moments later, alone.

I say, "I felt like someone was watching us. But I'm not sure whether it was her or not."

Logan grunts. "My guess is, if Emi is this afraid to come in out of the cold, maybe somebody was watching her, too."

"Well that doesn't make me feel better," I say. "At all."

"Come on," Ash says. "Let's just keep walking. If someone follows us, we're bound to spot them."

Logan says, "What you mean is that what just happened creeped you out, and you would very much like to leave. Don't think I didn't notice that you jumped behind me when Emi ran out from behind that tree."

"Oh, I totally did that," Ash admits. "Aren't you the one who's supposed to be everyone's bodyguard?"

Logan says, "I haven't been private security for a long time."

Although, to Ash's point, Logan does keep jumping in and saving people. Ash acts more indirectly. Both times he's helped save my life, it was from a distance where he wouldn't get hurt.

We follow Ash, heading off in the direction from whence we just came. He says, "There's a ninja amusement park this way."

Logan groans, "Even if it's open – which it won't be – that's going to be a tourist trap. It's probably completely cheesy."

"I don't care about cheesy," Ash says. "I'm looking for cool-looking backgrounds, where nobody gets upset if you are taking video."

Logan considers this. He says, "Fair. But couldn't you find a park or something?"

Ash says, "Not walking distance from where we are staying. It's wall to wall buildings here. The only park I could find has construction going on across the street. It's a lot easier to cancel noise in a controlled environment anyway."

His point is quickly proven when, as we're heading towards the Ninja building, we reach a construction area. It's a narrow lot between two buildings, but workers are breaking up old concrete and framing out something new.

It's harder to talk as we walk past. There's a sign I can't read, showing that it's going to be a multi-story building.

As we walk, I'd swear again that someone is following us. I whirl around again, and I catch the impression of a dark suitcoat as someone turns off into an alleyway. It feels somehow familiar, though I can't place why.

I whisper to Logan, "Did you see that guy?"

Logan admits, "Not really."

The rest of the walk is uneventful. If that guy had been following us, we scared him off. Eventually we reach the ninja amusement park, which is contained in a single brick building – but of course it's closed until 10 a.m. Logan seems more disappointed that the barbecue restaurant on the first floor is also closed.

And we have walked so far that we really need to head back if we're going to get there in time to get ready for the festival.

But I can't shake my worry. What if we were being followed by Noel's killer? The police aren't even looking for a murderer. I ask Logan, "How long, exactly, does Connie need to wait to file a missing person's report?"

Logan says, "She could probably do it today, considering everything that has happened."

Ash says, "Assuming he doesn't turn up."

With more vehemence than I mean, I say, "I know what I saw, Ash. He was dead."

Ash holds up both hands, as though warding me off. "Hey. I didn't say he was going to be alive."

Logan says, "Assuming he actually is dead, you have to wonder if the killer had time to move the body. Obviously, they would have stashed the poor guy somewhere when the police showed up. But they probably would have gone last night and moved the body somewhere else. But none of my contacts reported anyone contacting the police about a break-in. If the killer moved Noel, they likely had a key."

"How do we know who had keys?" Ash asks.

"Old fashioned detective work," Logan says. "We very discreetly ask."

Chapter Eight
Tuesday

As far as I can tell, the officials haven't decided to kick me out of the festival, and everything seems fine with the Greetings and Felicitations booth.

A bit before the festival opens, Henri, the chocolatier at the next booth over, takes the few steps needed to come check out our space. He has a couple of flat objects wrapped in white paper. He says, with a thick French accent, "I hear you have a refined palate and a fondness for sandwiches. I made these for my breakfast and made a couple extra to share with you."

"Oh, wow, thanks." Impressed at the man's thoughtfulness, I take one of the sandwiches. He hands Logan the other one. I unwrap it. It's a warm, melty grilled cheese, made with brie and fig spread. It's a combination I've had cold before, on charcuterie boards, but I never would have thought to make it into a grilled sandwich.

Logan asks, "How do you know that much about Fee?"

Henri says, "I often look up news about chocolate, and I stumbled into the podcast about your friends. It was fascinating."

I take a bite of the sandwich, and the sweet of the fig spread perfectly balances the saltiness of the brie. "Mmmmmm." I didn't even mean to say that out loud.

Henri looks pleased. "You should also try my drinking chocolate. I think it would suit your taste." He pours us little sample cups out of a big urn on his counter.

Ash takes one, sips it, and says, "It's like drinking a coconut truffle."

Henri nods. "Exactemente." He then starts looking at the contents of our booth.

He's kind of a big deal. Henri Martin trained in Switzerland and Belgum, traveled the world sourcing cacao, and now owns one of the most exclusive chocolate boutiques in Paris. He's had cooking shows and competed in filmed competitions.

It's almost embarrassing to have him perusing my bars.

He picks up one and examines the packaging. "It reminds me of the Kit-Kats, no?"

I immediately bristle. I'd already had one person accuse me of using commercial chocolate. Trying to keep my temper with such an important chocolatier, I ask, "Why would you say that?"

He smiles kindly. "Have you not seen the Kit-Kat wrapper, here in Japan? There is room to write a greeting, just like on your bars."

"Oh," I say. My irritation deflating, I muster a real smile. "I didn't realize."

I didn't think my idea to have chocolate bars double as greeting cards was unique. I just didn't know it was a thing in Japan.

Ash says, "Kit-Kats are huge here. They have over a hundred and forty flavors – including one partly made with cacao grown in Japan. The greetings thing is because Kit-Kat sounds like kitsu katsu, which means something like, 'Do your best,' so people give them to kids taking tests and such."

"Why do you know all that?" Logan asks.

Ash says, "Because Imogen has made it her mission to collect as many Kit-Kats as possible while we are here. She's already got the sake flavored ones, and the hojicha – roasted green tea – ones." He holds up a hand as though to stop my protest. "I already talked to her. She's not using them as wedding favors. We're ordering your truffles."

I nod my head. Darn right. Why serve candy bars – even cute ones – when you can have custom truffles done for free? "You know they'll be a gift, Ash." But then something clicks about what he said. "Wait. How is there chocolate being grown in Japan? The growing range for cacao is 20 degrees north and south of the equator. Japan is well outside that zone."

Henri says, "They are growing in greenhouses. There is a tiny island off the coast of Tokyo called Ogasawara. They have only 32 square miles of land. But they are doing interesting things."

Logan says, "We have to go see that while we are here."

Henri tuts. "It is 24 hours by boat, maybe."

"Oh." Logan sounds deflated. "Then maybe not."

I say, "If we did come back for our honeymoon, maybe there'd be time."

Logan says, "But would you want to spend that much of it on a boat?"

"If the cabin was nice enough," I say.

Logan gives me a mischievous grin.

But I don't have time to contemplate the implications, because there's a Japanese woman, in her late teens or early twenties, striding with purpose toward the booth. She is wearing a tee-shirt with the festival's logo on it. She looks nervous, and when she reaches us, the ponytail her long dark hair bobs as she talks. "Sumimasen, Koerberu Sensei. May I take samples of the chocolate you submitted to the contest? There are some minor points the officials would like to work out."

"Of course," I say. I hand her several of the bars I had hand carried in my backpack. I know for a fact nothing has happened to them.

After she leaves Logan says, "I'm sorry this is happening to you. I know how excited you were to be here."

I tell him, "I'm not going to let it ruin my experience at the festival." I gesture at the large floor. "I haven't even gotten a chance to look around."

"I'll go with you," Dawn says. "I've never been to this kind of event. It would be fun to see what a professional thinks of it, eh."

Is she serious? It wasn't that long ago that Dawn had called my chocolate making a frivolous endeavor and said Logan was wasting his potential taking part in it. She had urged him to quit and return to the police force. Maybe, since she's come to respect me after I saved her life, she wants to try to respect what I do. Or maybe since she's seen the level at which chocolate can be esteemed, she sees there's more to it than just a snack. Or maybe she just wants to low-key snoop.

Fisher says, "I want to see too."

"Of course, Love," Dawn says. She twines Fisher's fingers in hers and kisses his hand. His free hand comes up to touch her face. The way she looks at him – Logan was right saying he has her wrapped around his little finger. But that's not a bad thing.

And it's a lot like the way Logan looks at me. I glance over at him, but he's busy checking out the French chocolatier's booth.

Ash says, "Why is nobody listening to what I said about PDA?"

He's looking at a trio of ladies walking by with clearly disapproving looks on their faces.

Fisher lets go of Dawn's hand. Then they both collapse into giggles, like schoolkids who have been caught out. Which is a bit surreal, given how serious Dawn usually is. Or maybe that's just the only side I've seen of her.

"Come on," Dawn says. "As of two minutes ago, the festival is now open to the public. Let's look around before it gets crowded."

We make our way down the row sampling craft chocolate, confections, cakes, and cookies. When we can, we talk to the booth's owners about their businesses and their techniques. Sometimes I find myself pantomiming to try to communicate, or just scanning QR codes with my phone, to look at in translation. Fisher keeps buying things, and by the time we turn the corner, his messenger bag is half full of treats.

Fisher tells me, "I hope you're not offended that I'm buying from the competition."

"Not at all," I say. "You can get chocolate from me anytime you visit Galveston. Take home what's special from here."

"Then why aren't you buying anything?" Dawn asks.

"Because I'm collecting ideas." I gesture back around the corner. "Did you try that black sesame bar a few booths back?"

Fisher says, "Not only did I try it, I bought two bars of it."

"It was really good, right? But except for Logan's new chocolate bar line, and the occasional limited-edition bar I come up with, Greetings and Felicitations focuses on 2-ingredient chocolate for our main bars. That means only cacao beans and sugar, so I wouldn't make that exact same bar. Logan might, though he would probably add his own twist to the flavor profile. Probably some kind of beer, knowing him."

"Then what good does it do you to try it?" Fisher asks.

"I do truffles and, for special orders, filled shapes or bonbons. It would be an interesting variation to emulsify into a gianduja, which usually has nuts. Some people may be able to eat sesame who can't eat nuts – but there is a potential for cross reactions, especially with peanuts."

Fisher says, "Dawn and I don't have any food allergies, but we're friends with a couple where she can't have dairy and he can't eat eggs. And they're both sensitive to gluten."

Dawn says, "But Love, that's still not as bad as nut allergies. Sure, Keith and Jen might get sick, but anaphylaxis can kill you on the spot."

Fisher says, "Either way, it would stink to have to check every food label and menu detail like our friends do."

I say, "My chocolate factory uses a lot of nuts. We're not at the scale where we could reliably be allergen free. We would have to have a whole duplicate set of equipment. But we do make sure that potential allergens are clearly marked on our packaging. The good news is we're free of everything your friends need to worry about."

Fisher says, "Regional foods can be a bit crazy with the allergens. I'd never seen pecan oil before I came to visit you in Texas. The store was touting it as a replacement for olive oil. I thought about buying some, but we like throwing parties and I was afraid someone might be sensitive to it."

Dawn says, "Avocado oil is popular now too, but I haven't bought it for the same reason. I work with someone who is massively allergic to latex, and he got sick from one bite of a burrito where the restaurant forgot to skip the guac. What if I forget that avocado has latex and bring cupcakes to the squad room?"

"Are you likely to bring cupcakes to work?" I ask, smiling at the juxtaposition.

Fisher starts to say something, but then he gets distracted looking at the booth across from where we are standing. "Hey, what's that?"

We follow him over to where a Japanese chocolatier is standing next to a case of edible art pieces. They are all beautiful chocolate sculptures, of a leaping dolphin, a detailed camera, and a hot-air balloon suspended in front of a chocolate sky.

But Fisher is zeroing in on a chocolate game board with flat pieces.

The chocolatier gives a mini-bow. "Irrashaimase!" Basically, *Welcome to my business*.

I point at the dolphin and say, "Kawaii." But after that, I'm stumped.

I must look embarrassed I can't continue the conversation, because he laughs and tells me, "I speak a little English. Where you from?"

"Texas," I say. "On the coast."

He nods knowingly. "Where JFK got shot."

I say, "We're a few hours away from there by car. But yes."

Fisher says, "I'm from Minnesota."

The chocolatier turns to a guy in his late teens, who is sitting behind the counter reading a manga book. They exchange words in Japanese, then both shrug at each other.

The teenager says, "My dad doesn't know anything about Minnesota. Sorry."

Fisher says, "No worries. I don't know anything about Tokyo."

The kid laughs, and he and his father start talking again. The older guy looks relieved.

Fisher points at the chocolate game board. "What is this? It looks cool."

The teen says, "It's a shogi board. Japanese chess."

Fisher says, "I play American chess. Is it similar?"

The teen laughs at the seeming absurdity of the question, then looks embarrassed for belittling Fisher's game. "Sorry." He shrugs. "Some of the rules are the same. But in shogi, the pieces are double sided. My dad even molds them that way." He moves to the case and extracts one of the game pieces, placing it gingerly on a small plate. He comes around the counter and uses tongs to flip the piece over, showing Fisher both sides. He says, "This is a pawn, but if you advance it all the way across the board, it gets promoted to a gold general. A gold is a much more powerful piece."

"Okay," Fisher says. "Having pieces go up in rank is a cool twist. It's kind of realistic."

The kid nods. "And pieces are captured in shogi, instead of killed. You can actually put captured pieces back on the board, as yours."

Fisher says, "I gotta try this."

The teen says something to his dad and the dad nods. The teen says, "I have a game board with me in the car. Do you want to go up to the roof garden and I can show you how to play?"

Fisher looks at Dawn. "Will you hold onto my messenger bag?"

She holds out a hand to take it. "Don't be surprised if those macarons you bought aren't in here later."

After Fisher and the teen shogi aficionado leave, I turn to the dad and ask, "Does everybody in Japan play shogi?"

"Not everybody." He moves to put the chocolate shogi piece back in the case. "But those who do really like it. My son is smart. He loves games."

Dawn says, "My husband does too. Obviously. I couldn't begin to play a game like that."

"Me either," the chocolatier agrees. He hands me and Dawn each a business card. "I am more artist than logic man."

A couple approach the booth, so we step aside so let them interact with the display.

The booth next door has white chocolate sourdough, from a baker from Hawaii. There's one loaf with pumpkin seeds, and one with pockets of cream cheese and chocolate chips, but I sample the one studded with macadamia nuts and dried pineapple. It's so good I grab a second sample. Then I buy a loaf to bring back and munch on when I get a break. Though that will probably be later in the day. We do have to visit Nao soon and find out what she might know about our missing dead guy.

We sample our way back around the square – only a fraction of the total booths taking up this whole floor. When we come back around the corner to the row my booth is on, I see a girl bringing yet another book to add to the stack of mystery novels. The girl walks right past Meryl's booth to do it, not even glancing at the tray of samples Meryl tries to hold out to her. Meryl is obviously annoyed, and I wonder if this is part of why she's so upset at me. It's hard to put work and money into marketing, only to be passed over because someone else's booth is more interesting. I have to admit, we have sold a lot of chocolate to the mystery fans and the Youtubers, mainly from our Sympathy and Condolences super dark line.

At our booth, Logan is talking to someone who is livestreaming, and I catch the words, "Death by Chocolate Challenge."

I groan. Meryl hears and looks over at me. I think she realizes we saw her attempted interaction with the girl with the book. Her lips narrow into a hard line, and she stares at me in a challenging way.

I flinch back. I would apologize, if I had any control over any of this. Even though I don't, I'd apologize anyway, if I didn't think it would make Meryl dislike me any more than she already does.

As it is, when we walk past her booth I smile at her and nod, hoping to at least look cordial.

But her expression doesn't melt.

Once we're past, Dawn asks me, "What's a death by chocolate challenge?"

I look down at the floor, embarrassed. "It's stupid." I force myself to look back up at her. "After the murders that happened at my shop, I got a reputation with the true crime crowd for being a murder magnet, and a bunch of them started daring each other to eat my 100% dark chocolate. They developed a superstition that anyone who ate the whole bar might be next. Of course, that never happened. But it did sell a lot of chocolate."

We reach the booth just as the Youtuber is unwrapping the bar.

Logan says, "100% dark chocolate is a lot crumblier than the chocolate you're probably used to." He hands the Youtuber a bottle of water. "That's because sugar is an emulsifier, and there isn't any in there."

Undeterred, the Youtuber takes a bite of chocolate. "Hey, this isn't bad. It doesn't taste like chocolate as I know it, but you guys know, my motto is embrace things for what they are."

He proceeds to eat the entire bar, taking frequent sips of water between bites. Once he finishes, he says to the followers on the other side of his camera, "Okay. I've done it. I'm not a superstitious guy, but stay tuned to the channel, just in case. And in the meantime, give

Josh a follow. He's been so patient with me getting the split screen technology to work, he deserves it, am I right? Thanks Josh, for joining me from your location at the Greetings and Felicitation store in Galveston, Texas. And thanks to the 130 followers local to the Houston and Galveston area who joined Josh today to do the challenge. Peace!" He makes a peace sign, then pockets his phone, nods at Logan, and walks away.

Logan says, "I don't think we brought enough chocolate from the Sympathy and Condolences line."

I nod in agreement. "I thought the Death by Chocolate thing had all died down."

Dawn says, "No, yeah. It only takes one person to make something go viral."

If it's morning here, it must be the end of the day in Galveston. I try to imagine 130 people crowding into my shop right at closing, wanting to try the bar. I take out my phone to text Carmen and see how she's holding up, only to realize she's been texting me. The last text from her says, *I've called in Miles to get started on more 100% bars. He's the one with the most experience making chocolate of those of us left here. Of course, we may run out before the new bars are ready.*

Conching chocolate takes a minimum of three days. So even if Miles is there right now, roasting beans and winnowing off the outside chaff, Carmen could be facing disappointed customers for a couple of days. I am glad, though, that we'd taken the time to teach Miles how to make chocolate. He's a college kid, so I don't know how long he will still be around to help out. But he's a quick learner, and while we have him, I'm happy to share anything I know.

When I'd first opened my shop, I had been caught up in having everything the way Kevin would have wanted it. And then when I had realized owning a business was my dream on my own, I had a hard time letting go of control of even the smallest details. No one got to actually make the chocolate except me. If I had held onto that attitude, we'd be in an even worse crunch now.

I text back, *Tell him thanks and that I own him a favor when I get back.*

Carmen sends three laughing-face emojis. I'm not sure how that's funny. Maybe she's just reacting to all the stress of the unexpected rush.

Chapter Nine
Tuesday

A red-haired girl with red sparkle heart stick-ons surrounding one eye approaches the booth. She's wearing a short tiered dress, paired with long white gloves. It's also red, with white polka dots in some of the tiers. She looks like she escaped from a retro costume party. She smiles at me and says, "You must have had enough of the Youtubers today, right?"

I scrunch up my nose. "I don't know. Some of my friends are Youtubers." I gesture in the direction the Death by Chocolate Challenge guy had gone. "And that one was certainly good for business."

"Good," she says. "Because I'm Annabelle the Baker. Chloe said you would want to talk to me about Noel Bell. She wasn't really clear why, but she said you would feed me chocolate and get your pastry chef to be a guest on my channel."

My mouth o's open in surprise. "I can certainly handle the first part. But you will have to talk to Carmen about whether or not she wants to do an appearance." Annabelle looks disappointed, so I hastily add, "She probably will. She's in the middle of promoting the second Greetings and Felicitations cookbook. There's a lot in there about gluten free baking, and other stuff that's trending right now."

Annabelle says, "I'm more interested in her overall cooking style, how she takes classic recipes from around the world and finds ways to elevate them. I've lived in both Mexico and Japan, and I've been toying with an idea for a while of doing a white chocolate and matcha tres leches cake for my channel. It just feels like Carmen would be the perfect guest for that episode."

"That does sound like her," I agree. The only problem is that I don't know yet whether I should trust Annabelle. I don't want to match Carmen up with someone who potentially murdered Noel.

After all, it was Annabelle's marzipan perfume line that Chloe had been wearing at the crime scene – a crime scene that had smelled overwhelmingly of almond cake. "But I don't think Carmen has plans to travel for book promotion. Especially not as far as Japan. She didn't even want to come for this trip. Her boyfriend's kid had surgery, and she's been checking in at the hospital every day."

"Oh, poor kiddo," Annabelle sympathizes. "I totally get her wanting to stay put. We can do it virtually. We just split the screen, the same way your chocolate challenge guy was doing. I actually have time tomorrow, if it would work."

"In that case," I say. I type a quick summary of what Annabelle is proposing and text it to Carmen. Carmen asks for Annabelle's number and about a minute later, they are Facetiming to set the details of the show. Autumn is there at the shop, and Carmen ropes her into helping out with the shoot – even though Autumn doesn't do many recorded interviews, let alone a baking show.

They agree to do a couple of recipes, which can be released as different episodes. I listen to them brainstorm ingredients and techniques. They decide on the matcha tres leches and a ginger and citrus miso shortbread cookie that is a riff on a cookie recipe Carmen has in the first cookbook.

"But what should we do for the third one?" Carmen says. "We have a lot of good ideas, but nothing feels quite right."

I say, "What about something involving black sesame and coffee."

"Yes!" all three of them say in unison.

"Can we make it decaf?" Autumn says. "I'm off caffeine until I have the baby."

"Of course, mija," Carmen says, patting Autumn's hand. "We wouldn't torture you by making you smell coffee you can't have."

Annabelle says, "What if we did it as a roll cake? Black sesame cake with coffee cream."

"That sounds divine," I say. I'm glad they're having fun on this, and nobody is feeling left out, just because they weren't able to come on the trip. I think about the chocolate maker with the chocolate shogi board. Greetings and Felicitations has an artist, too, who has been doing amazing things with sculpture and 3D printing techniques. "Maybe you could show off some of Tracie's chocolate sculptures on one of the episodes."

That springboards them into a whole different conversation.

Having a mystery writer sit in on the livestream could actually be helpful – assuming we ever find Noel's body. Autumn might have an opportunity to ask Annabelle some innocuous-sounding questions that could lead to uncovering a motive.

While they're still brainstorming, I put together a plate of samples for Annabelle so I can walk her through some of my chocolates. I move to give them to her.

Autumn sees me come back on screen and says, "You better be taking all kinds of notes for me about Japan. This is only the second time we've talked on video, and this time we're inside a building."

"Sorry about that," I say. "We've been busy."

"Right," Autumn says. "I don't guess the dead stunt man ever showed back up after you two took a dive off the roof. Some of the stuff that happens to you would make for better plots than half my books."

"Dead stunt man?" Annabelle says. She hangs up on Carmen and Autumn. "Are you saying Noel is dead?"

Her voice is loud, and several people turn to look at us.

"I believe so," I say, much more softly. "But his body went missing, and at this point, the police haven't even officially filed it as a missing person."

Annabelle looks like she's going to say something loud again, so I take her arm and say, "Maybe we can find somewhere quieter to talk about this."

Logan starts to follow us as I lead Annabelle toward the elevators. I know he doesn't like me wandering off alone with potential murder suspects. And I understand why.

"It's okay," I tell him. "You don't have to come with. There's a little coffee shop on the second floor where we should be able to sit and chat."

Annabelle says, "It's okay if Logan wants to come. I don't have anything to hide."

Annabelle is quiet in the elevator. But once she has a cup of coffee in front of her, she murmurs, "Poor Noel."

I look down at my own cup. The cute latte art, of an owl on a branch, feels out of place for the moment. I take a sip just to smudge it. I ask, "What happened between you and Noel on the set?" Noel's wife had called it unprofessional, but I'd like to hear Annabelle's side of the story.

Annabelle swirls her coffee. "You've seen Noel. He's incredibly hot. And he was helping me with my scene. We're all fleeing from the second kaiju, and I had to dive under a closing door to get into a bunker. He gave me some tips on how to dive without getting hurt."

The café isn't busy, but somehow that makes it feel exclusive. We're the only folks sitting on our side of the space. It's got shiny black tabletops, with wrought iron legs. And there's a row of burlap coffee sacks in black lacquer frames on one wall, matched by black accent paint making swoops near the ceiling. Our table even has a black multi-section box with various sugar packets, honey straws, and those individually packaged damp napkins.

"How many kaiju are in this movie?" Logan asks.

"Three," Annabelle says. "Plus a few that only appear for a scene or two. The special effects guy even built a baby kaiju with these huge wings, just for one scene. It's adorable, kind of like a chicken smashed together with a hamster. Some of the scenes are shot with props like that, using the old-fashioned tokusatsu techniques. You know, scale models and monster suits, and stop motion. It's all paired with CGI, for a retro vibe that doesn't feel too cheesy. The director is a genius."

"Noel tell you all of this?" Logan asks.

"Some of it. I got to talk to Director Kudo too. He is obsessed with the kaiju genre and wants to tell a monster story for our time."

A guy comes in and takes a table a few away from us. He seems to be watching Annabelle, and then he looks at his phone. My guess is he's trying to decide if an internet personality he follows is really her. I hope he doesn't come over here to ask for an autograph. Although Annabelle doesn't seem the type to be bothered by a request like that.

Ignoring the guy, I ask, "So Noel was helping you. How did it go from that to you feeding him cake?"

Annabelle says, "Noel had a scene that day as one of the kaiju. It wasn't the full suit, since that would have been too cumbersome. In the scene, he had to grab onto a kaiju-scale helicopter that was supposed to lift him into the air, then he does a backflip dive into the ocean."

Annabelle may think that sounds genius, but I've started to wonder if Kudo's directorial vision is actually a little silly.

Logan says, "Since the studio is several miles from the ocean, I'd love to see how they shot that."

"Later," I say. "I think she's getting to the point."

Annabelle says, "Noel had already had his hands done with the prosthetics for his close-up. There was no way he was going to be able to eat without messing it up. I fed him some of the cake samples. I stopped when I realized Connie was getting upset. But I didn't think it would be a big deal, since he and his wife are separated."

"He told you that?" I ask. Because that hadn't been the impression I'd gotten from Connie.

"Well, yeah," Annabelle says. "His wife must be crazy if she's going to let him go."

Several of the cops I know have told me that when someone starts giving too much detail, it could be a sign they are lying. And Annabelle had certainly given a lot of information. Maybe she's just fascinated about the movie making process. Or maybe it's a misdirect.

I ask, "You're the one who makes the almond cake perfume, right?"

She beams. "You've heard of it? That one isn't supposed to be cake, though. It's marzipan and musk."

Logan says, "So it's not edible. I was thinking you might be using almond oil and cake-adjacent ingredients."

Annabelle giggles like he's said something vaguely scandalous and says, "There is food-grade almond oil, but it's a lot more common for spa treatments. People use it for massage oil and hair treatments, or even grind bits of almond in body scrubs. However, since I'm selling on the internet and people tend to get a little crazy, I try to steer clear of potential allergens and home-made concoctions. All my perfumes are synthetic, and they're produced at a lab in India. I do tie a bow with a little pouch of glitter onto each bottle myself. To give it the personal touch, you know?"

I ask, "Is it possible some of the perfume could have gotten spilled on the set?"

"I don't think so. Why would you think that?"

I study her for a moment. She looks genuinely confused. I say, "Because when I followed Noel into the building last night, it absolutely reeked of almonds."

Her eyes go wide. "Wait. Whatever happened to Noel – are you saying I'm a suspect?"

"Yes," Logan says, without hesitation.

Annabelle says, "I never even met Noel before the filming. And even if he and his wife weren't separated, I'd hardly kill a guy for lying to me. I have more self-esteem than that."

She's right. She isn't a strong suspect – unless there's something more connecting her and Noel than we know about. I discreetly text Autumn to try and find that out while they are planning the YouTube episode.

I tell Annabelle, "I'd appreciate it if you didn't say anything about Noel on your channel, until someone finds his body. It could make things weird with the investigation."

"I get that," Annabelle says. She gets up, leaving half her coffee. "I need a minute, to think about this. I'll see you tomorrow, for the livestream."

"Me?" I ask.

"Yeah. If Carmen has Autumn as a cooking partner, that means I get one too. And since I'm doing you a favor not mentioning Noel . . ."

"Then I need to do you one too."

After Annabelle leaves, I take the time to finish my coffee. I tell Logan, "I regret not taking a picture of this latte art before I messed it up."

Logan says, "I took one when I got it from the counter."

I grin at him. See? He gets me.

Once we're back upstairs, I start organizing things so Ash and Imogen will have an easier time handling the booth and then explaining how everything works to Dawn and Fisher.

I'm just straightening my business cards and brochures when someone else shows up with a book. Only this time it's an older guy with thinning hair. After a beat, I recognize him. It's Taniguchi, the special effects artist for the movie.

I tell Ash, "There's your special effects guy."

Ash moves around the booth and intersects Taniguchi. He says, "Can I get you some chocolate to sample? Or take that book for the stack? Felicity has been getting quite a few mysteries for her pile."

Taniguchi clutches onto the book. "She already has this one. I was just hoping to get it signed."

He's right. I got a copy of *Murder on the Orient Express* back when I had gone on that cruise where I had solved the murder of a cantankerous mystery writer.

Ash looks embarrassed. He's angling for an invite to look around the FX lab, but his efforts seem to be backfiring.

I grab a pen and move over to Taniguchi. "Of course I'll sign it for you."

Logan asks, "How come you know so much about Fee?"

Taniguchi says, "My niece showed me some pictures last night of your glass case of books. She's interested in true crime. Which is a bit troubling, since that interest has only intensified since she lost her mother and had to move in with me."

I ask, "So her dad wasn't in the picture?"

He cocks his head. "I don't understand that phrase."

Right. That's not a literal idiom, so I can see how it might not translate. I say, "So her dad wasn't around to take her."

Taniguchi looks sad. "He died when my niece was two."

I say, "I'm sorry to be bringing all of this up."

Logan says, "If you think the true crime thing is a problem, why are you bringing her Felicity's signature?"

"Who said this is for her?" Taniguchi asks. "I collect signatures of famous people I've worked with."

Ash points out, "You aren't working with Felicity."

Taniguchi says, "She is Chloe's guardian, and that is close enough. I will get Chloe to sign something too."

Logan jokes, "Too bad she can't sign Honda. Chloe's YouTube stardom started with her cat."

Ash blinks. "Your cat's name is Honda?"

"Not my cat," Taniguchi says. "Honda is Director Kudo's."

"Honda. Like the car?" Ash asks.

Taniguchi waves both his hands in an emphatic *no* gesture. "When it came time to make the first Godzilla movie, there were only two men who could do it – Eiji Tsuburaya and Ishirō Honda. If it had been my cat, I would have named her for Tsuburaya who is known as the father of tokusatsu. He invented techniques such as the iron crane used for elevated film shooting. And he worked with almost nothing to make such enduring classics as the early Godzilla films. You may know him more for the techniques in Ultraman."

"Ultraman was cool," Imogen says, from behind the counter. "That was the show that got me interested in someday visiting Japan."

Ash grins at her, then turns back to Taniguchi and asks, "Then what did Honda do?"

Taniguchi says, "He wrote the script. That note of drama and sadness in the first Godzilla movie – that was Honda and his tendency towards tragedy. Tsuburaya loved King Kong and wanted to make a movie about a giant whale destroying a city. Honda made the idea work. That's how you have the gorilla whale, which is what Gojira literally means."

Logan says, "It sounds like that little cat has a big reputation to live up to."

Taniguchi grins. "Our Honda has become the movie studio's mascot. Kudo even had the writers add two scenes with the cat, and I got to add laser vision effects for her."

I hold a hand out for the book, and when he gives it to me, I sign the blank front page, *My friend Taniguchi, this is one of my favorite books. Enjoy the ride! Felicity Koerber*

I hand it back to him, trying to think of a way to discreetly ask what I want to know – without putting him on the defensive. After all, Japan is a culture where coworkers stand up for each other – at least officially. "I was just curious. Do you know if either Noel or Connie Bell had a key to the studio building?"

Immediately, Taniguchi looks wary. I guess my questioning wasn't discreet enough. He says, "Most all of us have a key. Me, Kudo, the receptionist, the crew, the writers. So yes, Connie and Noel have keys, as do the main actors. Why do you need to know?"

"I told you, yesterday I went into the building after Noel did. The door was unlocked. And that's when I saw him lying there."

"What exactly did you see?" Taniguchi asks. For a second the question seems suspicious. But then I realize he's probably wanting to know if I actually saw Connie there.

"Not much," I admit. "I went outside, and when I came back, Noel's body was gone." I think about what Chloe had said, her impression of what might have happened to the body. "Does the janitor have a key?"

Taniguchi laughs and seems to relax. "Yes, he does. Should I arrange for you to talk to him?"

"I would appreciate that, actually."

Taniguchi says, "Are you certain that Bell is dead? I heard he was headed for Belize."

"Who told you that?" Ash asks.

Taniguchi gestures in the direction of the set. "It was someone on the crew. They speculated many things after you left yesterday, but that seems the most plausible."

Logan asks, "Do you know what is on the other floors of the building?"

Taniguchi starts describing the rough layout, with two floors for storage, plus the writer's room.

I'm only half listening. All that storage – Noel's body could be anywhere, if it is even still inside the building. Noel should have had a key when he disappeared – so the killer could theoretically have taken it off him, after following him inside. But then how could the killer have set up whatever was necessary to kill Noel and then make him disappear in the first place? It seems impossible.

Ash starts pestering Taniguchi with questions about the special effects for the movie. Taniguchi finally gives in and says he will show Ash around if Ash comes to the studio later today. Then the poor special effects guy beats a hasty retreat before he gets asked to do anything else.

Shortly after that, Meryl walks past, and I try to talk to her. After all, we're going to be here all week. I need to find a way to diffuse the hostility. She gives me a steely look and says, "I can't believe they haven't kicked you out yet. Cheater."

I swallow back a rude reply. I can't let her unhinged emotions get to me. So I take a deep breath, and focus on why I'm here. I sell some chocolate to happy customers, using a card Hudson had made that translates information on all the products into Japanese. I get to talk to chocolate aficionados from half a dozen countries. I even get to show off some of the sets of specially molded chocolates we've made just for this event. They are boxes of four, including two solid and two filled shapes. One set has my bunny Knightley, in four cute poses, including a 3D take on his silhouette pose that we use for our logo. The other has sculpted pieces of sushi. Both sets have been airbrushed courtesy of Tracie, the artist who teaches chocolate art classes at Greetings and Felicitations. My little chocolate shop really has grown into something I can be proud of, even here with this high caliber of chocolate professionals.

I try to enjoy that fact, and not worry about whatever the officials might be contemplating right now. And before I know it, Logan takes my hand and says, "It's time to go see Nao."

Nao is still an enigma to me. I've tried to puzzle out her possible connections to Noel. But what do a university professor and a stunt man slash thief have in common?

Chapter Ten
Tuesday

Nao's apartment is in a high-rise, and the floor-to-ceiling windows look out onto the city. We're not far from the festival venue. I've heard housing is more expensive in Tokyo than it is in Texas, so it is hard to see how she affords this place on a professor's salary. Maybe she inherited money. Or maybe she has a side gig. So many people do, nowadays.

In the corner, there's a small natural wood writing desk tucked in between the two windows. It must be glorious working there, surrounded by natural light.

Nao places a tray on her teak coffee table. The click of it touching down, and the soft rattle of china, breaks the silence. The tray holds three cups and a pot of tea. Logan and I are sitting on a sleek – and decidedly uncomfortable – sofa. Nao sits catty-corner to us in a springy-looking modern plastic chair. The chair is hunter green. It's one of the only splashes of color in this place.

Even at home she's dressed up, in a flowy pale green dress. As she leans forward and pours the tea, Nao says, "I suppose Noel is still missing."

"Unfortunately, yes," Logan says. "I'm sorry about your friend."

"We weren't friends exactly." Nao gestures for us to take our tea. "He came to me asking about some research."

"Research?" Logan echoes. "Was he interested in detective fiction?"

Nao shakes her head. "I'm also a sponsor for a traditional Japanese culture club at the University. Noel was interested in finding out about some sculptures he had found. I later found out he had stolen them. But they weren't really worth much anyway, since they were obvious reproductions." She hisses air through her teeth. "An art connoisseur, Noel is not."

Something sounds a little pat about all of this. But whatever she's hiding – if I'm not just imagining it – it seems improbable that she could have killed Noel. After all, she was still on the roof when we fell over, so it seems unlikely that she could have gotten into the movie studio building before he did. That's the frustration: all my possible suspects so far have a clear alibi. Unless whatever killed Noel was introduced to his system or put on his person before he entered the building. In which case – alibis become mostly irrelevant.

As I'm examining the beautiful taupe and gold cup, it passes through my mind that in a lot of the mysteries stacked up in my booth, tea is drugged or poisoned. And whoever the elegant lady is serving it is usually the murderer. I hesitate before drinking out of my cup, and Nao notices. She arches an eyebrow at me. I take a long sip of tea. It's a nice oolong, with just a hint of bitterness. And it should be safe. After all, it would make it a lot more obvious she's hiding something if she drugged us now, when we're just asking basic questions.

I ask, "Did you see what happened to Noel's jacket yesterday, before he went over the roof?"

"Before you both went over the roof, you mean?" Nao stands up. "I took it with me for safekeeping. I assume he will contact me when he turns back up. I also assume you want to have a look at it."

"Yes, please," I say.

Nao moves to a mirrored hall closet with a sliding door. She takes out the thin suit jacket, brings it over, and hands it to me. "It's nothing special."

I take a pair of latex gloves out of my purse and slide them on before I start going through the pockets. I don't want to contaminate evidence. Not that the police at this point even believe there's been a crime. But when they do find Noel's body and get around to searching the movie studio, they're going to find my fingerprints all over everything. It's too bad I hadn't had a pair of gloves on me yesterday. Let alone my purse.

It really is an ordinary jacket, without hidden pockets or anything sewn into the lining. There's no wallet in here, or his phone. Which is a shame, because it would have been useful.

Logan asks her, "What were you and Noel fighting about?"

Nao waves a dismissive hand. "Oh, that. It was nothing. He asked me to dinner and I said no."

That sounds like a poorly improvised lie. I say, "It looked like Noel was trying to steal your cell phone."

Nao huffs. "He was trying to put his cell phone number in it."

Okay. That at least sounds plausible. Maybe she's not lying, then.

"You know Noel was married, right?" Logan asks.

"Was?" Nao repeats. "Are you saying he and Connie split up, or that you think Noel is dead?"

"The second one," I admit. "Which is why we need to know your reaction when he asked you out."

Nao says, "It was nothing like that. He said he had a business proposal. I have no idea what it was. But surely it wasn't legal."

In one of the jacket pockets, I find a plane ticket to Belize, in Noel's name, dated for two weeks from now. I hadn't expected that. Had Noel bought it the night before he died, in an effort to actually get away from the fight he had had with his wife? For a brief moment, I wonder if Noel might have been trying to fake his own death. But that's impossible. No one could have faked it through the chest compressions I had done trying to revive him. Perhaps he had been trying to fake his death, and something had gone wrong. That still doesn't explain why the plane ticket was dated so far out. He would have wanted to leave the country as soon as possible, to prevent being discovered.

So that is probably a dead end. But it does bring up a good point.

I ask Logan, "Can you look into whether Noel had a life insurance policy, and who benefits."

Logan takes out his phone and starts typing a text. He says, "I probably should have done that already."

I realize why he didn't. He hadn't really believed I'd found a body. So that level of investigation had seemed premature. But Noel hasn't turned up anywhere – alive or dead – so my story is starting to sound more plausible.

Nao says, "Surely that's not necessary. Noel is good at disappearing. He always turns back up."

Logan looks at me, like, *You going to tell her you saw his body – which then disappeared?*

But I'm focusing more on how she's talking about Noel. Always doing something isn't how you describe someone who turned up at your door one time asking for research. Why is she hiding something?

I find mints and a pair of sunglasses in one of the other pockets. Once I take those out, I feel there's something puffy still in there. I pull out a small crumpled sheet of paper. When I uncrumple it, it turns out to be a typewritten message threatening revenge. The wording is a bit hazy, but Noel had clearly upset someone. He'd read the message and crumpled it. But then he had kept it. Why? Maybe he had been somewhere where he hadn't felt comfortable throwing it away, and then he'd just forgotten he had it.

So how long ago had the message arrived? There's no way of knowing. With the paper being under commonly used items like mints, it could theoretically have been shoved into the pocket yesterday. But I get the feeling that it had been there for longer.

The note ends with, *You know what you did. Confess now, before it is too late.*

Of course, it seems likely that Noel has done so many illegal things, he wasn't quite certain what he was expected to confess to.

Logan points to the words, *You know what you did.* He asks, "Could this be from the angry chocolatier from the festival?"

I think about it. But I don't see a possible connection between her and Noel. I say, "Surely not. But Dawn is already investigating her. If anything connects her to Noel, I'm sure your sister will find it."

Nao is listening to our conversation while she refills the teacups. She doesn't say anything, but she does look alarmed.

There isn't much else of note in the jacket. Just a second pack of mints, and a couple of 500-yen coins.

Nao says, "I guess if Noel really is missing, I will have to turn this over to the police. They will want to know that his plane ticket wasn't used."

I'm more concerned about the threatening note. I ask Nao, "Can you think of anyone Noel might have been afraid of? Or anyone he had wronged?"

Nao says, "Honestly, I don't know him that well." Probably to change the subject, she says, "I hate that you've come all the way over here for relatively little information. Let me make it up to you. I have the perfect kimono for you to take home."

"Aren't kimonos expensive?" I ask. I'd seen ads for renting kimonos to wear in historic parts of Japan, but they're not exactly everyday clothing, even here.

"Yes and no," Nao says. "People wear them for weddings and formal occasions, and if you buy them new, they can cost quite a lot. But at the same time, a lot of old people die with kimonos that nobody wants, and they wind up in landfills, or at best, thrift shops. These are special garments, that used to be handed down through generations, but now fewer people want old things. They want fast fashion and easy trends. The club I sponsor recently did a project rescuing unwanted kimonos and turning them into modern jackets, purses – even pants. There's a long tradition of kimonos being re-tailored into other garments to hide significant wear on the cloth. But we kept the ones that were in excellent shape, to share kimono culture with visitors to Japan at our next event. We want everyone to be able to try it."

I protest, "I'm not sure I'd ever have an appropriate occasion to wear something like that."

"You never know." Nao goes into her bedroom and comes out carrying a dress box. "If you want, I can show you how to put it on. There's a lot of layers involved, and you usually have to get someone else help you tie the bow in the back."

I don't remember actually agreeing to accept the gift, but somehow Nao is already explaining what an obi is – a wide belt worn higher than your midsection – and how many layers are involved in dressing, and how it's cool that the sleeves function as pockets.

Twenty minutes later, I come out of Nao's room dressed in a green and blue floral kimono, with a black obi wrapped around my body and poofed out behind me in a way that makes it difficult to sit down. I'm still not sure how Nao kept me from asking any more real questions during all that time.

Logan gives me an appreciative look and says, "You definitely need to bring that home."

"See?" Nao says. "I knew your fiancé would like it."

My new phone buzzes with a text. It's Patsy, telling me, *Chloe needs to be over at the film studio in thirty minutes. It looks like almost everyone wants to go. Ash said to tell you he's only ditching the booth because Dawn and Fisher are staying to watch it for him. Can you meet us there?*

I groan. "We need to be at the movie studio in less than half an hour if we're going to use Chloe's cameo as an excuse to look around."

Nao gives me a wicked grin. "That means you can't waste time changing. I guess you're going to get a chance to wear the kimono after all. Do it with confidence, and no one will judge you."

"Thanks for putting that idea into my head." I sigh. "I think we need a taxi. I already feel self-conscious enough that I'm not about to try wearing all this on public transportation."

Nao gives me a pair of cloth shoes to complete my outfit and neatly folds the clothes I'd been wearing into the dress box, which she thrusts into my hands. I don't have time to argue.

I text Ash, *Have you left yet?*

Ash texts back, *I'm getting in the elevator.*

I text, *Can you bring eight boxes of the assorted truffles? I find chocolate makes it easier to get people to talk to you.*

He texts back, *Sure. But I thought you wanted to snoop, not talk to people.*

I mean, can't both be true?

Chapter Eleven
Tuesday

"Nice dress," Ash says.

"It's a kimono, Ash." I say. "It's no big deal."

"Yeah, but if I say nice kimono, it sounds more genuine than I want to feel. What guy wants to tell their friend they're pretty? It's weird."

Imogen says, "I think it's beautiful. Do you think your friend could get me one too?"

I say, "She's actually a murder suspect. But probably." I text Imogen Nao's contact information.

Ash hands me two bags with *Greeting and Felicitations* written on the sides. The chocolates I asked him to bring are inside.

A *Quiet Please – We are recording*, sign is on the door to the sound stage. Chloe has already gone inside to do her scene. Ash and Imogen have waited for me and Logan, while Patsy and Arlo are watching Chloe. I know it has to be killing Ash to think he's missing anything.

I text Patsy to let her know I'm here, and to ask, *Will everyone freak if we open the door?*

She texts back, *We're about to take a break.*

Okay. So we need to wait.

Logan asks Imogen, "So whatever happened with that boat?"

Imogen had inherited a boat named *Santiago's Dream* from the writer who may have been responsible for her father's death. It had been bittersweet, a sign that he may have felt remorse.

Imogen says, "I kept it. Right now, we're renting it as an Air B&B. But, someday, Ash and I want to travel the whole Gulf coast." She takes Ash's hand. Which I guess is okay, despite his anti-PDA statements, since we're the only ones here. "At first, I didn't want anything to do with something Flint has owned. But me and my sweetie have both done a lot of healing since then."

Ash says, "I don't think I've changed that much."

Logan laughs. "You're still ducking out of sight whenever trouble arrives."

Ash says, "I did help you with that goat. And the mechanical room."

Logan says, "Don't imagine I don't appreciate it. But those are low-risk activities."

"I'm a low-risk kind of guy." Ash gestures around us. "I'd think you would appreciate the support."

The door opens and Arlo waves us inside. He says, "You guys should see Chloe. She was born to ham it up."

Some of the people we'd seen yesterday are here. The two Latino guys are still behind the cameras, fiddling with settings or something. Several of the other folks we had seen are conferring over a script in the corner. One guy is sitting on a kaiju suit, which is at waist height, with the front half flopped over backwards. The suit next to it has fallen over, basically curling into the lap of the third deflated suit.

In front of a green screen, there is an Asian woman with blue hair wearing a black track suit. Connie is standing next to her, wearing an identical track suit – though she is significantly taller – and a blue wig. Surprisingly, their features are somewhat similar. I guess with the right camera angle – and if her face isn't directly to the camera – she could pass for the actress she is doubling.

There's a craft services table over at the far side of the room, past the miniature city. The rest of the actors are clustered around it, eating sandwiches.

Patsy and Chloe are on this side of the room, standing near the wall. We follow Arlo over to them.

"So how'd it go?" I ask Chloe.

"It was great!" Chloe is wearing a headband with cat ears and an attached tiara. She's holding Honda. "I get to be the alien princess who brought the cat to help save humanity." She scratches the calico's chin, cooing, "Who's a good girl, Honda, yes you are. You made me look so good."

"Is it done?" I ask, a little disappointed that I'd missed Chloe's big moment.

"There's still my big death scene, at the hands of the villains who made the Kaiju hostile. Later in the movie, Honda avenges me with her laser vision." She looks down at the cat. "Right, little Honda Wanda?"

Patsy asks, "Do all of the Youtubers die at the end of their cameos?"

"Pretty much," Chloe says. "Hudson is supposed to be here when we're done with break, to do his scene. We'll probably get to see him act."

Connie comes over to us. She's holding a sandwich filled with whipped cream and strawberries. She addresses Patsy, "Hello dear, I don't think we've met."

"I'm Patsy, Chloe's aunt."

"She's your aunt?" Connie asks Chloe. She gestures at me. "I thought you said Felicity was your aunt."

"We both are," Patsy says quickly. Lies begetting lies.

Connie finishes her sandwich. She looks from me to Patsy and back again. "Sisters, huh? I can totally see the resemblance."

Arlo, who has dated both of us, goes beet red.

So sisters it is, at least for the duration of this case.

To deflect her questions, I hold up the Greetings and Felicitations bags and announce, "I've brought chocolate." I glance over at craft services, then I whisper, "There's not enough for everyone. Just a few of the folks I met yesterday." I take one of the boxes of truffles out and hand it to her.

Connie says, "Don't worry. I won't tell anyone." She holds up her phone with her other hand. "Want to see the stunt we're working out?"

She shows us an animation giving a rough idea of what's supposed to happen. She explains, "Kudo has a thing for shots up on the roof, and this time he's using this building. There's another stunt set up involving a crane arm, where the villain's main henchman is supposed to climb out onto it, while being chased by a baby kaiju. I'm supposed to reach out from the second-floor window and try to catch him while he's dangling from the hook at the bottom of the load line. He refuses the help and I turn away, shocked. The implication is that the little kaiju swoops in and eats him."

"That sounds complicated," Chloe says.

Connie says, "Not really. There's a fire escape leading to the roof, and I'm going to be anchored to it with wires. There's an air mat set up under the crane, in case anything fails. We're supposed to have someone arriving tomorrow who can fill in for Noel." Her voice catches. After all, her husband is missing, presumed dead. But she's trying to hide her worry and grief. She clears her throat and gestures across the room. "You should grab a couple of sandwiches from the table. The caterer is Director Kudo's aunt, and she makes everything with precision and love."

We all follow her over, not the least bit ashamed about swarming the table.

"Where is Kudo?" I ask. I don't see him anywhere.

Connie gestures at the door. "He had to leave unexpectedly. He had his assistant take over to finish the scene, but after that, we're breaking until he comes back."

That's disappointing. I had hoped to ask him a few questions privately, about Noel, and about the staff – all the while trying to gauge if he is the kind of man who would murder his love interest's husband. Because, so far, he and Connie are still my strongest suspects, and I really hope it isn't Connie.

"What am I looking at?" Arlo asks, gesturing to the sandwiches on the table, alongside salads and side dishes and little plates of cake. The sandwiches are stacked together vertically, each cut half facing up, showing off the filling.

Connie grabs one of the meat sandwiches and says, "Japanese sandos are on milk bread, so they're all going to be slightly sweet." She gestures with the sandwich she's holding. "This is a strawberry sando, with strawberries and whipped cream. It's completely sweet. The other two are savory. You have a katsu sando, with sliced pork cutlet and a tangy sauce, and egg salad sando, which is pretty similar to Western egg salad, except it uses Kewpie mayo and has a soft-boiled egg in the middle."

I pick up one of each. After I've sampled the fluffy fruit, the crispy pork, and the rich egg, I say, "I like the katsu best. The sauce almost feels familiar."

Connie says, "That's because it has both ketchup and Worcestershire sauce in with the soy and ginger."

"Makes sense," Logan says.

Ash basically inhales his sandwiches. Then he gestures over to the kaiju suits. "Do you think I could try one of those on?"

Connie turns and says something in Japanese to one of the guys standing by the table. He says something back to Ash, gesturing at the watch on his wrist.

"What did he say?" Ash asks.

"He said you have to wait until the writers are done with their script changes. Then someone can help you put the suit on in maybe twenty minutes."

Logan says, "I thought you said there is a writer's room upstairs."

"Well," Connie says, "One of those blokes thinks the upstairs is haunted. We've heard noises too, but I think it is just mice. Honda has caught a few, and left them as presents."

"Fair enough," Ash says. "In the meantime, point me in the direction of special effects. Taniguchi said he would show me around."

Connie says, "He's down the hall."

"I know where it is," I say.

Logan and Arlo both follow along as I escort Ash to the effects lab. We meet Hudson, who is on his way in. He joins us just as Ash knocks on the door.

From inside, Taniguchi said, "Hai! Douzo!" Which I think means, *come in*.

Ash opens the door just as there's a hissing noise. Taniguchi, who is holding a remote, spins around in a bucket seat chair, looking delighted until there's a crack, and the chair breaks from the upright holding it, dumping him on the floor. Taniguchi is middle aged, so I move forward, worried that he might be injured.

But the special effects guy smiles up from the floor and introduces himself to Ash. "Hajimemashite. I am Wataru Taniguchi. I'm in charge of special effects."

I try to make eye contact with Logan, but he is focused on helping Taniguchi up from the floor. I hadn't gotten Taniguchi's first name before. But Logan has to realize that Wataru Taniguchi must be Wataru T. Doesn't that make him the same guy who sent Emi that message? The one desperate to meet up with her?

But if Logan gets the connection, he's hiding it very well. He reaches into one of the bags I'm holding and takes out a box of truffles. Logan says, "We appreciate you taking the time to show us around."

Taniguchi takes the box and sets it on the table. He tells Logan, "Arigato gozaimaus! You seem to have caught me at an embarrassing time." He gestures at the tipped over chair on the floor. "Honda the cat will not be riding up into her spaceship on that thing."

Logan leans over to check out the broken piece. "I'd love to help you fix that."

"Me too," Ash says. "I'm good with a welding torch."

"I can help hold it," Hudson says. "I'm not really technical, though."

Taniguchi says, "Douzo." Which in this case is probably closer to, *have at it, if you want*.

I'm beginning to see that it is a very useful word. The three guys start working on putting the chair back together.

Taniguchi turns to me. "What a lovely kimono. I'm glad to see you embracing our traditional culture." He opens the box of truffles and takes one out. He says, "Unless there is something more to it. Perhaps *Murder on the Orient Express* really is your favorite book, and you are sending someone a message."

It takes me a second to put it together. There had been a kimono found on the train in Christie's book. It had been scarlet, perhaps a little joke on Christie's part signifying that it was a red herring. I tell Taniguchi, "This kimono was a gift. I hadn't intended to wear it today, but I didn't have time to change."

Taniguchi looks skeptical. He pops the truffle into his mouth. He looks pleased as he chews. After he swallows, he asks, "Have you heard the expression, there are no accidents?"

"I have," I admit. "But I don't believe it is true."

"I am curious," Taniguchi says. "How do you feel about the ending of *Murder on the Orient Express*, with the murderers not facing justice. Many feel that it is satisfying, since the man they killed was irredeemably evil."

I say, "That's the biggest flaw in the book. Poirot was working with the police, but in the end he decides to be judge and jury all by himself. It's too much power." I adjust the collar of the kimono. "Still.

I think a jury may well have acquitted them or given them a minor sentence. In America, there's a law that allows for a jury to nullify a case, because they feel honest justice contradicts the law. It doesn't happen often, but it is possible."

I try to read Taniguchi's expression. What is he trying to tell me? Whatever he has to do with Emi, he seems to feel that he is on the side of justice. Right?

Or, possibly, he's just an avid reader wanting to discuss an interesting book. Maybe he has no idea we have Emi's phone. Or maybe he's not connected to Emi at all, and it's just a crazy coincidence. But I can't discount the possibility that it's not.

Taniguchi says, "How do you even define justice? Is it not like trying to feel the breath of a butterfly wing?"

Now he's getting poetic. Which is even more confusing. Are we talking about Emi, or aren't we? And is he asking for an answer? He seems to be waiting for one.

I stammer, "It's when things are morally right. People who hurt others get punished. People who do good are rewarded."

Taniguchi laughs. "Such a simple view of the world. I wish to live where you do, Koerberu Sensei."

I say, "The world I live in isn't always just. You just asked me to define what justice is."

"True," Taniguchi says. He takes out his phone and asks, "May I have your number. I have spoken with our janitor, and he is willing to speak with you. I can share his contact information."

He sends it to me, and I nod, letting him know that I've received it. I say, "Arigatou."

Ash says, "Check this out." He sits in the chair, draws up his knees and spirals upwards as the device lifts towards the ceiling.

Taniguchi claps his hands. "Sugoi! Arigatou!"

There's a soft chime from Ash's pocket. Ash says, "Okay, now let me down. It's time to go back to the set."

Logan says, "You set a timer when we left, didn't you?"

Ash says, "How else was I going to know when twenty minutes was up?"

Taniguchi says, "Thank you again. I have several other props to build today."

Which I think is his way of telling us he is done chatting and we need to leave.

When we get out of the room and the door has closed behind us, I let out a nervous burst of air. I flutter my hands to get the others' attention. "This is the Wataru chasing Emi, right? The potential threat was from Wataru T. And he's T for Taniguchi. That's why he was asking me all those complicated questions about justice. Emi must have done something wrong, don't you think?"

"That's not necessarily the same guy," Hudson says. "Wataru is a very common name. I have three friends named Wataru. It's probably why the guy who messaged Emi included a last initial, so she'd know which one. But Taniguchi is a common name too. He might as well call himself John Smith."

"You think it may be an alias?" Ash asks.

"Also, not necessarily," Arlo says. "But it does strongly suggest he might be the guy we are looking for. Otherwise, it feels like one coincidence too many."

Ash says, "Want me to talk to him? I can tell him I want to interview him about special effect techniques for a special episode of my podcast."

"But your podcast is all about true crime," I point out.

"Then I'll start a second podcast," Ash says.

He'd do it too. I close my mouth, with nothing to retort. When Ash gets an idea, very little can stop him.

"You do that," Logan says. "Fee and I will keep looking for evidence of the body. Also, we need to figure out what's making the noises upstairs. It could be a clue."

Ash says, "Don't you want to see me in a kaiju costume?"

"Not necessarily," I say.

"I do," Hudson says. "I'm always up to take video of crazy stunts."

Logan moves towards the front of the building. Today, one of the women we met yesterday is sitting at the reception desk. That is why the door was locked last time. Everyone – the receptionist included – had been invited to lunch.

I nod at her and give a more confident, "Ohayo gozaimaus."

She replies, "Ohayo gozaimaus," back and smiles at us until it becomes clear that we are headed for the staircase, at which point she races from around the reception desk and manages to get between us and the stairs. She makes a *definitely not* cross with her arms. She sounds upset, but I don't understand what she's saying.

"Sumimasen," I tell her, another good general-purpose word that includes the meaning of *I'm sorry*.

We back away down the hallway, offering apologetic mini-bows.

Logan says under his breath, "We'll have to find somebody willing to escort us upstairs."

I say, "Maybe we can manage that later. It sounds like right now we are destined to help Ash dress up like Godzilla."

Logan points out, "Godzilla is a copywritten monster. Those three suits we saw in the corner were all unique creations. Personally, I like the one that looks like a turtle and a grasshopper had a baby."

I say, "But one of them kind of looks like a dinosaur. Which is what I always thought Godzilla was."

"Nope," Logan says. "Gorilla whale."

"You didn't know that until today," I insist.

"Did so," Logan says. "I told you I like monster movies."

"What else don't I know about you?" I ask. My tone is teasing, but I really am still worried I've been an unobservant girlfriend and now fiancé.

He says, "I hate wearing socks around the house, I failed fourth grade, and I'm afraid of snakes. So if we do ever get to take that guy up on his offer to visit origin in Brazil, I'm probably going to be the one hiding behind you."

I say, "As long as you're willing to squash the bugs." I shudder. "Not that I'm afraid of them. I just get all grossed out over the actual squashing."

"Noted," Logan says. "Anything else I should note for future reference?"

"Did you really fail fourth grade?" I ask.

Logan says, "I really disliked the teacher, so I spent a lot of time drawing planes."

"I can sympathize with that. I had this one English teacher that disagreed with everything I said in my papers, so I started just writing notes in class and turning those in as my assignments. I got an A on every one."

"Fee," Logan flashes me a mischievous grin. "Don't tell me you didn't actually read the books."

"Guilty," I say. I should be embarrassed to admit this, considering how much ribbing I've given Logan for not liking to read fiction. I've actually gotten him into reading, at least occasionally, and this morning, I noticed him perusing the titles in the stacks of mystery novels. But we're being honest, and that feels good.

Logan opens the door heading back into the sound stage. Ash and Hudson are still waiting for the writers to finish their huddle. By the time we walk over to join them, the writers are standing up, sharing a few last jokes, and heading off to turn over their work to the assistant director.

Hudson asks Ash, "So which one of these monsters strikes your fancy?"

Ash points at the one that had fallen over. "Who wouldn't want to look like a butterfly dragon?"

"I think that one's supposed to be a girl," Hudson says.

"So?" Ash says. "Help me figure out how to get into this thing."

Hudson improvises a phone stand out of the edge of one of the dessert trays on the craft services table. He starts recording.

Ash says, "This suit is heavier than it looks."

Somehow, the suit feels out of place, and I try to remember if it was leaned over like that yesterday, when I had been in this room. I don't think it was. Suddenly, I have a sense of foreboding.

Hudson and Ash both study the suit trying to find the zipper. When Hudson finally spies the tab and tugs on it, I can't believe how he spotted it.

I say, "That zipper was hidden so perfectly. I wonder why they went through so much trouble."

Logan says, "That's the thing about monster movies. If you can see the zipper, it ruins the illusion. Then you're just looking at some guy in a suit. Which isn't nearly so scary."

Hudson asks, "What's this crud on the zipper?" He tugs, then once the zipper gets past its stuck spot, it zips open with a *spppppppf*. The head of the suit flops forward, and there, encased up to his waist, is Noel. We all gasp, with the exception of Hudson, who recoils with a nauseated sounding, "Ugh."

He looks over at his phone, his expression horrified, then his shoulders slump in relief. "Thank goodness we're not streaming live." He moves over to the craft services table and uses the backs of his hands to press the side button that will turns the phone off. Then he squirts an excessive amount of hand sanitizer on his palms, from the bottle on the table.

Ash seems frozen in place, keeping the suit balanced so Noel doesn't take an undignified dive to the floor. Logan approaches and helps him lean Noel back against the wall. It looks awkward and unnatural. Most people are looking away. Arlo is calling the local police – again.

Logan tells me, "You must have been truly out of it, Fee, if you thought there wasn't a mark on this guy. Clearly, he's been stabbed."

"That's not right," I tell Logan. "And surely he couldn't have been in that suit last night. The police were all through this place. You have a missing human, the first place you look is the human sized suit."

I spot Chloe, standing with Connie and the actress Connie is doubling. Connie looks like she might faint again, and silent tears are escaping her eyes. She's still the one with the most to gain from Noel's death – but if she is faking shock right now, she's one heck of an actress in her own right.

The woman she's doubling for wraps her arms around Connie in a supportive hug. Connie grips the woman's arm so hard that the actress grimaces, but she doesn't let go.

I feel her pain, feel tears trying to form in the corners of my own eyes. But the best thing I can do for her right now is to keep things under control. Hoping she can understand me, I ask the actress, "Can you get her out of here, somewhere where she can sit down?"

"Ryokai. I mean, right, I can do that." The woman turns Connie away from the unsavory sight. Imogen and Patsy help lead her toward the door.

Chloe seems rooted to the spot, glancing between Connie and me, unable to decide if she should stay or go.

When I point at Chloe, she squeaks, "I didn't do this."

"I know," I say. "Give me your phone. You took footage in here last night."

Reluctantly, Chloe hands over her phone. I scroll back through the clips – and she's recorded a LOT of video since arriving in Japan – until I get to one that shows the wall. I show the phone to Logan and Hudson. "Look. The butterfly-dragon suit was sitting up. And it looked a lot more deflated."

"So Noel's body wasn't in it when we were here last night," Chloe says in a shaky voice. She still can't seem to look in the direction where Noel is propped up. "What does that mean?"

"I have no idea," I admit.

Chapter Twelve
Tuesday

I look down at my hands. You'd never know that the police just fingerprinted me. They'd done it electronically, using a hand-held device that could electronically match all of our prints with those at the scene.

This time, they sent a detective who speaks English. Small mercies, I guess.

We've all been separated, until the cops are able to interview us. Although it seems like at this point, it would be a bit late to try and get our stories straight. I can't imagine how Connie must be taking all of this, being alone and about to be interrogated. I feel helpless, not being able to change that.

I'm sitting in someone's office. It's the same one I saw the stack of file folders in yesterday. Only now, instead of on the desk, the folders have been filed into the desk drawer, alongside older more yellow file folders. I can't help myself. While I'm waiting, I start flipping through them. Some of them are financial statements, reporting to the company that actually green lit Kudo's vision. It looks like Kudo's last two movies didn't turn a profit. He must be counting on this one to turn things around for him. Given that – even if he really does have a crush on Connie – would he really have been impulsive enough to kill a guy on-set when it was bound to derail the movie?

All the evidence I have on him is circumstantial at best. A longing look that passed between him and Connie, and the fact that he has a key to this place and knows the layout better than most. It does seem odd that he'd disappeared from set right before Noel's body was discovered. Perhaps, if Noel's death really was an act of impulsive anger, Kudo realized in the clearer light of the next day that he had done something stupid, and he just ran.

But that's a ton of conjecture.

There are personnel files here on everyone, but most of the documents are written in Japanese. I start using that text translation app to figure out what I'm looking at. Noel has two notes in his file about him not showing up on set when he was expected.

Kudo has a weekly therapy appointment marked in his, though it's not clear what for. There's also a note about him having been involved in an assault, although the police later dropped the charges. But that does show him as having a temper – which makes him a solid suspect.

I look up the janitor. According to Taniguchi's text, the guy's name is Hiro Ito. The name order is flipped in his file, so I think Hiro is his first name. I didn't get a chance to call him, so I'm looking at his file blind. He's in his thirties, married, two dependents. So he's got kids. There's a note about him one time sleeping on the job. So maybe his kids are young and need a lot of care? Or else money might be tight and he's working a number of jobs. And then I move the camera, and the word *contractor* pops up in English. Which makes sense. Assuming that much of the building is being used for storage, it would be hard to justify someone cleaning here full time. He probably takes a number of cleaning jobs to make up full-time pay. So the big question is – was he even here yesterday? Or can he prove he was somewhere else?

Something touches my leg, and I flinch away. I look down, and there's Honda, her tail up and twitching happily like a rattlesnake's. It's definitely her, with the heart behind her ear. I'm becoming more and more convinced that there is only one calico related to this building – no matter how improbable that is.

"What about it, little cat," I ask, putting a hand down for her to sniff. "Are you able to walk through walls?"

Honda meows. I'm fairly certain she wasn't in this room when I sat down. She could have been hiding in the bookcase, or in the tall vase in the corner, but somehow, I don't think so. So how did she get in? And does it have anything to do with the way Noel died?

Honda jumps up onto the desk. I scratch her chin and she lifts her face, eyes closed and happy. Life is simple for a cat. I withdraw my hand, and Honda flops down on the desk. She is such a little cat. She sighs heavily as though all the weight of the world rests on her tiny frame. I get how she feels.

I tell her, "Usually when things go wrong, I cope by feeding people. That's not an option here, so what else am I going to do but snoop?"

She blinks. I decide to take that as agreement.

I send Janitor Ito a text, composed with Google Translate, asking him if we can talk. He replies that he is free tomorrow morning, if I can bring a translator. I agree.

Just as I hit send, the door to the office opens, and I freeze, the janitor's personnel folder still open in my hand. Detective Yamada looks pointedly at the folder and frowns at me.

I point at Honda, like it is all her fault. He rolls his eyes. I slide the folder back in the drawer and push it closed.

Yamada says, "Let's leave the cat here. I don't want her giving you more bad ideas."

I follow him to a conference room, where he joins the other detective on the other side of the table from me. Detective Matsumoto doesn't speak English, so I guess he's just sitting in as a formality.

"Can I see your travel documents?" Yamada asks.

I pass over my passport and my driver's license.

He looks at my passport. "You're from Texas. Where JFK got shot."

I don't even try to explain how far away Galveston is from Dallas. I just say softly, "That's right."

"And you claim that yesterday, you found Noel Bell's body."

Again, I say, "That's right."

"But you claim to have attempted resuscitation, despite the fact that Mr. Bell had been stabbed through the heart."

"Wait. No." I wave my hands at him, frustrated at not being able to express myself more clearly. "Yes, I attempted to revive him. But he hadn't been stabbed."

Yamada sighs. "I understand you have medical training. You more than anyone should understand that blood doesn't flow from a wound if the victim is already dead."

"That's true," I admit. "It must be some kind of illusion."

Yamada says, "What is not an illusion is your fingerprints on the victim's skin, and the injuries to the chest area consistent with punching. You admit to having a fight with Mr. Bell yesterday, and you claim he pulled you off a roof. Did you then follow him into this building and attack him?"

"No," I say. "I did follow him, but I found him collapsed and unresponsive."

I look over and notice that Detective Matsumoto is drawing a picture of a calico cat in his notebook.

Slowly, I say, "I administered aid. Chest compressions related to CPR can leave bruises on the body, and are even known to break ribs."

Yamada sighs, even more heavily. "What was the nature of your relationship with Mr. Bell?"

"He stole my cell phone. I happened to see him again, and I wanted it back. It's hardly the kind of thing I would attack him over. It would be difficult to find out what he did with my phone if he was dead."

Yamada says, "So there *is* a kind of thing you would attack someone over?"

"No, that's not what I was trying to say." I bring my thumb and forefinger to the bridge of my nose. I am starting to get a massive headache. Detective Matsumoto is staring at something across my line of sight. I look behind me, and there's Honda, sitting on a cabinet full of coffee supplies.

Yamada turns and notices the cat. He's clearly surprised, but trying to hide it.

I tell Honda, "Maybe you really do walk through walls."

Yamada gives me a disapproving look. I'm obviously not helping my situation any. He says, "It isn't hard to find information about you on the internet. You've been involved in solving multiple murder cases."

"That's true," I say, trying not to sound defensive about it.

"Why do you keep getting involved in these cases?"

I shrug. I can't help but notice that Matsumoto's drawing of Honda is really good. I'm not about to bring up the murder books, or anything else I can't explain. I say, "It just sort of happens."

Yamada looks skeptical. He says, "I might be arresting you right now, except that your fingerprints aren't on the knife – but there is someone here whose are."

I'm on edge, and now I'm getting frustrated. "You're not going to tell me who it is, are you?"

"Actually, I am. But only because she is a minor, and she told us you are here as her chaperone."

I feel a sinking weight in my stomach, and the strength has gone out of my arms. Taking a shuddery breath, I say, "Please, no." I had taken on a lot bringing Chloe here. I hadn't been surprised to find out she'd ditched Patsy to come to the movie studio building. And I know there's an assault on her record. But I know she didn't kill Noel. I say, "There has to be a trick to that too. Chloe was in that conference room for a while, and she couldn't have gone anywhere. It was a converted closet or something, because it only locked and unlocked from the outside. It seems likely her prints would have been on a glass or a water bottle, or even the door handle, from when she tried to get out. They could have been lifted and transferred."

"Maybe," Yamada admits. "But why go through all these complicated theories first, when the simple ones are far more likely? Mr. Bell left comments on a number of Chloe's videos. They are relatively innocuous, but given the complaint she made when she met Mr. Bell in person, it is possible that she felt threatened upon seeing him again and stabbed him. It could be considered self-defense, if he actually did threaten her. But it could also have been the unreasoned action of a scared kid."

I stand up. "Chloe did not kill Noel. The whole idea is preposterous."

Yamada says, "I'll be honest with you. We're afraid she's a flight risk. Convince me why I shouldn't take her into custody pending the outcome of the investigation?"

I remember what Hudson had told me about how the Japanese police rarely make an arrest if they don't think they could prove the case in court. Is Yamada bluffing? Trying to get me to confess to save Chloe? Or really hoping to not arrest a foreign kid?

I glance at the coffee cabinet for a moment to think, and to find the reassuring presence of Honda the calico. But, of course, she's not there.

I say, "We're here for the chocolate festival. None of us are planning to leave before the end of the weekend. Chloe is here helping out, and she has collaborations planned throughout the week with other Youtubers. There's a big one on Friday, with a cat toy company and about twenty Japan-based Youtubers. It's supposed to raise money for cats with FIV. I think she'd rather die than miss that. So there's no way she's going anywhere."

Yamada studies me. "How about we compromise, and I hold onto her passport. That way, it would be hard for her to leave the area."

I say, "I thought tourists have to carry their passports at all times. What happens if someone asks for Chloe's while you have it?"

"Then she will likely wind up at the station." He hands me a card. "But calling me at this number should straighten that out."

I take the card. It's not like I have any choice. I put the number in my phone and text both Yamada and Chloe, so that he has my number and Chloe has his.

I get a text back from her that says, *What's going on Aunt Fee?*

Poor kid. She must be terrified.

Chapter Thirteen
Tuesday

We all look a little bedraggled by the time we make it back across the street to the chocolate festival. Arlo has a cat carrier in one hand and a nylon bag filled with cans of cat food and assorted toys in the other. The police had sealed off the crime scene, and since Kudo hadn't been there to do something with the cat, Chloe had insisted we take Honda with us, since the film cast and crew obviously weren't in any condition to deal with the little calico.

I have no idea what we are going to do with Honda, though, since our hotel policy clearly states that service dogs are the only animals permitted in our rooms. Hopefully, we will be able to contact Kudo soon, and he can come get his pet. Logan has been leaving him messages. So far, he hasn't responded.

Hudson says, "Savannah is a huge cat person. Our apartment technically doesn't allow pets, but our landlady loves Savannah's banana bread, so we can probably bribe her to look the other way for a day or two, if Kudo doesn't come for Honda."

"I can add in some chocolates," I volunteer. "And we can make it clear it's just short term."

Chloe mumbles, "We have to get a litter box. I didn't find the one Honda was using at the film studio."

Chloe has clearly been crying, and her eye makeup has smudged out into dark circles. Patsy gives her a hug. I've given her several hugs, too. I've too have been accused of murder, and it was traumatic. But I can't imagine facing something that shocking in a foreign country, away from your family, at seventeen.

Patsy says, "Don't worry, we'll figure this out. The cat, and your passport."

Honda has been crying, too, giving high-pitched heartbroken meows ever since we left the movie studio building, and she's already sounding a bit hoarse. I guess she can't walk through walls, after all, or else she wouldn't still be trapped in the carrier.

Logan asks Hudson, "Are a lot of apartments in Japan pet restricted?"

He nods. "Apartments here are small, and the walls are thin, so loud pets can be a nuisance to your neighbors. There's a lot of wood and paper used in construction – especially in older apartments – that pets can easily damage. Our apartment has textured wallpaper, which I'm sure will be irresistible to a cat. The lack of pets allowed at home is one of the reasons why Japan is known for cat cafes."

Chloe says, "I thought cat cafes originated in Taiwan."

Hudson says. "True. But they became popular because of Japan."

Chloe's phone rings. Her voice raspy, she says, "It's my mom." She steps away to talk to her.

Patsy and Arlo wait on the sidewalk with her, while the rest of us go inside.

I start to go back to check on Chloe, but when I turn, I bump into a guy carrying a big cardboard box and he drops it.

"Sorry," I say, moving to help him pick his stuff up.

"It's okay," he says. "I work for one of the chocolatiers at the chocolate festival up on the sixth floor. You should check it out."

I quip, "Oh, I will." More seriously I say, "I'm actually a vendor at the festival."

"Very nice," he says. "I'm Jack Taylor with Beautiful Chocolate out of Tampa, Florida. I look forward to stopping by your booth."

I look back, seeing Chloe as small and vulnerable, despite her larger-than-life attitude. I know we had to tell her parents what happened. But I wish there had been a way to wait until after we fixed the problem. I feel guilty that this happened to Chloe on my watch.

Logan calls out to me, and I have to rush to meet the others at the elevator before the door closes. Only – there's something tickling at my brain that I've seen Jack Taylor before.

When we approach our booth, Dawn steps off to the side and waves me and Logan over. She whispers, "Emi was here. I saw her watching our booth from a row over. When she noticed I had seen her, she bolted."

Logan says, "This is getting frustrating."

Dawn says, "I followed her as far as the elevator. I watched it go up to the roof. But I can't guarantee she's still there."

Logan says, "Looking up there is worth a shot."

I step over to the booth next door and ask Henri, "Do you have any more of that hot chocolate?"

"Drinking chocolate, mon ami," Henri says. "And of course."

I know the distinction. Hot chocolate is usually made with cocoa powder, and is light and foamy, like hot chocolate milk, while drinking chocolate is made from melting chocolate and then thinning it out with milk or water, giving it a rich mouthfeel. I just have more important things to worry about right now than terminology.

Henri gives us three paper cups with lids, and we promise to pay him when we get back. He doesn't seem concerned.

Logan and I head up to the roof. I'm holding two cups of drinking chocolate, while Logan only has one. I find that my hands are trembling, and with two cups, there's no way to steady them. Am I scared to go back up to the roof garden after everything that happened up there yesterday?

Logan asks, "Do you really think you're going to lure Emi into talking to us with a cup of hot chocolate?"

Apparently, he's not worried about terminology either.

I shrug, trying to keep my hands still so he doesn't see how nervous I am. I say, "It seems like a better shot than offering her truffles."

I try to remind myself that Emi isn't the dangerous one in all of this. She's the one who got the message that she's in danger. Only – that stuff Taniguchi said is still rattling around in my head. Say there is something important about Emi's phone. Could she have killed Noel, either in self-defense or hoping to get her phone back?

When we get to the roof, I spot Emi standing near the glass. She's in profile, half looking out at the city, half watching the elevator. She's wearing a hat and sunglasses, but I can still tell it's her – partly from her model-straight posture and her perfect manicure. She didn't have to come here. And if she is still hanging around, she must want to talk to us. I just don't know why she's so scared.

Instead of heading straight for her, Logan angles towards an empty table. We both sit down on the same side of it. I place both of my cups down on the table, sliding one of them across to where I hope Emi will be sitting.

There are more people up here today, chatting and picnicking. Fisher is at a table over in the corner with the kid from the shogi board booth, and they are deeply absorbed in a game. But the table Logan chose is away from the crowd, enough that we should have privacy to talk.

I see Emi hesitate. I watch her shoulders draw up towards her ears. But if she doesn't approach us, then what's the point?

Logan takes a sip of his drinking chocolate. As though we're having a normal conversation on a normal day, he says, "This came out really well. We might have to start selling this in the shop."

"Maybe," I agree. "It wouldn't be the first time we'd offered some form of hot chocolate."

Emi forces her shoulders away from her ears and strides over to us. She sits down in her spot at the table. Without preamble, she asks, "Were you working with the pickpocket?"

"What? No," I say. "I don't know if you saw the news yesterday, but I chased him and he pulled me off this roof."

Emi nods. I wish I could see her eyes behind the oversized sunglasses. I can't really read her expression. "I thought it might be an elaborate ruse. After all, what are the odds of someone I recognize showing up, if not to get me to let my guard down." She glances over at Logan.

His eyes go wide with surprise, then narrow with hurt. He says, "I was a good guy when you knew me before. I'm still a good guy now."

Emi says, "You were a guy protecting me for money. Who knows where your real loyalties lie." She gestures down at the cup in front of her. "What's this?"

"Drinking chocolate," I say. "Kind of a peace offering. Although, I'm not sure what you think we did to you."

Emi reaches out and takes the cup. Then she swaps it with mine, saying, "You can never be too careful."

I take a sip out of the cup in front of me. Maybe I should have swapped cups with Nao at her apartment, when I'd been worried about the tea. Am I too trusting? The flavor of the chocolate registers on my palate, blooming pleasantly with berry brightness. I tell Logan, "Hey, this isn't the coconut-infused stuff from this morning." I see Emi tense, so I hurry to add, "It tastes just like our bar from that valley in Costa Rica."

Logan takes another sip. "Yep. Henri bought some of our bars to try out. He added just a hint of cherry liqueur to bring out the sweetness. That's why I was thinking we should have it at the shop – though without a liqueur license, we'd have to do cherry syrup or something."

Emi takes off her sunglasses and looks skeptically at Logan. "Really? This is what we're talking about?"

Logan gestures with his cup. "I'm a chocolate maker now. I thought proving that might put you more at ease."

Emi hesitates, then she takes a sip out of her cup. She can't help but smile, because it's a delicious drink. "Let's say I'm convinced."

Logan says, "We want to help you, but we can't if we don't know what's going on."

Emi asks, "How did you wind up with my phone?"

I think about how to explain that one. Whatever I say is going to spook her. So as calmly as I can, I say, "Noel died and I grabbed a nearby phone to call Logan."

Emi starts to stand up from the table.

Logan reaches out a hand across the table. "We didn't kill him."

Emi sits back down. "Well, I didn't either."

"We figured that," I say. "Otherwise, you would have just taken your phone back. We were worried you might be in trouble, since your phone had been stolen, but you never deactivated it."

Suddenly alarmed, Emi reaches across the table and grasps my wrist. "You have my phone on you, right? You didn't deactivate it, did you?"

"No," I stammer. "It's right here, data intact."

Logan draws the phone out of his pocket and sets it on the table.

Emi grabs it. "Let's hope you're right." She goes into the files on the phone and pulls up a PDF. When it loads, she sighs in relief. "It wouldn't have been safe to upload this to the cloud. If someone hacked my account, it would have been simple for them to delete it from all devices."

"What data are we talking about?" Logan asks. "I went through this phone and I didn't see anything out of the ordinary. I don't think that file was even in the list."

A couple of people come off the elevator. They walk past us to find tables.

Emi drops her voice to a whisper. "It's the whistleblower file. I never imagined the phone being stolen. I should have made a backup, but there wasn't time before I had to get on the airplane."

"I'm confused," I say. "Didn't the whole whistleblowing thing happen years ago?"

Emi starts to reply, but one of the passersby doubles back and jostles her arm, trying to force her to let go of the phone. Emi squeaks in protest, and then in pain as the guy twists her wrist to force her to drop the phone.

He scoops it up and starts to move back towards the elevators. I jump up to try to block his path, but Logan is already on the move. He grabs the guy's arm, and the phone drops, skittering back towards me. I grab it, glancing down to make sure the screen isn't broken. It isn't, thanks to a sturdy phone case. I toss it to Emi, then try to help Logan stop the guy, but the would-be thief times it just right and slips into the elevator as it closes. Logan tries to wedge his hand into the door to keep it open, but he just misses and winds up sliding his hand down the seam between the closed doors.

We turn back to Emi. She is still sitting at the table, clutching the phone to her chest. Tears are leaking from her eyes, and she's trembling, and somehow that vulnerability only makes her look more beautiful. Whereas when I cry, I look like a full-on terror. But this isn't about me – or about me imagining past Logan having a crush on Emi.

Something is worrying at my brain, a hint of recognition. Right when the elevator doors had closed, I'd caught a glimpse of the guy's gray jacket. It had been the same style jacket I'd glimpsed yesterday. I gesture in the direction of the elevators. "That was the same guy who was following us yesterday. At first, I thought it was you, Emi, but then later I caught a glimpse of the gray coat."

Color drains from Emi's face. "He followed you to get to me. Or really, to get to the phone. After he tried to kill me last night – he knew I'd come here to get my phone back."

Logan sucks in a breath. "Are you hurt?"

Emi lifts her sleeve, revealing a white bandage wrapped around her forearm. "Nothing too bad. Just a gash."

Sympathy shines in Logan's eyes. "Whatever is going on is worse than I thought."

Emi says, "My case as a whistleblower was so public that a girl who wanted to do the same thing reached out to me. She works for a manufacturing company back in the States that has been illegally dumping chemical waste into the nearby lake. We were supposed to meet up, but she never showed, and then last week, she sent me this file, with proof."

I say, "So this had nothing to do with the people who were threatening you back when Logan was protecting you."

Emi asks, "So why didn't you use your own phone?"

"What?" I ask.

"You said you found my phone, but the thief stole my phone right after he took yours. So if you found the phones, why didn't you call for help on yours?"

"Mine wasn't there," I say sadly.

Emi looks suspicious again.

I take the loaner phone out of my pocket. "I've been using this."

Emi nods, like she finally believes me. Maybe because it's such a basic old phone.

But thinking about that moment when I had met Emi while leaving the airport, I finally realize why I thought I had recognized Grey Suit Guy yesterday. He was the one following Emi out of the doors at the airport. If he had been after her phone, and potentially trying to hurt Emi, having Noel steal said phone at the airport had potentially saved her life. Noel couldn't have known that – or could he? Maybe he had become a hero.

But news of Noel's death must have put the guy back on the trail. Assuming he is the bad guy here, and that Emi isn't the one who killed Noel.

Logan is busy scanning the crowd, looking for other threats, so I keep this thought to myself. It's clear that Emi doesn't trust us. So it's only fair that I don't completely trust her. We only have her word that she's helping this other whistleblower. For all we know, she might be looking for the girl for nefarious reasons.

I ask, "If there was so much danger, why come to Japan?"

"My contact for releasing the data told me that if I didn't want to meet him in the same area as the company doing the dumping, where they would be in a strong position to stop us, he had friends in Japan who would help process the data and get it into the right hands. I wanted to keep my husband and my kids out of it. We already had to uproot everything once. So I told them that I wanted to go visit my family. You should have seen my kids. They have a lot of screen time with their grandparents, but they've never met them in person. They were doing all sorts of things to try and get me to take them with me."

"But of course you couldn't," Logan says.

Emi says, "I really did intend to go to the countryside in Sendai. I doubt anyone knows I have family there, so it seemed the best place to get entirely off the grid. But then my phone got stolen, so I decided to stay around for a few days and get a new one, and replace some of the stuff that had been in my bag. I couldn't believe that right after seeing you get your phone snatched, the same guy ripped me off, too. It was like he wasn't even worried about getting caught."

Logan says, "So you weren't entirely lying to us. You were planning to visit your grandparents. You just omitted the reason why."

"I didn't tell anybody. Even Ricky didn't know anything about what I was doing. He would have wanted to come with me to try and protect me, and if anything happens to me, the kids are going to need him to be there more than ever."

I say, "He must be worried sick, having been unable to reach you for days."

I think about those missed calls that had come in while I'd had the phone off. Why hadn't he left a message? And why had the calls stopped?

Emi says, "I sent him an email that I'd lost my phone, and that I would be in touch once I got a new one. Besides, he knows that the area where my grandparents live doesn't have great phone reception. So he's probably feeling more left out than worried."

"But you really are in danger," I point out. "There was that threat from Wataru T. that came in on your phone. And I'm afraid he may be closer than you think."

Emi cocks her head. "Wataru wouldn't have been threatening me. He's my contact for the news outlet that wants the exclusive on the chemical leaks. And I doubt he's even in this country. He lives in Seattle."

I blink stupidly at her. I take a long sip of my drinking chocolate, trying to recalibrate everything I'd been thinking. Finally, I manage to say, "So Wataru T. isn't Wataru Taniguchi, special effects artist on any number of creature features, including the upcoming *Kaiju's Day Out*?"

Emi scrunches up her face, trying to understand. "Why would you think that?"

I take a deep breath, trying to think where to even start. "I thought that maybe Noel had been killed because he had possession of your phone, and then right in the same building where I found his body, there was a Wataru T. working down the hall. I was trying to make it all fit together."

Emi says, "I applaud your imagination. But my Wataru T. is Wataru Tanaka." Emi does a quick search on her phone, then shows me a picture of a Japanese guy in his thirties with a prominent red birthmark on one cheek. He has thick hair that flops into his eyes, and a round affable looking face. He's cute in a teddy-bear kind of way.

In other words, he looks nothing like Wataru Taniguchi.

I say, "I feel terrible now. I've been suspecting the other Wataru for no reason, just because of his name."

Of course, I don't exactly have a shortage of other suspects. And there's no proof that the guy chasing and threatening Emi – whatever his name is – didn't attack Noel. Maybe he is the killer and had heard me coming and hid when I'd found the body. If so, I was fortunate to have escaped the same fate when I had taken the phone he was after and gone outside.

But Noel wasn't exactly a sweet guy. Even his wife admitted he flirted with too many people and wasn't reliable at work. And he may or may not have told Annabelle the Baker he was separated from Connie. And there was the plane ticket to Belize, and the threatening note that had been in his jacket pocket. *You know what you did.* Presumably Noel had done something to upset someone, and he may have been planning to leave the country to leave the consequences. Unless I have all that wrong. For all I know, Noel might have written that note and then crumpled it up instead of delivering it to the person who had upset him.

I bring both hands up to my face. Here I've been investigating since yesterday, and I'm not sure if I've actually narrowed down anything. If I'm going to solve this in time to help Chloe, the first thing I need to determine is whether Noel was killed because of something he'd done to someone in his life, or if he might he have been killed because he was the one in possession of the phone.

I think the key here is figuring out how he was killed – twice. Clearly, Noel was already dead when he was stabbed, no matter what trick had been used. So what had actually killed him? Since I hadn't observed a clear cause of death, I'm assuming it was a poison, or perhaps something involving electricity. But who would have done such a thing?

Since Taniguchi is now cleared of having any connection to Emi, and he couldn't have been the one following us near the cat billboard, I have to discount him as a serious suspect. Assuming Emi herself is telling the truth, my main suspects now are Kudo, Connie, and Nao. And, of course, the guy in the gray suit. But with the movie set closed down, how am I supposed to effectively keep investigating?

Emi says, "You look like you're thinking so hard you might have an aneurism."

I say, "There's just so much going on. Remember the teenage girl with us at the airport? She is being accused of murdering Noel."

Emi says, "Oh, my."

Logan says, "We should go back inside. Figure out a safe place for you to go until you can get the meeting re-set with your contact here. I already blew the meet, so I'm not sure what you are going to need to do to get in touch."

My phone buzzes with a text. It's from Dawn. *The festival officials want to talk to you.*

I show the text to Logan.

He says, "Well, that can't be good."

Emi asks, "Is that why you are so dressed up?"

I tell her, "No. It just happened. I've been meaning to change all day, and there hasn't been time."

Emi says, "Don't worry about it. You look great."

I say, "As long as they don't ask me to sit in a chair with a back."

Emi giggles. "That's why I'd rather wear a formal than a kimono, given the choice."

Logan needs to stay with Emi, so I go alone to the officials' office, which is a conference room set up at the back of the event space. There is a long table, surrounded by chairs. Four people are seated on one side. The woman on the end gestures me to a chair on the opposite side of the table. Not only does it have a back, it's on rollers.

I carefully make my way over to it and sit down. The bow at my back pushes me forward, so I look like I'm leaning aggressively against the table. There is a tray in the middle of the table, with two of my chocolate bars on it, along with two bowls of samples.

I look at the people across from me. There are two men and two women, all watching me curiously. The men are wearing suits and one woman has on a red dress, while the other is wearing the official festival tee-shirt – which is probably issued to lower status employees or volunteers.

The woman in the dress smiles and says, in English, "I am Mrs. Kobayashi, organizer of the Tokyo Fête du Chocolat. These are my colleagues, Mr. Watanabe, Mr. Ishida, and Ms. Kondo. I am glad to see you are embracing the culture of Japan. I understand you are from Texas."

I wait for her to say *Where JFK was shot*, but she just makes eye contact, waiting for my response.

I adjust myself in my chair, trying to push the lower half of my body forward so I can sit up straighter. I say, "My chocolate shop and factory are in Galveston. That's a small barrier island on the coast-"

"I know where that is," Mrs. Kobayashi says. "Galveston just happens to be sister cities with Niigata, the area where I am from. The two celebrated their fiftieth anniversary of being sister cities in 2015. I visited your beaches at that time."

"I was living in Seattle that year," I say. "I am sorry I missed it. I didn't even realize Galveston was big enough to have sister cities."

"Japan has a number of sister municipalities in Texas," Mr. Ishida says. "For instance, Sendai is a sister city with Dallas."

"Dallas?" Mr. Watanabe says, looking like he just picked a single familiar word out the flow of foreign conversation. "Where JFK was shot."

I have to stifle a giggle. This is serious. My reputation is at stake.
I ask Mrs. Kobayashi, "What did you enjoy about Galveston?"

She says, "The seafood gumbo. I've never tasted anything like it."

I say, "I'm more about chicken and sausage gumbo myself. But my aunt makes a delicious seafood one."

Mr. Ishida clears his throat. "Mrs. Koerberu. The chocolate bars we retrieved from your stand are clearly different than the ones submitted for judging. Do you have an explanation?"

"I don't. We do all our own packaging, in the same small factory where we produce the chocolate. I apologize for making this suggestion, but there must have been a mistake once you received the bars. Perhaps they were mixed up with someone else's submission."

"We have considered that," Ms. Kobayashi says. "And we are prepared to accept that."

"Really?" I say before I can stop myself.

Mr. Ishida laughs. "Yes, Mrs. Koerberu. For two reasons. A) the bars we received were made using a slightly different mold and b) your chocolate is much better than the submitted sample."

"Arigatou." I nod a mini-bow. "That is kind praise." I hesitate, but I can't overcome my curiosity. "May I see the design?"

Mr. Ishida picks up one of the chocolate bars from the tray. It's one of my wrappers, featuring the profile view of Knightley, with the place to write a message on the back.

I unwrap it. It's the right size for one of my bars, with the subtle pyramiding that gives it visual appeal and makes it easier to break in straight lines. And there's the outline of a bunny in the oval at the center of the design. Only – that bunny isn't Knightley.

I point at the silhouette. "My bar design is inspired by my pet rabbit, Knightley. He's a lop. This one isn't."

"We noticed the ears," Mrs. Kobayashi says. "It is strange. None of the other contestants have a design involving a rabbit. And the mold is so similar, it is hard to believe that a bar that looks so similar was submitted entirely by mistake."

Mr. Ishida says, "It almost appears that someone sabotaged your entry. But we cannot figure out how that might have been done. We are willing to let the matter go, if you are willing. The bars we received directly from you will be presented to the judges."

Ms. Kondo tips her head forward. "I will see to it myself. I am in charge of coordinating the samples and the judging. I apologize deeply for the mistake."

I say, "I'm just happy to still be included for consideration."

Mr. Ishida walks me to the door. He says, "I look forward to presenting the awards at the end of the festival. I hope I will be able to announce your name as one of the winners. Ganbatte."

When I step into the hall, he gently closes the door behind me. They must have more business to discuss.

I lean against the wall, as best I can given the kimono, trying to get myself together before I have to cross through the festival booths.

I know I just said I would let it go, but this meeting has left me with so many questions. How would Meryl have even known what the fake Greetings and Felicitations bars tasted like, to compare it to a specific commercial brand? She might claim that she just overheard the judges talking, but that seems far-fetched.

The officials realize that someone switched the chocolate bars, but they are willing to believe it wasn't me. They can't fathom who would have done such a thing, because the chocolate community is filled with artists who take pride in their work, and wouldn't want to win on anything other than merit. But I have a pretty good idea who sabotaged me. I just can't prove it.

And where am I even going to find the time to try, when I already have to solve a murder and keep tabs on Chloe? Thank goodness I have friends here willing to help.

When I get back to the booth, Meryl is waiting there. Her arms are crossed over her chest and she starts tapping her foot as I approach. I guess she already got the news that I haven't been disqualified.

I wave, trying to look friendly and avoid engaging in conflict. I've learned that people sometimes make assumptions about how you feel about them based on how they feel about their own actions. And the misunderstanding this causes leads to even more conflict. I've been on the receiving end of that before – and I've been the defensive one, too. I'd love to avoid repeating that experience.

Meryl eyes my kimono, from the collar to the hem. She says, "Don't think dressing like that is going to help you fit in."

I say, "I'm obviously a visitor. I'm not trying to do anything presumptuous. I just want everyone to have a good time at the festival."

Meryl huffs. "Why don't you just drop the innocent act? We're all here to make money, not friends. And I'm not even sure you're serious about the money. Or the craft of chocolate making. That niece of yours practically got arrested for murder. And you've been spending half the time you've been here chasing – something. At first I thought it was publicity stunts, making a mockery of our field. But now I don't know what it is."

"Now wait a minute," I say.

Meryl isn't listening. "I plan to make another complaint, that you are putting the festival attendees in danger by harboring a potential murderer."

I almost hope she does. Wouldn't that make it obvious to the officials that she's made this personal, and is using any excuse to try and get me removed from the festival? Only – maybe they won't see it that way, no matter how obvious it is to me. It would be humiliating to be so sure they'll back me up, and then get escorted off the floor. I swallow a harsh retort. Instead I say, "I assure you I am passionate about the craft. I've worked hard on developing my palate, and on developing the technique that goes into my chocolate."

"Oh yeah?" Meryl says. "Why not put your palate where your mouth is?"

Dawn stifles a laugh at the unintended turn of phrase.

Meryl shoots her a glare. "What I mean is, let's see what people think when you give your chocolate making class."

And now I'm anxious that she's going to try to sabotage that too.

Chapter Fourteen
Tuesday

Patsy, Chloe and I take the cat to get settled in at Hudson and Savannah's apartment. Honda has at least stopped yowling, though when Chloe lifts the carrier into Hudson's borrowed van, the cat lets out a few raspy meows.

Chloe says, "I know how she feels."

Hudson, from the driver's seat, says, "Savannah is working from home all day, so at least Honda won't be alone."

Chloe puts her fingers through the carrier's bars and says, "Honda is the most sociable cat I've ever seen. She needs to be on the stream for the collab I'm doing with the cat toy company."

Patsy says, "You're going to have to ask Director Kudo about that one."

Assuming he gets in touch.

Honda starts licking Chloe's hand, grooming her.

Chloe says, "They do that when they feel comfortable, like you're part of their colony."

Hudson says, "But she barely knows you."

Chloe says, "We spent a lot of time together yesterday. After I realized I was locked in, she came and sat on me and purred until I calmed down a bit. A lot of cats like to be helpful, and Honda really gets into the role." She starts talking to the cat. "Don't you widdle sweetie. Such a good girl."

I scoot around to get a better look. Honda glances up at me, then starts purring, loudly. Maybe she's signaling that we should both support Chloe in her time of stress. The cat butts against Chloe's fingers with the top of her head, demanding more pets. She's certainly a confident little cat.

How had she been jumping from room to room at the studio building? It had almost felt like she was trying to tell me something, maybe about how the building works. Of course, maybe she just liked having the company, and wanted to follow me from room to room. Maybe she had scratched holes in the wall in hidden places. I need to get back into the building and explore how the offices connect to each other to see if it's a material she could have clawed through. Of course, that's going to take some time. It's a big building, and the police are going to want to explore it before they release the crime scene.

As soon as we park, Chloe throws open the door. She says, "Honda's been without a litter box for a long time today. That can be bad for a cat's kidneys. She also needs access to water ASAP, for the same reason."

Hudson says, "Savannah got the box, as you requested. I'm sure there's also bottled water."

I tuck the dress box filled with my ordinary clothes under my arm, and then I get out of the van.

We follow Hudson up two flights of stairs to an apartment that looks modern and airy, despite the dilapidated building exterior. The entire kitchen had been remodeled, and there's a laundry room with one of those single unit washer/dryers. By combining the two devices, this has left an open space for the litter box. Chloe opens the carrier, and without hesitating, Honda steps out. Chloe picks the cat up and deposits her on top of the clean litter.

Savannah has a computer setup in the apartment's second bedroom. It has three monitors and takes up most of one wall. The rest of the room is decorated in deep reds and browns. She's sitting in a gaming chair with red piping on the edges of the leather. Her shoulder length brown hair curves in towards her face. She's wearing a gold-toned blouse and jeans, with furry leopard print slippers.

"Hey," she calls, without getting up. "I'm glad you stopped by. I wanted to see how you are holding up, now that everything with Noel has hit the news."

"I'm doing pretty well, all things considered." I go into the room. "Thanks again for helping Chloe out."

Savannah says, "No problem." She gestures back towards the living room. "Hey, where's Logan?"

I say, "He had to help out an ex-client. Emi has someone trying to get information from her, so he's getting her a safe place to stay while he works to get that information somewhere safe."

"Really?" Savannah's wide eyes look shocked.

"What?"

She picks up a coffee mug from her desk. "Your fiancé walked off with a femme fatal, and you're not even worried?"

"Why should I be?" I ask. "I trust Logan. And besides – Arlo went with him. They're going to take turns keeping watch and trying to set up a meeting with her contact."

Savannah asks, "And Patsy's not worried either?"

"Not that I'm aware of."

Savannah says, "Maybe I'm just jaded. Or I've watched too many bad movies with convenient plot devices. I'd like to think I could trust Hudson too, in the same circumstances. But would I be doomed to repeat the insecurities of so many movie heroines?"

I say, "Hudson seems like a loyal guy. Granted I haven't known him that long."

"He's complicated, but yeah, loyal." She taps her computer monitor. "Check this out."

The image on the screen is Connie and Noel's wedding picture. They look young and happy. But the article headline says, *Did Money Crack the Celebration Bells?*

Scanning the text, I gather that the Celebration Bells was the media's nickname for Noel and Connie, as a stunt artist power couple.

The article supposes that, facing the possibility of losing the house that appears in the background of the wedding picture, Connie and Noel were about to split up, leaving them both destitute – until Noel's murder "conveniently" happened.

I'm conflicted. Connie is pretty high on my suspect list. It makes sense that the media will speculate. But I know what it is like to be low-key accused of murder. If you are innocent, it can make you feel worthless, and like everyone is belittling your grief.

But the part she's actually pointing at is at the bottom of the screen, where my name is mentioned as the amateur sleuth who is on the case. And the article makes it sound like me nosing around in their lives is what had likely led to Noel's death. It's all vague enough that the author can't be sued for libel. It's not the worst thing that has ever been printed about me. And, to my surprise, I find I don't really care.

Look at me, with all the personal growth and self-awareness. But it's such a freeing feeling. Anyone who knows me will know this article is utter rubbish.

"Somebody is fishing for clicks," I say. I sigh. "You get used to people thinking what they're going to think, even if there's zero evidence. You really can't change their minds."

"I wish I had that kind of confidence," Savanah says. She gestures at my outfit. "You pull that off with ease, while the one time I rented a kimono in Kyoto, I felt like people were staring at me the whole time."

"I'd actually like to change into my regular clothes," I say. "Any chance there's somewhere here I could do that?"

"Sure," she says. "Use the master bathroom. It's through our bedroom."

I go to change, and Honda follows me. The bedroom features more leopard print, from the blackout curtains to the comforter. There's even a sculpture of a black cat on the tall dresser.

When I shut the bathroom door, Honda is inside with me. She starts crying to be let out. Yet when I open it for her, she goes out and I shut the door, but she immediately starts crying to be let back in. Tough. She's just going to have to wait until I get the kimono in the dress box. The small room smells of vanilla and musk, probably a body wash given the wet shower area behind me.

A paw comes under the door, and there are plucking noises as Honda tries to pry her way in. She's actually a very stubborn cat. But when I open the door, and she sees I'm leaving, she doesn't want in anymore. My guess is that I'm familiar, and she's in an unfamiliar place.

I put the dress box down and pick her up. "It's okay," I say. "We're going to figure out what's going on with your owner."

My phone buzzes, and it's a text from Kudo asking about his cat. Which is just a wild coincidence. I show the cat the phone, though I know full well it is meaningless to her. "Look, he wants to come get you later tonight. You don't have to hold on too long, and then you can go home."

Honda meows, a sound clearly resonating with excitement, and then she makes little noises, almost chirping like a bird. It seems crazy, given it was just text on the phone, that she could have recognized her owner was worrying about her. But then I realize Chloe is standing behind me with a clump of feathers on a string, and that Honda could not care less about what I'm telling her. Honda suddenly races past me and does a backflip, following the feather lure, trying desperately to catch it. What ensues highlights her determination to follow the feather low or high or spinning in a circle. She eventually snatches the toy out of the air, only to become bored with it shortly after her success – right up until it starts moving again. After a bit Honda flops on her side on the floor, breathing heavily, clearly tired. But when Chloe starts moving the toy to put it up, Honda springs for it again.

We all laugh, and finally the toy winds up on top of the fridge, out of the calico's reach.

Chloe tells Hudson, "I'm going to come back over later and spend some time with her."

Hudson says, "You could just stay here if you want. I'm taking Mrs. Koerber and Ms. Nash to their appointment, but Savanah's here and you could just hang out on the couch."

"Absolutely not," Patsy says. "She's not leaving our supervision. Look what happened last time."

I say, "We can come back after we talk to Connie and see if that leads to any other suspects."

Patsy says, "Won't that look odd? If Chloe is the prime suspect, and she's digging around, couldn't it look like she's trying to prejudice the investigation?"

I say, "I had thought about that, but what else are we going to do? Logan and Arlo are who knows where trying to get Emi settled, and Dawn and Fisher are manning the booth." I gesture toward Hudson's sofa. "You could stay here with Chloe and the cat, if you want. I guess I would be okay going by myself."

"What about Ash and Imogen?" Chloe says. "You're supposed to be visiting Connie to get stunt woman tips. They're the ones who would be excited about that."

"You're right." I've spent so much time trying to dissuade Ash from interviewing people – it hasn't occurred to ask him to help. I text Ash, *You up for an investigation?*

He texts back, *Heck yeah. It's today, though, right? I just got invited to go on a Japanese talk show tomorrow.*

Yep, I reply. I send him the address where we're meeting Connie and ask, *How soon can you and Imogen get there?*

He texts, *Imogen's invited? She'll be chuffed. Right now we're finishing eating. So maybe like half an hour?*

I show the text to Hudson and ask, "Is that reasonable?"

He says, "Our apartment here is in Nakano City. Connie lives in Oiamachi, which is on the other side of Shinjuku. So probably closer to an hour."

I let Ash know and send him more details on what we're planning to do.

It's a long drive, just me and Hudson, and I keep checking my phone to make sure Chloe's Find a Friend location hasn't changed.

We mainly listen to music and chat about ways I can improve my social media.

But at one point, Hudson touches the scar running down his face and says, "I thought I'd never get a part in a real movie, after the botched plastic surgery. It was kind of Kudo to invite me to participate, even if it is a cameo. I hope he has nothing to do with the murder."

I can't tell if Hudson is telling me this, or if he is asking me to reassure him. I don't know enough yet about what's going on to know what to say.

I ask Hudson, "Is Kudo a nice guy?" By which I mean, is he the kind of person who might kill someone to get that person out of the way of his own happiness.

Hudson says, "I don't know him that well. He seems patient with the cast. I've been hanging around when I have free time, watching parts of the filming, and I've only seen him lose his temper once. There was a malfunction with one of Taniguchi's props, and no matter how many times Taniguchi tried to fix it, it kept moving backwards instead of towards the camera. Kudo finally shouted at him that if he wasn't competent, he should just quit. I thought Taniguchi was going to cry, but he just picked up the machine and took it back to his lab. They must have talked it out later, because the next time I visited the set, they were acting like friends again."

I ask, "Did Noel have any enemies on the set? Or anywhere else in his life?"

Hudson says, "Not that I know of. He was friendly to everyone. Keiko – the receptionist – didn't seem to like him all that much. But that was because he used very informal Japanese when speaking with everyone, which can come across as rude. But I think he learned Japanese from watching anime, and most of that is going to be informal. One time, I saw Noel try to sneak upstairs, and she got short with him."

"What is upstairs, anyway?" I ask.

Hudson shrugs, never taking his eyes off traffic. "No idea."

It was worth a shot.

"Okay, what about anyone Noel was friends with?"

Hudson thinks about this for a long time before saying, "Like I said, he seemed to get along pretty well with everyone. I don't think any of them had any idea he was a thief. Juan and Franco, the cameramen, are from Belize. Noel spoke Spanish, and no one else does, so they seemed to gravitate towards him. They came to Japan for this project, and considering, their conversational Japanese is pretty good. But it can get lonely operating with a limited vocabulary. My first six months here was miserable."

The ticket in Noel's jacket pocket had been for Belize. I wonder if they had anything to do with him buying it? It's too big of a coincidence for them not to, right?

Okay. So I need to talk to Juan and Franco – and to Keiko – as soon as possible. But with the movie shut down, there's no easy way to find them. When Kudo comes later, maybe I can talk him into sharing all their contact info.

After that we lapse into silence, and I pull out my phone to read a few virtual pages of *The Honjin Murders*.

Hudson stops at a red light and glances over at me. He looks back at the road, but says, "Inspector Kendaichi. That one's a classic. You know there's an anime starring his grandson?"

"I did not know that," I admit. "I never heard of Kendaichi before someone handed me a Japanese-language copy of this very book when I was minding my own business at the chocolate festival."

The light changes, and we start moving. Hudson says, "Uh oh. They flat out gave you a murder book out of nowhere, huh?"

"Pretty much." I close the book app and lower my phone to my lap. "I wouldn't have taken it, only I was blindsided."

"Ouch," Hudson says. He gives me a brief sympathetic glance. "Don't blame yourself, okay? Noel would still be dead if you hadn't taken it. There would just have been nobody looking for him." It sounds like Hudson really believes what he's saying. And it is comforting. He adds, "One of my friends is a booktuber. She has a video that breaks down the first couple of Inspector Kendaichi books. I can send you the link, if you want."

"That would be very helpful," I admit. "So much is going on, I'm having limited time to read."

Hudson glances briefly at me again. He says, "If that book might offer some clue to the murder, why don't I put you in touch with my friend, and she can walk you through it."

He pulls over and sends a text. Two minutes later, my phone rings, and a bubbly girl named Vanessa introduces herself then explains to me the important things about the book. One, that the murder of two newlyweds involved mechanical means to create a stabbing machine that somehow left the sword outside of a locked room, standing up in the snow. Two, that the villain had help. Three, that the idea for the murder came from the characters' love of the mystery genre and ideas used in those books. And four, that the love between the courting couple soured shortly before the wedding day, and that one partner considered themself betrayed.

I have no idea how any of this relates to the case at hand. Or if it even does. A part of me still believes that the idea of the murder books could be in my head. Maybe I just try to make connections, and any story could give me the jumping off points I need. But part of me believes that there is something from *The Honjin Murders* specifically that I need to understand. But which part?

I am just hanging up with Vanessa when we arrive at the building where Connie wanted to meet up to offer us stunt tips. I had asked if she still wanted to do this, since everything had happened, and she had said that she welcomes the distraction, so here we are at a Sports Center. I've never been particularly athletic, so the whole thing fills me with dread.

Imogen and Ash are already here, sitting on a bench outside the building. Imogen is wearing yoga pants and a long tee-shirt, and Ash has on a matching track suit. I can't remember seeing Ash in anything but a button-up shirt, with long or short sleeves, no matter the occasion. Honestly, it's weird.

And wasn't Imogen wearing a dress when she'd left the chocolate festival? Had they stopped somewhere to buy clothes for this?

I'm still wearing slacks and flats. Maybe I can use that as an excuse to just watch the stunt training.

Hudson asks, "You good?"

"Yeah. Sure." I start to get out of the van. I turn back to him and say, "Thanks. For everything. You've been amazing this whole trip."

He gives me a double thumbs up. "Don't look so grim, Mrs. K. You got this."

I wave as he drives away, then I turn to Ash and Imogen. Right. We're doing this.

Connie had left us guest passes at the desk, and it only takes a little awkward pantomiming for us to use our basic phrases to retrieve them. We also get a facility map with a big X over the room where we are supposed to meet Connie.

My shoes echo down the hallway, while Ash and Imogen's sneakers are silent. Had they bought shoes too? How could they shop that fast?

We open the door and find Connie standing at a ballet bar in front of a mirrored wall. She has one leg on the bar, stretching. The floor of half the room is wood, but the other half is covered in mats. Connie is barefoot, so I guess we're not actually doing ballet.

Connie finishes the stretch, then she turns around, tuts at me and says, "Okay, come along dear."

She leads me to the locker room where she gives me jogging pants and a tee to change into. At that point, I stop trying to resist. I'm going to have to actually train, if I want the chance to ask questions.

We go back to the training room. Connie demonstrates a forward roll. She has to be kidding. She's a few years older than me, and I haven't been that flexible in more than a decade.

I say, "Remember, I'm still sore from falling off a roof two days ago."

Connie says, "We'll deal with safe falls in a little bit. First, let's see what we have to work with."

Ash says, "I'll go first!"

Connie grunts agreement. She tells Ash, "Try to do as many rolls as you can in a row."

I ask her, "Can I ask you a few questions?"

She gives me a sad smile. "I wouldn't expect anything else, if you are really trying to figure out what happened to my husband." She turns to Ash, who finishes his last roll and stands up on the mat. "Great job! You did seven." She turns back to me. "Let me make it easy for you. At the time when you claim Noel was killed, I was at lunch with the others. The police already asked for my alibi during the more generous time frame they have, given their forensics. After we had that fight and Noel left, I didn't want to be alone at home, so I went to an onsen and spent the night there, watching movies with my headphones on in the quiet room. Then in the morning, I came here – they log entry and exit time – and then I went to the set. I had a stunt to review with Haruko – she plays the protagonist."

"My turn," Imogen says. She moves into place at the edge of the mat.

"What was the stunt?" I ask.

Connie says, "She is supposed to climb up the Kaiju's leg and implant a device in the spine that will allow her to communicate with it telepathically, ending the rampage behavior. The prop leg moves back and forth the whole time, trying to shake me off. There are rock climbing handholds disguised as skin bumps, but it's still difficult."

Imogen reaches the other edge of the mat, pivots back towards us and raises her hands like a gymnast. "How'd I do?"

"That was eight," Connie says. She looks at me and gestures with her chin at the mat. "Come on. At least try."

She coaches me into position and through the movement, and I manage to flop over in a less than graceful roll.

"Again," she says.

I manage a total of three, with a big pause in between each to reposition myself. When I finally pull myself up to standing at the end of the last roll, all three of them give me a round of applause. Which is a bit condescending, when you think of it, but their expressions show they clearly mean well.

I look at Connie. She had had a fight with Noel. Could she have gone to the onsen on purpose, to have an alibi, and then snuck out to set a trap for Noel, something she knew he would trigger when he grabbed his keys? Potentially, he could have been poisoned when the keys cut his elbow, finishing him off quickly, instead of a slower death from skin absorption. That would clearly explain how he had gone from hobbling one minute to flat out dead the next.

But could she have snuck out? Would she have been able to, without someone remembering her, given that she's British with distinctive hair? Although, being a stunt woman, she could have gone over a railing or climbed a fence out of the pools.

If it was poison, she could have even applied it to the keys before he left home – and then she'd gone to the onsen because she didn't want to be alone with the guilt, while her husband was slowly dying.

Only – she seemed so clearly distressed when she found out he was dead.

I ask, "Did you still love Noel?"

"Of course," she says, her eyes flashing with fierce emotion. "Every day and with every breath."

Connie gestures all three of us over to the bar and has us hold it while leaning forward and then making swooping movements with our upper bodies and arms. The stretching feels good – but at the same time, it is reminding me how sore my muscles already are.

I ask, "Did Noel ever flirt with Haruko?"

Connie laughs so hard she has to wipe a tear from her eye. "Um…no. Haruko would probably have kicked him in the face if he had tried. She expects to be treated like a princess by any man who approaches her, and Noel . . . he might have been my prince, but he wasn't exactly Prince Charming. Besides, she goes for younger guys."

Imogen says, "We've been doing the research. I've found records of multiple times you've had divorce papers drawn up, but the paralegal I talked to said Noel always managed to talk you out of filing them."

Connie's lips narrow. "I'll have to have a word with my lawyer."

Imogen says, "Please, don't. You have to understand the power to be wooed that comes with the mention of a true crime podcast – and a potential movie."

Connie says, "I'll consider letting it go – if you turn those skills to finding other suspects. But only because I want to know the truth." She sighs. "Noel never took anything seriously. He could be a total flake. A month ago, he threatened to quit the production to go surfing in Australia. He often does random, stupid stuff like that, just for the thrill of it. Sometimes, I couldn't take it and I threatened to walk away. He would commit more to our relationship – and the life we built – for a while. And when he got too far out of hand again, I would draw up another round of papers."

Ash says, "You'd found a way to make the relationship work."

Connie nods. "Exactly."

Hmmm. The guy who was at the bar where Emi was supposed to meet Nichijo had an Australian accent. Now that one, surely, is a coincidence. What's more interesting is how Imogen is contributing to the investigation. I didn't even find out who Connie's lawyer is – let alone reach out.

Imogen says, "It worked even given the huge insurance policy."

Connie says, "Noel and I have both worked in a dangerous career for decades. It only made sense to have life insurance. The kind of life we lead doesn't lend itself to having kids, and Noel's family back in Yorkshire have all passed on, so yes, I'm the only beneficiary."

Changing the subject, even as we change stretches, this time bending over and reaching our hands to the floor, I ask, "Since I know you didn't approve when Noel flirted with other women – what's up with Director Kudo flirting with you? Is there something going on between you two?"

Connie snaps upright from the stretch. "Don't be daft. Kudo is such a reserved man, that would be like flirting with a tree."

Imogen says, "Maybe he was just respecting the fact that you were married. Felicity says she saw something in the way Kudo looked at you. Maybe he just couldn't hide his feelings."

She stares at me, and I reflexively touch my face, like maybe the scratches have started bleeding again. They haven't. Finally she says, "Do you really think so?"

So much for my theory that the two of them might have been working together to eliminate an unwanted third party.

"I have one last question," I say, and it's my turn to share a bit of information Imogen doesn't know yet. I say, "We found Noel's jacket. And there was a note in the pocket that said, 'You know what you did.' Do you know if Noel blamed someone for something? Or if someone blamed him?"

Connie turns away and says, "Let's practice some falls, yeah." She pulls a mat over to the mirrors, then she climbs up onto the ballet bar, saying, "Don't tell the gym guys we did this."

She jumps off the bar and lands dramatically in a heap.

I let out an involuntary squeak and move towards her, with the trained instinct to help.

She laughs. "No worries. I'm fine. Notice how I landed hips first, then rolled across onto my chest? That reduces the overall impact. I read somewhere you used to be a physical therapist. That should make sense to you right?"

"It does," I say, wondering what I'm going to have to do to get the answer to my question about the note.

Connie says, "It's okay, love. You don't have to jump from the bar if you don't want to. You can just fall on the mat from standing."

Imogen says, "But I want to try it from the bar."

Connie says, "Try it from the mat first."

We do. Even with the technique, falling still hurts. Imogen does try it from the bar. Ash and I give her a round of applause, though neither of us want to follow her example.

Connie says, "That forward roll technique we practiced? You learned how to tuck your chin. Now we're going to take that to a backward fall that involves a roll."

I try. I really do. I can do the backward roll from a squat – with help. But I can't overcome the fear of falling backwards enough to just let go from a standing position.

"It's okay," Connie says finally. "You tried – and what more can you ask for?" She leans back against the bar. She takes a deep breath.

And then another. And then she says, "That's not the first time Noel has received that kind of note. I found one crumpled up in his jeans pocket, maybe a month ago. I was sorting laundry, and he came in late with a gash on his chin, and when he'd gotten some painkillers in him, he started talking. His words were vague, but the implication had been that someone held Noel responsible for a death – even though Noel didn't believe he had anything to do with it. Falsely accused, he kept saying. But he looked scared. I asked him if there had been other notes, and he just said, 'A few.' And then when we got up in the morning, he acted like he didn't know what I was talking about. So I thought – maybe he made it up. Maybe it was one of the girls he paid too much attention to, or one of their boyfriends or husbands, telling him he'd gone too far. Or maybe someone on set, upset that he wouldn't back down about how a stunt should be done, or that he was delaying the production. Whatever he was hiding – I know he wasn't capable of killing someone."

I tell her, "I've only worked on solving seven cases before this one, but still – I have seen a lot of people pushed to their limits, with reasons to commit murder. And some of them snap. It's rarely the most straightforward psychology for who or why. Maybe something did happen."

Connie shakes her head. "Even when he was out of it, he said he didn't feel he was responsible." Then she blinks. "Really? You've solved seven murders? The podcast only talked about two."

Ash says, "That's seven murderers, actually. There were more victims in a lot of the crimes. So she's probably solved dozens. We're just getting into the second case on my podcast."

"Not by myself," I amend. "Logan and Arlo have both helped me get information, and backed me up." I gesture at Ash, "This guy has even indirectly saved my life at least twice when I was in over my head." I lean back against the bar, next to Connie. "All I ever wanted was to be a good chocolate maker, to put my life back together after

I lost my husband. I set up shop and an employee died at my grand opening. And things snowballed from there."

Connie says, "It sounds like you're the one holding your group of friends and helpers all together."

I say, "I've actually had to work on that. I've had more people support me in ways I didn't deserve than I could count. They deserve most of the credit."

Connie looks shocked at my easy dismissal. "What a life you have led. And here I thought cooking was boring."

I start to explain to her that chocolate making and cooking aren't the same thing.

But Ash says, "Boring is not a word in Felicity's vocabulary.

Chapter Fifteen
Tuesday

With Hudson off to run his YouTubery errands, we take public transit back to his place, which involves a twenty-minute walk to the train station. My hair is still wet from showering at the training center before changing back into my regular clothes. My muscles are so sore from our little training session that at some point I threaten to just sit down and let them go on without me.

Imogen says, "I'll buy you a nice hot tea at the station. We're almost there."

It had been a few more blocks, and when we get there, she buys me not only a tea but a packet with a hot fried chicken cutlet in it. It is surprisingly good, for something that came out of a hot case.

We are fortunate enough to find a seat on the train, and Imogen insists I take it, while she and Ash stand holding on to the straps suspended from the roof. Every time the train lurches unexpectedly changing direction, I groan aloud, until Imogen says, "You know, we could go find a place with a private onsen. If you rent the whole bath, nobody cares if we all wear swimsuits. It's part of the Japan experience I don't think you should miss."

Is that her way of saying she feels sorry for me? Seriously. Ash must have told her how intimidated I'd been when he'd suggested the idea to help with my aches from falling off the roof – which have been magnified from all the exertion I have put my body through today.

Even if it is a pity offer . . . is it weak that I'm wondering if I should take her up on it? If only there wasn't so much to do. I say, "I wish I had time for that."

"Okay, I'll book it for Friday night, then," Imogen says. "For all us girls."

I give up trying to resist. "Sure. It will give Chloe something to do."

When we finally make it back to Hudson and Savannah's apartment, we find Chloe asleep on the sofa, with Honda curled up on top of her.

I close the door, and Chloe wakes up, jolting Honda, who jumps to the floor with a thump. Chloe sits up and stretches. "Oh, good you're back."

"You have a good nap?" Imogen asks.

Chloe says, a touch defensively, "It wasn't as much of a nap as you think. I spent the afternoon putting together the clip I took of the movie studio building, and the snippets I've gotten of people working on the film." She gestures towards the kitchen. "Hudson sent me his stuff too."

I go through to the kitchen. Patsy is sitting at a table, working on something on her tablet. Hudson is sitting opposite her, reading a book. When I ask him if I should drink water from the tap, he hops up and grabs me a cold bottle of water out of the fridge.

He says, "You guys can have whatever you find in here."

Imogen comes into the room and sets the rest of her train station bento finds on the counter. She says, "Here's dinner for everyone, since none of us have had time to cook."

That's thoughtful of her. I haven't even thought about dinner. That makes me wonder what Logan is doing for dinner tonight.

I text him, *Miss you, Babe.* I realize that's the same pet name my aunt uses for her husband. Maybe that's why it feels so natural to me. I ask him, *You taking care of yourself? Make sure you eat some protein and take your turn getting some sleep.*

There's no immediate response. Which I find disappointing and a little worrying. Even if it has only been two minutes, and there are a million reasons why he might not be answering. There had been one time I had tried to call him – only he had left his phone in Minnesota.

Hudson tells Imogen, "You didn't have to do that." But he picks up a plastic container of curry and rice and takes it back to the table.

I take my water back to the living room and sit down on the opposite end of the sofa from Chloe. Ash is sitting in the oversized chair nearby. Imogen comes and squishes into the chair next to him.

Chloe asks, "How did it go today? Did you come up with any new suspects?"

"No, but that's okay. We already have so many." I start to outline what I've uncovered, giving the others time to chime in with their thoughts. While I'm talking, Hudson comes in to listen. But it's all still circumstantial.

Assuming that Noel had somehow been poisoned before he went into the building, Nao is the most promising suspect. She was on the roof, close enough to have put something on his skin or stabbed him with a micro-needle. And I still have the distinct feeling that she is hiding something.

Only, I can't understand what her motive might have been. From what she told Logan and me, she barely knew Noel. But if she knew him at all, it doesn't make sense that he would be trying to steal her phone. After all, she presumably knew what movie set he was working at, so wouldn't he have expected her to just turn him in? Unless something else was going on. Could Nao have been showing him something on her phone? Could she have been the person Noel had wronged – who whether justly or not believed he had killed someone she cared about? But if that was true – why show us the jacket with the incriminating note?

Somehow, though, Nao having a mystery motive seems more likely than Connie having killed Noel, even though Connie had more concrete slights and built-up years of conflict behind her own motive. She claims she hadn't seen him for a significant amount of time before his death, so any method of poisoning would have to have been delayed. And I can't figure out how she would have moved the body, when she was with the group who had gone to lunch. Unless there was a trick to it, which I haven't uncovered.

Kudo is still a viable suspect, too. Even if Connie was unaware of his unrequited love, his feelings could have been enough to tip him over the edge. He could have been sending notes all along, to pave the way for the idea that Noel had been killed by someone he had wronged. Maybe he – or Connie – had somehow left the lunch group, and gotten back to the set, then rejoined them.

And I can't forget Annabelle the Baker. She had seemed to be hiding something. But why? Might she have another connection to Noel that she isn't admitting? She is certainly audacious enough to have hidden somewhere on the set and attacked Noel as he came in. And she'd been in the building before. With that strong-yet-quickly-dissipating smell of almonds, it's a strong possibility that she and Noel fought, and somehow a couple of bottles of her perfume got broken. If she took the broken bottles away with her when she exited the set to spirit away Noel's body, it would make sense why the smell would fade.

Chloe says, "I hate to think Annabelle might be trying to frame me. She's working on the pet collab, and anyone who is as kind to cats as she is can't be a bad person."

I say, "Cat lover or not, we can't discount a viable suspect. We need to look closely at the footage to see if we missed evidence that she – or someone else – might still have been hiding on the set, unable to get away once a bunch of people showed up."

Chloe pouts, but seems to accept this.

I tell everyone that I still need to talk to Keiko, the two cameramen and the janitor. Not to mention the wrench that Emi's appearance – and the fact that Noel chose her phone to steal – throws into all of this. All the movie-related suspects could be innocent, and

Noel the victim of a death intended for Emi. Which means I should be even more worried about Logan's safety than I already am. Him, and Arlo, too. I glance at Patsy.

She says, "I'm sure the guys are fine." But there's a note of worry in her voice.

Hudson points out, "There's always the possibility that Emi's the one who killed Noel, to get back the data on the phone."

"I doubt that's true," Patsy says. But the worried expression in her eyes seems deeper. Patsy shrugs. "Oh, heck, while we're spitballing, we can't forget Meryl. After all she had phrased her contempt to me in the same words as the note in Noel's pocket. You know what you did."

There're too many suspects, and I don't have the clues to eliminate any one of them. I rub at my eyes. They feel gritty and dry. Honda jumps on the sofa next to me and tries to climb onto my chest. She starts purring loudly. I give her a gentle push to let her know she should keep going. I don't mind her sitting on my lap, so I try to position her where I actually want her.

Chloe says, "Cats like to sit on your chest and purr when you're sick or sad. There's actual evidence that the vibration of purring can be healing for inflammation, wound healing, muscle repair and pain relief, among other things."

"I could use all of those things," I say. When Honda tries to climb up to my chest again, I let her, cradling her with my arms as she loudly purrs.

The calico stands up in my arms, stretching her back and turning in a circle. Then she angles herself so as to stick her butt in my face, thwapping me on the cheek with her tail.

Chloe looks delighted. "Mrs. Koerber," she says, "That means she trusts you."

I put a hand up to stop the tail thwapping me again, realizing this very determined cat is small enough to hold in one arm. Honda settles down, still purring, and starts making biscuits against my sleeve. I have to admit that holding her is making me feel more relaxed. As for the pain relief and muscle repair – I *think* maybe I feel better. But there's no concrete way to measure it.

Chloe uses an HDMI cable to hook her phone into the apartment's giant TV. She says, "Maybe the video I put together can clear some of this up."

Hudson says, "I'd rather skip it, if you don't mind. If you need me, I'll be downstairs, in the gym."

I hate that he's headed off alone, but Chloe puts a hand on my arm to stop me following him.

Chloe says, "Hudson sent me the clips he took, in the building, and of him and Ash finding the body. He said he deleted it all off his phone, because it creeped him out too much."

Hudson had been at the hotel in Galveston a few months ago, when another murder had taken place, and he had dealt with it pretty well. But it's different actually discovering a body. If he's this bothered, I hope he talks to someone about it – maybe his wife, or a therapist – before the effects of trauma really set in.

I tell her, "You're pretty wise for a seventeen-year-old. "

Imogen says, "Sometimes, maybe. But she got her passport taken away for being impulsive. There's that."

I give Imogen a look to make it clear that she's not helping.

Imogen ignores me and asks Chloe, "Did you touch the murder weapon? Or were your fingerprints somehow transferred onto it later?"

Chloe's face goes red, all the way to her hairline. She says, "Before they sent me to the conference room, I was on set waiting for Director Kudo to get back. There were a bunch of weapons on a wall, in a part of the set that was supposed to be the inside of a study. I touched a lot of things. But I assumed they were all props. How was I supposed to know someone was going to use one of them to frame me for murder?" Chloe shudders and crosses her arms over her body. "I'm going to jail, aren't I? You don't have to make me feel worse about it."

"I'm sorry," Imogen says. "Sometimes when I notice things that don't seem right, I don't think before I talk."

"You are not going to jail," I tell Chloe. I lean forward, and Honda gives me an unhappy mmmrrrppp at being jostled. She jumps off of my chest with surprising force. I gesture at the television. "Let's look at the clips you took."

"Ryokai," Chloe says, trying to sound upbeat. "I learned that today. It means *got it*, or *good to go*. I think it's my favorite Japanese word."

Chloe starts the first clip. Having the video magnified to the size of Hudson's giant television screen makes it feel more vivid. Honda does a few more circles, getting comfortable being on the floor, then flops down against my foot. Maybe she's still offering solidarity, because I know my blood pressure just went up, looking at the screen, feeling like I'm mentally back to the moment where I tried to resuscitate Noel.

Chloe had taken some close-ups of the small buildings on the set. I know that at least one of the structures is hollow. I had seen Noel's stash of stolen purses and phones inside it. But do they all open? If so, who knows what might be hidden inside the others? Any form of gear could have been stashed, in preparation for the murder.

I don't think a person would fit, though, especially someone as tall as Annabelle, who is currently the most probable suspect to have been hiding nearby at the time. I try to imagine her crouching behind one of the buildings. Could she have been there, watching as I tried – and failed – to save Noel. Maybe? It's hard to tell for sure. Of course, if Noel had indeed been poisoned, she would have found my attempts humorous, since it was a completely pointless effort.

I had been in shock when I'd actually been on the set looking at a body, so I hadn't really thought much about the details of my surroundings. And today, I hadn't been there long either before we discovered Noel. I study the scene now, with more clarity.

The floor of the set is made of large sheets of plywood, painted gray and green to resemble pavement and grass. They are strategically covered with large model-railroad scale greenery to help sell the illusion. The buildings have doors and windows, and some have small models of people. It is a lot of work for something that is bound to be smashed before filming is over.

Noel had been lying at the very edge of the set, with the front of the building he'd been using as a hiding place swung wide open. I hadn't noticed any plants around him at the time, and I don't see any in the footage. It looks like all of that starts once you get past the first row of buildings. Maybe that has something to do with the filming techniques they are planning to use.

Chloe's camera moves past the open front of the scaled down building. There's something small just inside it.

"Wait." I ask Chloe, "Can you zoom that in? And maybe lighten it a little?"

"Sure," Chloe says, her fingers moving swiftly over the screen of her phone.

We both squint at the television. The small object looks like it might have been used to prop the door of box-building open, something that would only be necessary if whoever put it there was afraid that the structure was going to be moved or disturbed.

"What is that? Chloe asks. She zooms the image in more.

"It's a shogi tile," I say, recognizing the distinctive shape I'd seen at the festival. Of course, this one isn't made of chocolate. I can make out the character printed on it. It's a pawn, with the potential to become a gold general.

I'm pretty sure I would have noticed it yesterday, when I had reached into the de facto dollhouse to grab a phone to make the emergency call. That tile hadn't been there. Which means the killer must have placed it there, after moving Noel's body. They must have wanted to make sure that the door to the small building remained open, that the police looked inside and realized it was empty.

Hudson comes back in. "I forgot to grab my water." He goes through into the kitchen and comes back with a black Stanley cup. He sees what's on the screen and asks, "What are you guys looking at?"

Once I explain, Hudson says, "This sounds like something right out of Detective Conan." In response to our puzzled faces, he explains, "It's a family-friendly manga and anime about a teenage detective who gets drugged and becomes a little kid. A number of the plot lines involve a shogi piece, and how it moves or where it belongs on the board. I only started playing shogi myself after looking something up that was a crucial clue in the show."

Savannah comes to the doorway of her office and says, "You know Hudson. He's such a people person – and when he applies himself to something, he remembers everything. After playing for six months, he entered a shogi tournament and placed tenth. And now, we're friends with a meijin."

Before I can ask, Hudson says, "A meijin is a shogi master. I don't think I would ever be able to compete at that caliber."

"You never know," Chloe says. "Just imagine what that would do for the follower count on your channel."

They start discussing this, speculating whether or not Hudson would be allowed to stream at a shogi tournament.

Meanwhile, I'm trying to figure out how this development fits into what I know about the case. It's one more thing implying that the murderer is intelligent and logical. I'm not sure that supports

Annabelle as the suspect. She seems more a force of nature, much like Chloe or Imogen.

But the chocolatier with the sculpted shogi board had said that the majority of people in Japan don't even necessarily know how to play. I text Fisher and ask, *Can you try to figure out who from the movie set plays shogi? Or anyone suspicious at the chocolate festival who also plays? You should be able to make it come up naturally, since you are trying to learn the game, right?*

He texts back, *I'm not sure where to even start, but tomorrow I will give it a try. How's Logan? Dawn is worried sick about her brother, though she won't admit it.*

I have to be honest. I text, *I'm still waiting to hear from him. I'm sure everything's fine.*

We review Hudson's footage. He takes his water bottle and goes down to the gym before we watch the unzipping of the kaiju suit.

Ash, on the other hand, can't seem to look away. He says, "I looked into what it takes to actually act while wearing one of those suits, and it's difficult. It also takes a while to get in or out. One of the actors playing a secondary kaiju in Godzilla vs. Hedorah actually had appendicitis while wearing his suit, and they didn't have time to get him out. They rushed him to the hospital still dressed as a kaiju."

"And you still want to wear one of those?" Chloe asks, gesturing towards the screen.

"Obviously not that one," Ash says. "The police took all three suits into evidence, anyway."

The other clips Hudson collected are more interesting. There are a few of Noel. In one, he is practicing a flip using a horizontal bar. He lands on a mat, where Connie comes up behind him and puts her hands over his eyes. He pulls her hands away, and winks at the camera. Then he swings Connie around and kisses her, passionately. Hudson rapidly turns the camera away.

But I guess Connie wasn't lying when she said, one way or another, their relationship works.

In another clip, Noel is working out, doing bicep curls while facing the camera and talking to Hudson. He says, "My philosophy in life is to live every day as alive as you can. Whether that means scaling a mountain, paddling down a creek or gazing at the stars. Or maybe you're the kind of guy who gives your all every day to your job. If you mess up, say you're sorry. Move on, no regrets. And it's the same when you die. Move on. No regrets."

None of these clips provide any insight into why he died. Had he broken his own rule, refusing to take responsibility for harm he had caused someone? If so, why? He didn't seem the type to be afraid of facing the law, or even death.

There are clips of the cast and crew, too. At one point, the two camera guys are talking about fishing in Belize, which is right outside the Gulf of Mexico. I can understand parts of what they are saying in Spanish, but Hudson has helpfully added auto-generated subtitles to all his clips. They notice Hudson filming them and Franco starts telling the camera about being a kid living on Ambergris Caye, an island off the coast of Belize, in the 1970s when Jacques Cousteau showed up to document the 407 foot deep Blue Hole and associated cave system. He doesn't exactly strike me as a murderer. But he does spin a good yarn, and I can see why Noel might have wanted to visit Belize after talking to him for a while.

There's a clip of Haruko karate kicking the camera, her thick purple boot sole pausing in close-up, mere inches from the lens.

And Connie running across the set wearing a kaiju head over her head and shoulders, but otherwise dressed in a navy power suit. I'm not even going to ask what that was about.

Annabelle the Baker is in the background of one of the other shots. She has a tray of cupcakes in her hands, and she is in profile to the camera. Hudson zooms in on her only to have her put the tray down and hold up her hand, asking him to go away. She wipes at her eyes. I guess even Youtubers want their privacy sometimes. But I have to wonder why she was crying.

The doorbell rings and Chloe pauses the current clip. It's frozen on the face of one of the girls who had been in the group outside the movie studio building. She's one of the ones we didn't get to talk to. She has her mouth open, and her eyes look angry, and she is in the process of hurling a lemon at someone. Which looks terrifying. I doubt she's the murderer. She looks like the type to take more direct action than poison or whatever subterfuge had befallen poor Noel.

Chapter Sixteen
Tuesday

Savanah answers the door to Kudo.

He gives her a dashing smile and says, "I'm here to claim my cat. I hope I am at the right place."

"Come in," says Savannah, as she moves out of the way to let him inside.

He smiles at the group of us, but when he glances at the TV screen and sees the angry woman he flinches and gets a sour look on his face.

Chloe picks up Honda, cradling the calico upside down in her arms like a baby. She asks Kudo, "Does Honda have to go home already? It's been a stressful couple of days, and she's been such sweet company this afternoon."

Director Kudo's brow wrinkles as he stares at Chloe. "And that's supposed to help you how?"

Chloe says, "It's nice to have a cat to hold when all is falling apart in the world. Their purrs have proven to be healing, you know."

Kudo says, "Gomennasai. But I think I would like to take my cat home with me. You must understand."

Chloe looks heartbroken to have Honda leave her side, but when Kudo picks up the cat carrier and opens the door, Chloe puts Honda into it.

Kudo says, "I also like to have a cat to hold in times of stress. The police still have the movie studio taped off as a crime scene. The future of the movie is uncertain. And I have a terrible headache."

I say, "Come into the kitchen and I'll get you a bottle of tea."

I try to sound helpful, even though what I really want is to get him alone so I can ask him some questions. Basically acting like this is my fridge, I take a bottle of tea out of the door, and an onigiri from the bento stash Ash and Imogen had brought over.

"That would be nice," Kudo says, taking both.

Savanah comes into the kitchen and hands Kudo a little paper packet of pain relievers, which he swigs down with the tea, before saying, "Arigatou gozaimasu."

Savanah nods at him and then goes back into the living room. Kudo unwraps the rice ball. His eyes are red-rimmed, like maybe he has been crying too.

I say, "I'm sorry things have been so stressful." I gesture towards the cat carrier, which is on the floor beside his chair. "Honda is such a sweet cat. I love that she notices when people are feeling upset, and that she tries to help."

Kudo says, "She's always been that way. Maybe it's because she was bottle fed as a kitten. She was the runt of her litter, and her mother rejected her, but my aunt was determined to save her. I had never thought of myself as a cat person, but I was over there one day, and my aunt handed me Honda, wrapped in a blanket to keep her warm, and showed me how to feed her. She worked her way out of the blanket and buried her face against my elbow. And I was hooked."

I say, "You two seem to suit each other." I look at Kudo. I know he's dealing with a lot, but I can't waste this opportunity to ask questions. Trying to sound casual, I say, "I was at the studio earlier today. I wanted to talk, but they said you had an emergency and left." I let my expression make it clear that I'm hoping that he will fill in the details.

Kudo grimaces. "It wasn't an emergency, exactly. I had forgotten I had promised to meet my cousin. Her father-in-law passed away earlier this year, and we went to change out the flowers for his urn."

"Oh," I say softly. "I'm sorry." It's a long shot, but I can't help thinking about that note claiming Noel was responsible for something horrible. So I ask, "Noel didn't have anything to do with that did he?"

Kudo looks at me like I've lost my mind, and the intensity of his gaze brings home how hot he really is. He smolders. How could Connie compare him to a tree? That's one more thing that doesn't add up. He says, "Why would you think such nonsense?"

I lean back against my chair. "It just seems like maybe you had a problem with Noel for some reason."

Kudo snorts a laugh. "I have no reason to hold a grudge against Noel."

My next question is harder to phrase. I ask, "But were you jealous of him? What about Connie? I've seen the way you look at her. You're halfway to being in love with her."

Kudo's cheeks go red as he gets charmingly embarrassed. He looks down at the table and mumbles, "Not just halfway." But then he looks up at me and says, "But that was my secret and my pain to bear. I would never dream of acting on my feelings, as long as she was married."

Surprised, I ask, "Did you have a reason to believe she wouldn't remain married?"

Director Kudo closes his eyes and draws in a long breath. When he opens them again, he says, "Not one that's going to look good for me, while the police are looking into Noel's death."

I say, "It might make you feel better to share it."

"It probably won't," Kudo says. "But here it is, for what it's worth. I was reluctant to take a chance on Noel. He had broken contracts and been dropped by several large Hollywood studios, mainly by being arrested for stupid adrenaline-chasing stunts. But Connie San approached me and politely asked that we hire both of them as a pair – or else she wouldn't feel comfortable working on the movie. It was all about saving his ego – or so I thought. And it felt like Connie was being very sweet. It wasn't until later that I realized they needed money, and Connie wanted me to hire her husband so they would both be drawing a paycheck."

"But by then you were already smitten."

Kudo crumples the plastic wrap from his rice ball. "It wasn't like she had lied to me. And needing money doesn't make her any less of a good person. I admire the way she used to motivate Noel, encouraging him to work hard and to consider the feelings of others. I imagine that without her, Noel would have self-destructed years ago."

I say, "I take it you and Noel had some problems on set."

"A few. He showed up on time, and he could manage any stunt I assigned to him. It was mostly his attitude. Noel knew that he had messed up so many times before, he didn't deserve another job on a significant film. But he was completely ungrateful, almost to the point of being belligerent. I would have fired him – only Connie would have gone too, and I needed to protect her."

"From what?"

Kudo sucks at his teeth. "From the truth of what Noel was. From heartbreak. From getting hurt in a production with another studio not so committed to safety. I was always telling myself something different. But then Noel came to talk to me. And there was nothing I could do."

"He was planning to quit, wasn't he?" I ask.

Kudo says, "He told me he wanted to quit the movie halfway through to go treasure diving in Belize because Franco has a cousin he could stay with. And the way he explained it to me – he wasn't planning on taking Connie with him."

"So what did you do about it?" I ask.

Kudo presses the plastic wrap ball to the table. "I told him I wouldn't let him out of his contract. He said what I said didn't matter. He said it wasn't just the treasure diving. He wanted to be a dive guide for a little while, on some of the more challenging sites. I told him he was likely to kill himself, because when Connie isn't there, he stops being careful. I've seen it on set. He sprained a wrist a couple of weeks ago because he didn't check the length of a rope he was working with. If it wasn't for his natural talent as a stunt man, it could have been much worse."

I say, "But you worried about his safety for Connie's sake. It always comes back to her."

Kudo says, "I was worried about the studio's insurance, too, to be fair. And it didn't matter, because he showed up on set the next day. I guess he decided not to become a treasure diver after all." He gives me a sad smile, "But yes, it was mostly about Connie. Seeing him hurt – even a little – made her sad."

I say, "You know that gives you a motive, don't you?"

Kudo says, "I told you it was information the police are not going to understand."

I ask, "You didn't kill him, did you?"

Kudo looks scandalized. "Of course not. I'm a vegetarian. I can't stand the idea of hurting any living thing. Especially not a person."

I tell him, "I hate to break it to you, but earlier I saw Connie eating a chicken katsu sandwich. That I was told your aunt made."

Kudo waves a hand. "I know most people are not vegetarian here in Japan. One statistic I read when I decided to change my diet said only 2 percent of people eat the same way. I don't expect other people to have the same sensitivities I do. I mean, Honda's not a vegetarian. I feed her cat food that has meat in it, because she needs it to survive."

"She looks like you take good care of her," I say.

"Thank you. That's not the point." Though he looks down at the carrier and makes eye contact with his cat. Honda blinks at him. "The point is that I need you to figure out who really killed Noel. It can't have been that young girl who wants to keep my cat. I'm sure it won't take long for the police to figure that out, too. And then, I am afraid they will assume that Connie killed him. She can't go to jail, Mrs. Koerberu. Please. My heart would break."

The passion in his voice has me suddenly near tears. I wipe at the corner of my eyes, then I tell him, "I'm already doing the best I can to put together the clues. It could help if you could give me contact information for the two cameramen and for Keiko, your receptionist."

Kudo says, "What reason could any of them have to kill Noel?"

I say, "I'm just trying to get a clearer picture of what happened."

"Hai." Kudo takes out his phone and forwards me the information. He says, "I will instruct them to cooperate with you."

He types something longer and sends it as another text. About a minute later, I get a text from Keiko saying that she will bring the two cameramen to my booth at the chocolate festival tomorrow.

"Wow," I say. "Your receptionist is truly efficient."

Kudo's expression shows he's proud of his employee. "I strive to hire only the best. With the exception of Noel, obviously."

I ask, "Do you know when the next shoot using the kaiju suits was scheduled?

Kudo taps his finger on the table, thinking. Finally, he says, "It wouldn't have been until early next week."

I say, "So theoretically, Noel's body wouldn't have been discovered for four or five days, if Ash hadn't opened the suit. That's interesting."

I extrapolate from that mentally, rather than sharing more out loud with Kudo, who is still a suspect. Five days is a long time. Maybe that's what the Marzipan Musk perfume had been used for – covering any potential odor. But why delay the discovery of the body? Had the killer intended to move it? Or was the delay more about obscuring some particular detail?

Kudo says, "I wouldn't exactly call it interesting."

I ask him about the knife Chloe had touched, saying, "Why did you use real weapons on the set? Isn't there always a danger of someone getting hurt?"

Kudo says, "First off, I had no idea that Chloe was even there. Or that she had touched anything. Second, there isn't a knife missing from the set, at least not according to the photo the police made me review. And third – they are all prop weapons. I'm not looking for liability, am I?"

Chloe at least has the consolation that she hadn't put her own prints on the frame-up murder weapon. I ask, "Do you know anything about the actual knife he got stabbed with?"

Kudo shakes his head. "I didn't get to see it. The police were more concerned with why Chloe was on the set in the first place. They didn't understand why I would have Youtubers do cameos in my movie. It's obviously to reward them for being such loyal fans to the kaiju genre over the years. And even the ones who aren't the biggest monster movie fans are still out there sharing positive things about Japan and our culture. I believe that should be rewarded too."

I say, "I thought it would be because each Youtuber would encourage all of their followers to go see the movie."

Kudo says, "That is a good strategy too. And it will help a good deal with our marketing budget. But for me, it is about making a film that is a love letter to a genre I love and including the fans. Parts of it are self-deprecating homages to classic scenes. My vision is for it to be exuberant, with just a touch of farce. After all, when a mommy kaiju entrusts her baby to the wrong person so that she can have a shopping day, you can't play it subdued."

I ask, "Does everyone working on the movie feel that way?"

"Mostly," Kudo says. "At the beginning of the project, Taniguchi was hesitant to embrace so much camp. Even though his cinematic idol Tsuburaya was the one who did the effects for King Kong vs. Godzilla, and that movie had the two kaiju playing catch with a boulder. There was less angst than in the first few Godzilla films, and more goofy elements to create effects for, and Tsuburaya loved it."

"But Taniguchi came around?"

Kudo says, "Eventually. First he tried to get me to put a mystery in it, so he could do something atmospheric. Then he wanted to make a cyberpunk world. But he woke up one morning and came to the set whistling and told me if I was set on calling the movie *Kaiju's Day Out*, he might as well embrace it. That's when he started working hard on the set."

"Nobody else complained?" I ask.

"No one," Kudo says. "Honestly, most of the actors are there for the paycheck. Sometimes they will make suggestions about how to make their characters more consistent, but mostly, they do what the script tells them to."

In the doorway to the kitchen, someone clears their throat. I look up and it's Logan. He asks, "Am I interrupting something?"

"Absolutely not." I get up from my chair and rush to embrace him, rules about PDA be darned.

Logan says, "It's okay. I've only been gone half a day."

Still holding him in a hug, I say, "I know. But so much has happened. And you weren't answering your phone."

He says, "I turned the ringer off because Arlo fell asleep. Which means he gets to stay up all night and make sure Emi's safe."

Kudo says, louder than strictly necessary, "I'm going now." He looks clearly uncomfortable as he picks up his cat carrier and makes his way around us and into the living room.

I move away from Logan and tell Kudo, "Let me know if you think of anything else that might be useful."

Logan adds, "But don't forget to tell the police, too. We're not trying to interfere with their investigation."

Once Kudo leaves, Logan and I sit down at the kitchen table. He says, "We've figured out a plan involving Emi."

"Okay," I say. "Let's hear it."

Logan says, "Arlo will bring her to the chocolate festival tomorrow. We've arranged to meet her contact in the coffee shop, late in the afternoon. I'll already be in the shop, watching. Arlo will be somewhere outside the door."

"I want to be there with you," I say. "It will look more natural to someone walking in if we're there on a date than if you're alone watching the door."

Logan grins and leans over the table to twine my fingers in his. "How about a date tonight? We should just have time to get to Sky Tree Tower before they close. I hear the view of the city from up there is spectacular."

I squeeze his hand. "It would be nice to have a little time together, that isn't centered around work. Or murder."

"Yeah?" Logan asks. "You mean I can just put an arm around you while we look at the city lights?"

"Yeah. But that doesn't mean I'm not going to the coffee shop with you tomorrow, too."

Chapter Seventeen
Wednesday

Walking into the festival after having been up for hours is starting to feel like a routine.

This time, I brought canned coffee from the konbini to share with Henri. I had hoped to get him a cup with the cute latte art from downstairs, to thank him for the great job he had done with our chocolate yesterday, but the café isn't open yet.

He still looks grateful for the caffeine and pops open the can without hesitation. He says, "The jet lag, she is a vicious beast. I know being French – and a chocolatier – you may assume I only like refined food and drink, but I don't care if you know, I have been drinking these like they were water since I arrived in this country."

"Your secret is safe with me," I say.

"What secret?" Henri downs half the coffee. "Tell everyone. They may bring more of these."

We both laugh, then I tell him, "I teach my class today. It's still hard for me to believe I'm on the program for such an amazing festival."

Henri says, "It may be more difficult for some certain ones to believe. But I think you will do well when you explain to others how you make your chocolate. Something you are so excited to share will be interesting to your listeners too."

I pop the top on my own coffee. "What do you mean? More difficult for certain ones to believe."

Henri leans in and says softly, even though there's no one else near either of our booths to hear, "Meryl McAdams from Butterfly Chocolate has taught the chocolate making class at this festival for the past three years." I gasp, but Henri continues, "I for one do not understand why she has been chosen to do this. Maybe she has a friend involved with organizing the event? Or perhaps she was blackmailing someone, and now they have broken free."

He gives me a significant look. Now the way Meryl has been behaving makes much more sense. He probably would have shared this information yesterday, if there had been a moment when we had found ourselves alone.

The implication is clear. Maybe if I get kicked out of the festival, or my reputation is tarnished by cheating, she'll get pulled in last minute to present, which would mean she'd probably get reimbursed for her booth. She has to have been the one who had sabotaged my entry into the contest. But how could she have switched the chocolate bars?

Henri turns and lifts a glass cloche from the counter of his booth. He hands me a pain au chocolate – croissant dough that has been twisted around two chocolate rods, into the shape of a flattened scroll. I can see specks of herbs in the dough. He says, "When I am having a bad day, un pain au chocolat always turns it around. This one has herbes de Provence, which makes it even more special. Think of it as a speck of my homeland."

"Well then, merci beaucoup." I take a bite of the pastry, and it is heavenly. The dough is flaky, with the herbs making it almost savory. The bittersweet chocolate provides a balanced counterpoint.

If only it really could turn my day around – or preferably my entire trip, from the moment I met Noel in the airport and he tried to take my backpack.

"Where are your friends this morning?" Henri asks.

I say, "All over the place. Ash is going to appear on a Japanese morning talk show, so of course Imogen went with him for moral support. Dawn slept in, and when I left, Fisher was sketching the view from the hotel. The police have more questions for Chloe, so Patsy went with her to the station." I don't mention that Arlo is busy guarding a whistleblower with people actively looking for her. Sharing that info would defeat the point of keeping her safe by putting her in an undisclosed location. I say brightly, "Logan will be here in a minute, though."

It had been nice to have an actual date last night, even if it had been difficult not spending the entire time talking about theories on what had happened to Noel.

My phone rings with a request for a video call. I assume it's Logan and answer without even checking the ID. Instead, Carmen's face fills the screen. She's talking to someone else, like she called me then got distracted.

"Hey," I say, when there's a lull in the conversation on the other end of the phone. "Everything okay?"

Carmen says, "The news has reported about you being involved in a murder halfway around the world. We've tried to prepare, but between that and the chocolate challenge people, we're being overwhelmed. I really should spend time baking for tomorrow morning's rush. Does this cooking stream have to be tonight?"

I tell her, "I don't think Annabelle is going to take no for an answer. Plus, she's a suspect in the murder, and I want the opportunity to ask her questions without her getting suspicious."

Carmen sighs heavily into the phone. Then she says, "Okay. I'll figure something out."

I turn, looking at the festival slowly coming to life around me. I hate that I am so far away from my shop that I can't help out. I say, "Call in whoever you need to help. I'll make sure they get paid."

"Who's that?" Carmen asks.

"Where?" I ask, then realize that I've turned so that Henri's booth is in the background.

Carmen says, "That looks like Henri Martin. Only one of the most famous chocolatiers and pastry chefs who ever had a television show inspiring a generation of young chefs."

VANISHING INTO THE 100% DARK HOLDER 197

I say, "That's because it is Henri Martin. Do you want to talk to him?"

Carmen squees as I hand the phone over, but drops silent when she sees Henri's face on the screen. I've never seen her speechless before. I can't help but giggle.

Henri asks Carmen about the new cookbook, and Carmen gives him a flustered description. He and Carmen chat for a while. I finish my canned coffee and re-arrange the items on my counter. By the time I have everything ready, it's only a few minutes before the festival starts.

Henri hands me my phone back. He says, "There is a Japanese gentleman on the line for you."

"Oh, thanks." It has to be the janitor, finally returning my call. I was supposed to have a translator, but Hudson hasn't arrived yet. I answer the phone. "Hello?"

"Koerberu Sensei?" an unfamiliar deep voice says.

"That's me," I say. "Are you Hiro Ito."

"Hai," Hiro says. "Nice meet you. How . . . help?"

He's trying to converse with me in English, but he's obviously struggling.

I move into the aisle, looking for someone who can help.

I spot a group from the film studio, heading this way. Keiko and the two cameramen have shown up right at opening. I do have to say Kudo does hire prompt people. Keiko has even brought her own translator – Wataru Taniguchi. He looks half asleep and not at all excited to be here.

"Just a minute," I tell Hiro, and I rush over to Taniguchi. I hold out my phone to him. "Kudasai. You know Mr. Ito. Can you explain that I want to talk to him about when he was at the movie studio on Monday?"

"Of course," Taniguchi says. He takes the phone and puts it on speaker. He starts talking to Ito in Japanese.

I gesture the group over to my booth, so we will be less obtrusive. I hold up a finger to Keiko, signaling *wait*, and I step over next door, where I buy four of the pan au chocolat from Henri. He puts them in little paper bags. I offer them to my guests. The two cameramen each take a pastry and start eating them. Keiko takes one, nodding politely, but she just holds the bag.

Taniguchi says, "Hiro says he came to the studio building around ten that night."

That's not anywhere near the time Chloe had the impression of a janitor being in the building.

I ask, "Is he sure he wasn't at the building during the day? Maybe he dropped by for a minute? Or picked up something?"

Taniguchi relays this into the phone. After a brief exchange with Ito, he says, "Hiro usually does his cleaning jobs at night. I've only met him because he comes in person to get his check, or sometimes we make a huge mess demolishing props on set and he will come in to help clean up. He says that he was at his mother's house in Chiba for most of the day on Monday, fixing her plumbing."

Well, shoot. I had hoped he would have some information about what had been going on in the building, maybe even seen something about whoever had moved Noel's body. Not that it isn't good to definitively scratch someone off my suspect list in this case where everyone seems to have an alibi, and no one feels particularly suspicious.

A little deflated, I say, "Tell him thanks for calling. And that I hope his mother enjoys her new plumbing."

Taniguchi makes small talk with Ito before he hangs up and hands me back my phone, holding it carefully with both hands.

Keiko tugs at Taniguchi's sleeve and says something to him in Japanese. He tells me, "Keiko wants to make sure you get the answers to your questions. She is very loyal to the movie studio."

I ask, "Do you know why?"

Taniguchi turns and asks her. Her expression lightens and her eyes glimmer with emotion I can't understand until Taniguchi translates, "She says that five years ago, her husband left, and as a stay-at-home mom, she had such a long gap on her resume, she couldn't find a job. She found herself working part time washing dishes at a restaurant where Kudo's mom liked to eat, and one thing and another, Kudo took her on as a receptionist. It's a good job, with people she likes, and she can afford a good apartment. She doesn't want anything to jeopardize that."

Keiko nods emphatically.

I ask her, "Did you notice anything out of the ordinary before you all left for work on Monday?"

Taniguchi asks and translates back, "Everyone had already gone outside when she realized she'd left her purse in her desk. She went back in, and she thought she heard someone tap dancing."

Franco, one of the cameramen who has been patiently, listening, says, "But that's not right, idn't it?" His first language is Spanish. He must have picked up English somewhere in the United Kingdom. He says, "She says she heard someone banging, like using a hammer or turning a crank."

Keiko is nodding along to both of them, and she demonstrates by banging her fist into the palm of her open hand.

"I was paraphrasing," Taniguchi says.

Franco and Juan look at each other, and Juan mouthes, *That's not the same thing at all.* Franco nods.

Taniguchi tells Franco, "Your Japanese is very good."

Keiko continues, and Taniguchi translates, "She didn't see anything out of place, so she put up the closed sign and locked the front door."

That at least makes sense with everything else I've heard or observed.

I ask, "How did you feel about Noel? Do you know anyone he was having problems with on the set?"

Taniguchi translates back, piece by piece, "She thought Noel should be more professional at work, but now she worries that maybe she was too hard on him. He would wander somewhere he wasn't supposed to be on set, or track mud into the building, and then he would try to make it up to her the next day, by bringing her a slice of crepe cake from the bakery she likes, or bottled hojicha, because he knew it was her favorite. He reminded her in some ways of her son, who she does not see since he went to live with his dad. Maybe that is why she was so hard on Noel. She wanted him to live up to his potential."

Franco nods, agreeing with either the sentiment or the accuracy of this translation. He says, "I haven't seen my mom in a long time either. When we're done here, I should go call her."

Taniguchi continues translating. "She thinks Noel had an argument with someone in the conference room last week, but she didn't see who. She just heard Noel's voice, talking about integrity and him being married. Then he stormed out of the conference room and left for the day – even though he had another scene."

Could he have been fighting with Annabelle the Baker, maybe after the cake cubes incident? Maybe she had made advances, and when she'd been rejected, she had killed him. An overreaction on a massive scale, but that almond perfume ties back to her.

Of course, Noel could also have been flirting with someone else in the cast, or another one of the Youtubers. If he had no intention of being disloyal to his wife, his mixed signals could have been very upsetting to someone. But honestly, if it was someone he just met, Annabelle or anyone else, it seems an unlikely motive for murder.

Juan says, "One day, I saw Noel fighting with the lead actor. He didn't like the way Daiki was coming into the shot. Noel was going to have to match it for the stunt, and he got really upset. He said he wouldn't do it, because he might hurt himself. He was always careful like that."

I blink at Juan, trying not to show my surprise. Kudo had painted a completely different picture of Noel, saying he tended to be careless when Connie wasn't there. Could it be that Kudo was only paying attention when Connie was on the scene? Maybe he didn't have a great understanding of what was taking place on his own set.

Maybe Noel hadn't hurt his wrist because he was careless or depressed. Maybe he'd been distracted, by a threat or a complicated relationship.

I ask all of them, "Was there anything else going on involving Noel?"

"Not really," Franco says. "Only – last week was when Noel started asking us about Ambergris Caye. He was into all kinds of adventure sports. I mean, he climbed Mt. Fuji the first week he was in Japan. He mentioned a while back that he had dive experience, too. But suddenly he wanted all the technical information on the caves, and on the cost of living and the nightlife. I gave him my cousin's email address, since he runs a tour guide agency out there. I assumed Noel was thinking about getting away from the missus, since it was clear they'd had a fight. But it could have been that he started asking for alternatives after whatever had happened in the conference room."

They start discussing amongst themselves the time and logistics of what they had seen, and come up with a consensus that yes, that could very well be the case.

"Poor Noel," Taniguchi says. "I had no idea he was going through so much."

Franco says, "That's because you spend all your time in your lab, tinkering with the props. You should go out with us for beer sometimes, have a little fun."

Taniguchi makes a noncommittal noise. I hope he does go and build some connections.

None of them can think of anything else to add. I recommend that they stay and have a look around at the chocolate festival, since they obviously had to pay to get in. I doubt they will stay long enough, but I also let them know I have a class later, if they want to attend. After all, I could use a few extra friendly faces in the audience.

Logan is heading towards us, carrying yet another konbini bag. This one says 7-Eleven. He hands it to me, saying, "I saw this and thought of you."

"What?" I say. "An onigiri? Am I that predictable?"

But when I look in the bag, there are half a dozen objects wrapped in old newspaper. Logan says, "Don't unwrap them all. The guy at the vintage shop spent ten minutes wrapping them well enough to survive the plane ride home. Just open the big one."

I give him back the bag and unwrap the object. It's a teapot, with a maroon background and a delicate teal and gold design.

Keiko and Taniguchi both gasp in delight. Keiko says, "Sugoi!" and mimes clapping her hands.

Taniguchi says, "That's a real antique."

Logan tells me, "I never gave you an engagement gift. I wanted you to have something beautiful to remember this trip."

I say, "I never got you anything, either."

Logan gives me a sweet little smile and says, "Well, you did get me the ring. And I can't wait to wear it. Speaking of which, Fisher will be here in a moment to man the booth because I found a department store downstairs that actually does have a wedding registry. And they offer a discount for registry guests. Whenever he gets here, we can go." Logan turns to Keiko and Taniguchi. "In the meantime, would you like for me to show you around the festival?"

They agree, leaving me alone at the booth. As they walk away, I hear Juan ask Logan, "Are you saying that *she* proposed to *you*?"

That's exactly what he's saying. And the fact that he's not embarrassed about it makes me happy.

I start humming as I move back around my counter and put some truffles on a plate, then move back to the front to offer them to passersby. From where I'm standing, I can see Meryl, at the Butterfly Chocolate booth doing the same thing. I stop humming. I give her a tentative wave. She glares back at me.

She has to realize that I didn't accept the invite to be on programming here just to spite her. But she seems to think I did.

Surely she's not this harsh with everybody. I pull up Instagram and find her company account. It links to her personal account. It doesn't take long scrolling through pics of family dinners and cherry blossom viewings to realize Meryl lives in Japan, and her daughter-in-law is Japanese. There are shots of Meryl's daughter-in-law teaching her to make mochi, and of the two of them each walking a pair of matching toy poodles. Every third or fourth picture is of Meryl's tea or coffee at a different café. She likes walking on the beach, holding her granddaughter's hand, and touring the vineyards between Tokyo and Mount Fuji with her son. From everything I'm seeing, by all rights, Meryl and I should be friends.

There's no mention of a spouse or significant other. At least not until I scroll back a couple of years. Meryl doesn't post that often, so within a few minutes, I get to a pic of Meryl with her face pressed against the face of a handsome black guy. The caption reads, *It's been a year since we lost him.*

My heart breaks for her. Even if she cheated to try and get me thrown out of the awards. Even if she hasn't been very nice. Because nobody deserves to have to deal with that level of loss. And it explains a lot about why she's so desperate to have her usual spot at this festival. Part of it is probably money. That memoriam pic was taken in Japan, and Butterfly Chocolate has been operating here for ten years. It can't be cheap to live in Tokyo, and to suddenly be the only income when you were relying on two. It's not surprising she doesn't have a storefront.

But more than that, when your life is shaken up so much, you tend to cling to things that feel familiar. There's always an element of survivor's guilt that makes you feel the need to justify your existence. It's considered prestigious to be asked to participate in programming at a conference or festival. To have a festival where you are a regular presenter suddenly choose someone else has to be a blow to your self-esteem. And if my math is right, the first year she got asked to participate was the year after she lost her husband. I get it.

I'm just not sure what to do about it, since talking about any of this with her would be a disaster.

Logan comes back and notes my change in mood. "Hey," he says, "Why so glum?"

I start to hide my distress and say that everything is fine. But I want to have a relationship where we can really talk about things. So I show Logan Meryl's Instagram feed and explain what I've found out.

He says, "That has to be hard to see, considering your own loss. We don't have to go do the wedding registry thing right now, if you're not in the mood."

I take his hand. "How could I miss watching you pick out which of those katana sword looking umbrellas you want to go in the hall tree?"

"We're getting a hall tree?" Logan asks.

My dad is in the middle of renovating my suite at the hotel to join with Logan's. A lot of what he is doing construction-wise is going to be a surprise to both of us. "Last I heard, yes."

"Cool," Logan says. He checks the time on his phone, obviously wondering why Fisher isn't here yet. "I'm glad you're on board, because I spent several hours this morning finding a place with a wedding gift registry. Apparently, that's not usually a thing here. Traditionally, people just give money to help defray the costs of the reception. But I finally found one department store that offers a Bridal Club, which includes a registry, and lo and behold, one of their locations is this mall."

A few of the detective fiction club members I'd seen trickle in yesterday all show up again, in a group. It makes sense. If they bought tickets, they'd have access for multiple days.

This time, instead of leaving books for me to read, they've brought a canister of matcha. And they're hanging around instead of just scurrying off. From their body language, I can tell they want something. There are four girls and three boys, and they're straightening skirts and putting hands in pockets like middle schoolers at their first dance.

Finally I ask, "What's going on?" Surely one of them speaks English.

One of the girls steps forward and gives a mini bow. She says, "I'm Isa Yui, president of the Detective Fiction Club. We heard that Diaz San is interviewing people in Japan for his podcast. We were hoping that you would put our names forward to be interviewed as some of his biggest fans." She bows her head, and brings her hands together in a pleading gesture, though I see her angling her face to look up with one eye to gauge my response.

"I can talk to him," I say, "But I think his plan is to interview people who have been part of the various cases."

"Surely you can change his mind," one of the guys says. "We are the members of the club who read novels in English, so we know enough about western investigation work – real world and fiction – to make for interesting subjects."

I ask, "Does Suzuki Sensei know that you are here?"

Yui says, "It is difficult to contact Sensei outside of her office hours or our club meetings."

"What do you think she does with all that time?" Logan asks.

The guy who spoke before says, "There are rumors-"

The guy standing next to him elbows him in the ribs, effectively cutting off his statement.

Yui says, "It is inappropriate for us to speculate on what our teacher does. She is head of two student clubs at our school. That must keep her very busy."

She gives me a contact information list for the group, and they all walk away, half of them giggling.

A few minutes later, Yui comes back by herself, with the outspoken guy in tow. She says, "I don't want you to have any misgivings about Suzuki Sensei. Or to think that the rumors about her are dark or point to scandal. They are actually quite funny, when taken in context." She turns to the guy. "Kenji, say what you had to say."

Kenji doesn't look quite as brash, but he still hurries to speak. "Suzuki Sensei is a wonderful teacher. But there is a rumor that she is actually The Cat with A Thousand Names, a serial burglar who has been active in this part of Tokyo for the last seven years. The name was given to this thief by the police as a play on the name of one of Edogawa Ranpo's most famous villains, The Fiend with Twenty Faces. Edogawa Ranpo is one of the first writers of Japanese Detective fiction, and the one who popularized it. The Fiend with Twenty Faces is a gentleman thief and a master of disguise. Many subsequent characters of this type have been inspired by him."

"The reason this rumor is ridiculous," Yui says in a pained tone, "Is the only reason anyone can give for thinking she is The Cat is just that she took Kogoro as her Detective Club name. And Kogoro is actually the arch nemesis of The Fiend with Twenty Faces. Is Suzuki Sense mysterious – yes. Is she shockingly beautiful – yes. Does anyone know how she affords her fancy apartment or extensive designer wardrobe on a professor's salary – absolutely not. But none of that makes her a cat burglar."

Kenji says, "She seems to know too much about heists and burglaries when we discuss books at our meetings. The way she describes lockpicks and glass cutters, it seems like it might be from personal experience."

Yui rolls her eyes, belying the professional image she's trying to maintain.

Logan asks, "What are detective names?"

Yui said, "It started out as something the characters did in the Decagon House Murders. Each of the characters was called by the name of a detective instead of their regular name. It was a bit confusing to read, but it helped the writer hide the identity of the killer until the very end. While discussing that book, we all started talking about what our own detective names would be and why. I took Melody, from Autumn Ellis's first series, because I love to sing."

"Hey," I interrupt. "Autumn is my best friend."

Yui blushes in a way that makes it clear she already knew that.

I tell her, "I'll get Autumn to send you a signed book."

I want to tell her that Autumn is working on a book set in Japan, but it's not my place to do so, since it hasn't been officially announced yet.

Kenji looks totally jealous. I wind up promising that Autumn will send Kenji a book too. I'm sure she won't mind.

The two of them rush off to find the others, nearly crashing into Fisher, who has finally arrived. Today Fisher's tee says, *Easily Distracted by Plants*, with a half-finished painting of an ivy on a canvas set on an easel. I groan at the horribleness of this visual pun.

Logan asks, "Do you think Nao might really be The Cat with a Thousand Faces?"

"Part of me wants to believe she is," I say. "I know the theft part is awful – having recently been a victim. But there's something about the cool factor involved. Of course, that whole gentleman thief thing probably doesn't exist outside of movies."

Logan says, "When she was helping get you into that kimono, I had a look around. She does have a credit-card style set of lockpicks in her purse."

I point out, "You have a set of lock picks in the glove box of your car."

"And I taught you how to use them when we were breaking into a house, if I recall."

"That was different," I say. "We were gathering evidence."

Logan says, "Now we get to gather evidence on whether Nao is more than she claims."

I say, "What if she is and Noel found that out? Maybe he was blackmailing her. Do you think she might have killed him over it?"

"I hope not," Logan says. "That would completely negate the cool factor."

"What cool factor?" Fisher asks as he goes behind the counter and plops his messenger bag on a chair.

"The cool factor that appears when somebody says gentleman thief," Logan says. "Or in this case, gentlewoman."

Fisher says, "Don't tell me there's a gentleman thief in a kaiju movie. That would be too cool."

"Unfortunately, no," Logan says. "I'll explain it to you later. Right now, my fiancé and I are going to take a moment to daydream."

We go down three floors to the store Logan found for our registry. He says, "Of course we will have to register somewhere back home, too. Not everyone will want to order online or pay shipping."

"Obviously," I say. "And we need to make sure to pick some super cheap stuff, so that nobody feels obligated to give us anything. Honestly, I don't care if they bring a gift or not, as long as we are surrounded by friends and family."

Logan says, "Speaking of that. I think you should invite Kevin's family. It's an opportunity to redefine your relationship with them, and let them know you still care."

How did Logan know I'd been thinking about that, but worried to bring it up? Heat builds behind my eyes, and I think I might cry, it is so sweet he considered that. Sudden emotion makes it hard to speak, so I just nod.

Logan leads me into the store, and then on through to the back, where there is an alcove with fancy jewelry displays. In the corner, an over-the-top wedding dress hangs from a high bar so that the train flows onto the floor. And in front of us, there is a long desk with several sets of chairs, where couples can sit for consultations. This is the first real wedding planning we've done, and I find myself excited in a way I didn't expect – especially because I had just been on the edge of tears. This is actually my future. I feel fluttery and light, like I'm flying into a blissful dream.

I know there will be difficulties, and less-than-perfect days, but in this moment, my life with Logan becomes concrete. We sit for the consultation, get signed up for the club, and get instructions on scanning bar codes on our phones to register for items. The woman helping us emphasizes several times that we should be discreet and not bother other customers. I get the idea that while she is happy for us, she expects we will run up and down the aisles telling people we're getting married and demanding they buy us gifts. Who knows? Maybe that has happened to her before.

This is a very posh store, and after checking out a few price tags, I tell Logan, "I feel guilty putting any of this stuff on the registry."

Logan says, "Like you said, we can do a cheap registry too. Think about what you want our life to look like. If you want to give someone a few options for a total splurge for you, what would it be?"

I try to think. "I would love to have a luxurious bathrobe, and maybe a foot massager. But this floor is housewares. I know we tend to use the kitchen at the hotel back home, but wouldn't it be lovely to have our own espresso machine in the enlarged suite, without having to go downstairs? And maybe a wine fridge?"

"Lead the way," Logan says. "I know you live frugal, so it's good to see you daydreaming big."

To find the appliances, we walk through a whole section of Japanese-style dishware. I ask Logan, "Do you have a set of dishes you like?"

Logan says, "Nothing I'm attached to. My mom keeps saying that one day, I'm going to inherit the good china, because Dawn got the set my grandparents had as a wedding gift. But that's not something I like to think about. Besides, when would I use it?"

"You never know. We might be dinner party people."

"Were you and Kevin?" Logan asks.

"Sadly, no," I say. "I would have liked to have been, but he was more of an introvert."

"Then we had better register for dinner party dishes. Just in case."

Once we've found a pattern we both love, Logan says, "You know what my splurge would be? A nice set of Japanese knives. But I wouldn't put it on a registry. Too many of my extended relatives are superstitious."

"Then lead on," I say. "You can buy them for yourself, as your souvenir of the trip."

Once we're in the knife section, I notice one blade with a distinctive pattern down the sides of the handle, like the swirl of a giant wave against a blue background. It looks familiar. At first I think it is because it has a similar look to a famous painting. We've seen The Great Wave of Kanagawa printed on lots of touristy items. This isn't an exact copy, but it has the same vibe. But then I realize – this is the exact model of knife used to stab Noel.

I bring this to Logan's attention.

"Look at that," he says. "It wasn't a prop, after all." He snaps a picture of the knife and sends it to somebody. He types out a message to go along with it.

"What are you saying?" I ask.

He says, "I'm finding out if anyone from the film studio might have purchased one of these knives recently."

I say, "It's such a distinctive piece. Why would anyone have bought it right here, only to use it to confuse the evidence in a murder? Wouldn't it point right back to them?"

Logan says, "Not much about this case has made sense."

All of my bubbly pre-wedding excitement has dissipated, and I can't look away from the display knife. What business do I have spending time on myself when Chole is in danger of being arrested?

Still, I don't want to disappoint Logan, so we finish out our registry. It's nice to realize how much our tastes mesh. And by the time we're done, and Logan his checked out his purchase of a full set of Japanese chef's knives, he has a reply to his text. Against the list of names that Logan had given his source, it turns out that several of the suspects have been in this store and been drawn to the distinctive knife. Including Kudo. And Meryl.

There's also one guy from the editing department of the movie crew who bought one. As has Ash. I wonder if he has noticed it was the same one as the murder weapon. If so, he hasn't said anything.

Chapter Eighteen
Wednesday

Annabelle the Baker has an amazing kitchen. It's in her house, and has a whole array of camera equipment surrounding it. But the modern chrome and glass look of the cooktop and counters is a huge contrast to the rest of the structure, which is in the traditional Japanese style.

She has both Logan and me take our shoes off at the entrance, but even from here we can see the focus on the kitchen setup. It's open to a tiny living room, with a loveseat and a single chair. Obviously, the kitchen had been expanded and the living room shrunk during the remodel.

"Do you like the place?" Annabelle asks. "I got it for almost nothing. But it was a pain getting it up to code. Took most of my spare time, for a year."

"The part I can see is lovely," I say. "My aunt flips houses, so I know how much work goes into something like this."

Annabelle beams, obviously proud of her hard work. "You can't flip one of these properties. To get the financing, you have to agree to live in the house for a couple of years. But I'm not planning on going anywhere, so this is perfect."

She gestures me over to a rack of aprons, so I can choose one to wear during the filming. I pick one that has vertical stripes in fuchsia and teal. It's a bit brighter than the clothes I usually wear, but I don't want to get drowned out by the camera.

It will be good for Greetings and Felicitations – and Carmen's cookbooks in particular – to get publicity on Annabelle's channel. But I can't forget why I'm here. I need to figure out if Annabelle was the one in the conference room that day at the movie studio, having a fight with Noel. But how to approach it?

I gesture at her camera setup. "Kind of reminds you of the Kaiju set, doesn't it?"

She says, "You'd be surprised how many Youtubers have green screens, editors, and entire camera crews. The demand for higher video quality has forced a lot of us to step up."

Okay. This isn't going in the direction I need it to. I say, "Oh? I had no idea. That sounds like more than a full-time job. I'm surprised you found time to cameo in a movie."

Annabelle says, "I was only on set for a couple of days."

I ask, "Were you there last week, on Thursday?"

"I was," Annabelle says, looking surprised. "How did you know that?"

I shrug and try to look casual. "I heard there was a fight in the conference room on Thursday. I just thought you might have seen who it was."

Annabelle shows no reaction. She says, "No idea. I know Connie seemed really upset on Thursday. And at that point, it wasn't at me. One of the writers told me he saw her tearing up some papers and throwing them into the trash. And before you ask, no, I don't know what they were. But my guess is it was an eviction notice for that huge mansion they own back in the States. Or something to do with her side business."

"Side business?" I ask.

Annabelle turns and starts arranging spoons and scoopers on her counter. She says, "Connie sells atomizers. You know, like the things for dispersing air freshener in your house? I actually use a small version for my perfume line."

I say, "That seems like a weird side business for a stunt woman."

From what I know about Connie, she likes things on a large scale. She had admitted that she would rather Noel had committed a heist than continue stealing phones.

Annabelle says, "She inherited a family business. Gossip on the set is that she and Noel thought it was going to be their financial salvation – until Connie found out the business was getting sued because one of the models had a piece that could break off, becoming a choking hazard. That's why they're about to lose the house." Annabelle waves a whisk. "The diffusers are produced in India, and at some point, Connie is going to have to go there to deal with stuff. She was trying to wait until the movie was over."

Why hadn't Connie mentioned any of this? And what papers had she been destroying?

I like Connie, and I don't like suspecting her as a killer – but I can't help but wonder – can poison be atomized? Could Noel have been dosed with something that would absorb through the skin, but take a while to take effect, giving Connie an alibi?

I need to talk to her again – as soon as I can wedge in the time.

I remind Annabelle, "I can only stay for the first half hour of filming. I have a class to teach today at the chocolate festival."

And so much else to do after that – including helping protect Emi at her meet.

Annabelle's cooking stream goes well, at least the part I'm present for. Carmen gets to plug her books and show off Knightley. I miss my little bun, so it's nice to see him happy and healthy, munching parsley in his cage, once he's made his close-up appearance for the camera.

Autumn is also there, talking about her books. She admits that cooking isn't her thing, but gamely takes a turn with a whisk and measures out ingredients. I start having fun, interacting with my friends and playing around with flavor profiles. I almost don't want to leave.

I mime that I'd like to visit the restroom before I head out, and Annabelle points me at a rickety set of stairs. Logan has fallen asleep on the loveseat, waiting for me. So I try to go up the stairs quietly, so as not to wake him or to interrupt the recording.

There are three doors at the top of the stairs. I open the first one, and it is a linen closet. The second leads to Annabelle's bedroom. I start to close the door, but then the collage of posters on the far wall catches my eye. It's a jumble of actors and stunt men. There's Jackie Chan and Tom Cruise – actors known for doing their own stunts. But there are also a half dozen images of folks standing next to actors like Jason Momoa and Ryan Gosling, dressed in the same clothes, and ready for stunt performances. I guess it's easier to find those kinds of images than posters of the stuntmen. She does have one fan poster, though, and it's of Noel. It's signed – and there's a heart drawn around him.

There's a creak on the stairs behind me. Startled, I jump. I turn, pulling the door closed behind me. But Annabelle clearly saw me close it. She's not smiling anymore.

Is she the killer? If so, I'm clearly in danger and Logan is fast asleep downstairs, not likely to rescue me in time. I start looking for an escape route from this second story landing. There was a window in Annabelle's room. What are the odds of me climbing out of it?

Annabelle says, "The first episode is done. I was just coming up to check that I had remembered to change the TP in the bathroom."

"That's thoughtful," I say.

There's something in her hand, but I can't tell what it is. Is it a weapon? Or a roll of toilet paper. She comes up onto the landing, still between me and the stairs. If I push her at the linen closet door, can I scoot around her and make for the steps? It depends on what she is holding.

Annabelle says, "You look terrified. But you don't need to be. Yes, I have a thing for stunt men, and yes, I lied about not being disappointed that Noel wasn't into me when we were on set together. But no, I did not kill him."

"What's in your hand?" I ask.

She opens her hand, and there's a diffuser. She says, "It's also for the bathroom. Which tends to hold odors."

I want to believe her. I want to feel safe. But if poison can be atomized, Annabelle had just as much access to the means for Noel's murder as Connie did.

I say, "I'll just use the bathroom at the festival. I can hold it."

I scoot around her and head down the stairs. She lets me go. I wake up Logan, and we head out, saying a tense but superficially polite goodbye.

When we get outside, Logan asks, "Do you want to tell me what that was all about?"

I tell him, "I need to find a way to narrow these suspects down, so I don't have to go around being paranoid of everybody."

On the way back to the festival, I explain everything that had happened while Logan had been napping.

He says, "You think Annabelle is a crazed fan, unable to differentiate fantasy from reality. Sort of an If-I-Can't-Have-Him-No-One-Can murderer?"

"Maybe," I say hesitantly. "But Connie looks more suspicious now too."

During the taxi ride, I spend some time Googling my suspects, trying to get a feel for anything I might be missing. I start with Nao. Could she really be a cat burglar? I do a search for her name and Cat with a Thousand Names. Surprisingly, there's a Reddit thread with people supposing that she is the Cat. There are a couple of photos, some clearly taken from surveillance camera footage, of a blurry figure, and one seen from an extreme distance. I mean, it *could* be Nao. But none of them are clear enough to say it's probably her. It's impossible even to say for sure that the figure in most of them is a woman.

Searching Nao's name by itself doesn't give any hint as to how she affords her lifestyle. She grew up in a small town, became an orphan at age fifteen, and attended college in the United States on a full scholarship. She's only had one job, at the university where she currently teaches.

I search for Annabelle the Baker, and I find out that she has a restraining order against another Youtuber, who apparently decided they were dating after he was a guest on her show. Really, would she do the same thing to Noel, having experienced it herself? It seems unlikely. Even if she does have a poster of Noel on her wall – one she hasn't taken down even though he is dead.

Once we get back to the festival, Logan grabs a box of supplies from our booth, and we head for the screened off areas where the classes are being held. There wasn't an event scheduled before me this morning in the "room" where I'm teaching, so we can go in and set up.

I swoop aside the curtain and notice that Arlo and Emi are already inside. Arlo turns towards the motion, half standing, ready to defend Emi.

When he realizes it's us, he visibly relaxes.

Emi is wearing the sunglasses again, and she has a silk scarf covering her hair. I'm not sure how much of a disguise that is, given that she is hanging out with us.

There's a table set up on a small stage, maybe a foot high and carpeted to blend with the rest of the room. Logan brings the box in and sets it on the table.

Emi jumps up and rushes over to hug me. She says, "Thank you for being patient with me. Logan talked about you so much yesterday. It's hard to believe all the things the two of you have been through together. Seven murderers behind bars, because of you two."

I say, "If I hadn't lived it, I wouldn't believe it myself. My friend Ash calls me a mega murder magnet. He said once that I find myself in the middle of these crazy circumstances because the universe can sense my empathy. I don't know how much I believe that, but I don't have a better explanation."

Emi steps back and studies my face. "Whatever it is, I'm glad that I have your empathy – without getting murdered."

I'm still not a hundred percent sure she didn't murder Noel, trying to get her phone back. But I'm willing to set my suspicion aside for now.

Arlo says, "Remember my friend who is now a consultant for the Tokyo police? He was able to get me a copy of Noel's toxicology report."

He shoots a gloating look at Logan. Logan hadn't had a source able to get him Noel's forensics. Now, suddenly Arlo can get information Logan can't. Apparently the rivalry between them hasn't died out.

Happy to one-up Arlo when it comes to information, Logan announces, "Did you know that there's an assault charge on Kudo's record?"

Arlo looks a little less gloaty. I don't mention that I already knew this.

Logan says, "But he's not the only one. Keiko does too. The dates don't match, so the incidents aren't related."

Now, I didn't know that. Kudo's incident had likely been in his work file because it had happened at work.

"Details?" Arlo asks.

Logan says, "When Kudo first started working for the studio, he punched a director and almost got fired. He claimed it was in defense of one of the actresses, who was being bullied on set. He tends to get passionate about people he cares about."

This news only reinforces the idea that he might have killed Noel to protect Connie. I keep coming back to the idea that they both had so many reasons for wanting Noel gone, they might have been working together – no matter how much Kudo insists his affections were one-sided. He seems like the type who would take the blame for the murder on his own, just to protect her.

Randomly it occurs to me – if he was lying about other things, could he even be lying about being a vegetarian?

"What about Keiko?" I ask.

Logan says, "She gave her ex-husband a black eye after he said he was moving to Hokkaido. It had to do with the fact that he had custody of their son. She pushed the taxi driver, and he claimed a back injury from falling on the sidewalk."

Emi says, "As a mom, I excuse her for that one. It sounds like he told her he was moving while the move was actually in progress. I would have smacked him, too."

"Fair," Logan says. "I don't think it makes her more of a suspect."

"Maybe the toxicology is more helpful." Turning to Arlo, I ask, "What kind of poison did they figure out it was?"

Arlo says, "Noel wasn't poisoned. They found a broken epi pen in Noel's pocket, and there were signs of anaphylaxis in his body. It's possible Noel died from an allergic reaction. But my friend says the stabbing must have happened at the same time, or soon enough after for someone to have been able to confuse the results. Because without your testimony, they wouldn't have looked close enough to realize the stabbing wasn't the cause of death. The initial theory was that the anaphylaxis was caused by something on the blade."

That leaves me stumped. I'd been counting on Noel having been poisoned with something that had a delayed effect. Both Kudo and Connie had been out at lunch at the time the murder was committed. How could either of them have introduced an allergen – let alone moved the body, and stabbed Noel, which suddenly seems time sensitive – while in a group with all the other suspects? It's impossible. There has to be another solution.

It might have been a coincidence that the epi pen Noel carried broke when he plunged off the roof. But it is also possible that someone who knew about his allergy sabotaged it. The only person I can think of who could have done that would be Connie. Unless Annabelle or Nao broke the pen immediately before dosing him with the allergens.

I hate to admit it, but we don't have any accounting for Emi's whereabouts. But neither Logan or Arlo seem to have a problem with her sitting here listening to us discussing the details surrounding Noel's death. Neither of them seem to consider her a suspect, despite the fact that Noel took the phone with the secret file on it, so I keep that suspicion to myself.

Nao would have been in a position to hit Noel with an allergen – if she knew something he was allergic to. But would he really have gotten across the street if he was going into anaphylactic shock? And what would have been her motive? I suppose if she really is a master thief, Noel could have been cutting in on her territory. If he had refused to stop, it could have been enough to drive her to eliminate the competition.

Annabelle could have been in the building. She had said her perfume was made with synthetics, but what if she dumped her perfume and filled a diffuser with almond oil? Then the synthetic scent would have been reinforced with the real thing. Which would explain why the smell I had experienced had seemed more like almond cake than almond and musk. Maybe Logan had been right about Annabelle having lost touch with reality. So much of her life is filmed ... maybe she couldn't handle deviating from the narrative she was trying to project.

I ask, "Does anyone know if Noel was allergic to almonds?"

Arlo consults his phone. "That information isn't here."

People start filing in for the class. Hurriedly, Logan and I turn back to the box, setting up our equipment and pulling out trays of samples, featuring chocolate at different stages from the dried bean, to roasted nibs, to eating chocolate, from different regions in South America.

My translator shows up and introduces herself as Jodi. Her accent says she's clearly from the Southern United States. I'm guessing Georgia. But when she turns and speaks to someone in Japanese, her accent completely disappears.

Emi moves to the back corner of the room, pretending to be absorbed in her phone, while keeping her head down behind the sunglasses. It is a bit inconsistent that she has sunglasses on indoors, but maybe the sunglasses will pass as prescription, or maybe the kind with a camera built in. With the draped cloth walls, she at least has an exit if she gets too nervous.

There are a few familiar faces. Connie walks in, chatting with Taniguchi. They must have run into each other while exploring the festival. Chloe and Patsy show back up. I'm relieved that the police didn't arrest Chloe. I haven't really overlapped with the detectives this time in my investigation. I'm fine with that. I don't need to see Detective Yamada – or even Detective Matsumoto – again.

Only, I've spoken too soon. The two detectives walk in and take seats in the back row, on the opposite end from Emi. Then Keiko takes a seat on the other side of Taniguchi. Hudson and Savannah even show up. Savannah makes a heart with her hands, a clear message of, *You got this!*

By the time I start presenting, there are only a few empty seats. Arlo moves to stand by the wall, in case more people come in.

I hold up a dried cacao pod and ask, "Does anyone know what is inside this?" I shake it and the cacao beans in it rattle.

Hearing this, a little kid on the front row raises his hand. When I call on him, he says, "M&Ms."

This gets laughter from most of the room. "Close," I tell the kid. "Those are actually the beans that chocolate comes from." I address the audience, "I wanted to bring y'all a fresh cacao pod, but I couldn't really do that flying here, so I brought a dried pod and a wooden model of a fresh one."

I take out the model pod, showing how the size and shape is similar to a Nerf football, then I take off a piece, and show the inside, which looks like a swollen corn cob. The translator mirrors each step. I say, "Each one of these globs of pulp has a single cacao bean inside. It takes around 400 beans to make a pound of chocolate."

A few audience members make impressed noises. Excited that they are actually engaging with my presentation, I grab a double handful of cacao beans, and explain that they've been fermented and dried, and that we're going to roast and winnow them to develop flavor and then remove the husks, and then start the conching process to grind the nibs down further to make a texture that is pleasant to eat. I say, "Of course, fully conching chocolate takes three or four days, and I don't expect you to sit that long. So there's a second tabletop conch with a batch that's ready to mold."

That gets me a laugh from the audience. I relax a little more, feel the smile on my face get wider and less forced.

Someone walks in late and moves to take the single empty seat on the front row. My smile weakens as I recognize the guy. It's Wataru Tanaka. Emi's contact for her whistleblowing attempt. It would be hard to mistake him, with that birthmark on his face. He makes eye contact with me, and something in his expression makes me shudder. Tanaka is supposed to be in the United States, orchestrating Emi's meet with whoever can help her. So what is he doing here?

He turns around in his seat, clearly scanning the audience. Emi sees him, but instead of waving, she shrinks back in her seat. Does she feel like something is off, too?

I try to keep talking, putting a hand on the roaster, and explaining how roasting transforms the dried beans from something tannic and unpalatable, to something nutty, with the many flavor notes of chocolate. I ask for volunteers to come up and help put beans into the roaster. Without waiting for me to call on him, Tanaka steps up onto the stage and comes around the table to stand next to me. He whispers, "Where's Emi? I need to get a message to her."

I resist the instinct to look over to where Emi is sitting. Instead, I hand Tanaka a pair of gloves and whisper, "Why don't you just text her?" I gesture for him to put the beans in the roaster basket and place it in the roaster. I turn it on.

He whispers back, "Something spooked her. She blocked me. I got worried and hopped a plane."

On one level, that makes sense. Theoretically, he would have had time for a twelve-hour flight if he went to the airport the minute Emi missed her meet at the bar. But if he's here now, who is Emi supposed to be meeting in the coffee shop?

Trying to maintain a professional demeanor despite the fact that the hairs on my arms are on edge and fight-or-flight is making my legs want to shake, I start to explain winnowing, and how, as soon as the roasting is finished, we will crack the beans into nibs – smaller pieces that will go in the winnower.

Logan subtly moves between us and Emi, while Arlo is edging towards the table. Tanaka keeps scanning the crowd, but he hasn't zeroed in on Emi, despite her weak disguise attempt. I'm guessing he's never met her in person.

The moment of tension is like a blister ready to pop.

Suddenly, Emi stands up and makes a break for it, swishing the white sheet up and aside as she rushes into the exhibit hall. Logan follows her. Tanaka's hand goes to his pocket, presumably to draw a weapon. Emi's gone, but he could easily hit Logan. Without thinking of the consequences, I push down on the table, flipping it over against us. The chocolate that has been conching spills everywhere, splashing up all over me. The roaster hits Tanaka's midsection.

The weapon that was in Tanaka's hand goes skittering as he grabs at the roaster. It's a gun with weird edges, like it has come out of a 3D printer. It looks so fragile, I'd be afraid to fire it.

People in the audience are shouting, trying to get away. Adrenaline is pumping through me, making the noise seem distant, as my heart races and I make a grab for Tanaka, who shakes me off. I slip and fall into the chocolate coating the carpet.

Detective Yoshida vaults over several sets of chairs, then rushes forward and recovers the gun, while Detective Matsumoto races after Emi. Presumably, they don't know what's going on, and so are trying to cover all their bases.

At the same time, Tanaka drops the roaster and leaps over the table. Arlo moves to tackle him, but Tanaka turns and kicks him in the chest. Tanaka runs out into the festival. Everything is moving so fast, I can't keep it straight. Arlo looks hurt, but he's running forward too.

I smell something burning and realize the toppled roaster has caught the carpet on fire. I yank the cord to cut power to the machine. Then I grab an insulated hand mitt out of the upended supply box and start beating out the flame. I'm still thwapping at the carpet, making sure there's nothing smoldering, when Connie grabs my hand.

"It's okay, Fee," she says, using the nickname she's heard for me. Somehow, her face and blouse are smeared with chocolate too.

"We have to find her," I say urgently. "If she disappears, we can't help her."

Despite an unconvincing noise of protest from Detective Yamada, Connie helps me up, and we exit the room.

Connie is probably the one who murdered Noel. But that doesn't matter now, if she's willing to help. Much to the shock and disapproving glares of everyone nearby, she swings up onto a pillar, looking over the booths to see where everyone went.

She jumps easily to the floor and points in a direction that is very much not the exit. She says, "The guy with the gun went that way. I think Arlo might catch him." Then she points to the emergency exit sign in the opposite direction. "But the woman and Logan went out that door."

I nearly swoon in relief. "Good," I say. "It's okay. Logan will keep her safe and figure out what to do."

We backtrack to the classroom, but it's mostly empty. Patsy, Savannah and Chloe are already trying to get the chocolate out of the carpet. Detective Yamada is talking to Hudson, who is trying to explain what happened – even though he doesn't know who Emi is, or why she's in trouble.

All I know is, Emi isn't going to make her meet at the coffee shop.

I turn to Patsy. "You're about the same size as me. If I give you my credit card, can you buy me a change of clothes?"

"Here?" Patsy asks. "It's going to be expensive."

I gesture helplessly at my chocolate-covered clothing. "What else am I going to do?"

I take my credit card out of my purse and hold it out.

Chloe snatches the card and says, "I'll help, Aunt Fee."

I look at her skeptically. "In exchange for what?"

"Because I just want to help," Chloe says, though her face shows she's dying to ask for something. Finally, she breaks. "Okay. I've been talking to the group of Youtubers I'm supposed to do the cat toy collab with on Friday. They're all going down to Content Corner, to plan out who's supposed to cover what, and to get to know each other. I got invited to go."

"What is Content Corner?" Patsy asks.

Chloe says, "It's just a space outside a Family Mart – everybody calls it Famima, because here, they have an abbreviation for everything. It's where a lot of people stream from."

"Let me look into it." Patsy pulls out her phone and starts Googling.

I turn back to Connie. "Can I ask you a favor?"

Connie laughs. "You look just like Chloe did a minute ago. What is it?"

I glance at Detective Yamada. He is looking at the curtain, which is moving. It swishes open, and Mrs. Kobayashi comes in. Arlo limps in after her.

Here we go. She's about to kick me out. Meryl will be delighted.

Instead she bows deeply and says, "Moushiwake gozaimassen deshita!" Which is a way of saying you are very formally sorry for something. "Koerberu San, we are horrified that our security was inadequate. Please accept our apologies." She turns towards Savannah, who is still half-heartedly wiping at the chocolate mess. "Please do not feel you must do that. We have a cleaning crew on the way."

I say, "Thank you for taking care of everything. Of course, you couldn't have anticipated something like this happening." I don't mention that maybe we should have anticipated it, by bringing Emi in here.

Mrs. Kobayashi turns to Detective Yamada, and the two begin conversing in Japanese.

Patsy holds up her phone to Chloe and says, "Absolutely not. Look at this video of Content Corner. It looks like some of these people are drinking, and they're all just standing around near a railing outside the store while several uncomfortable-looking cops lean against said railing. You are a minor, and the police still have your passport, and even if you don't get asked for ID, if anyone streams this your mother is going to see it." Patsy draws breath, and as though she has almost forgotten, adds, "Plus it's all the way in Shibuya."

"Fine," Chloe says. "You make many good points. Even though I don't think it's that big of a deal."

Patsy and Chloe head out to find me some clothes. I can't help but wonder if we're going to be bailing her out of jail in Shibuya later tonight for not having ID.

Connie says, "About this favor?"

I say, "Logan and I were supposed to wait for someone in the coffee shop downstairs – in about an hour. It could be dangerous, but I was wondering if you would be willing to go with me?"

"It sounds important," Connie says, "so of course I'll help."

I smile at her with relief. She's such a nice person. I still can't see her as a killer, no matter which way the evidence leans.

Chapter Nineteen
Wednesday

This is the second time I've sat at the same table in this coffee shop. Only this time, I'm too worried about what is going to happen to care about the latte art. Much, anyway. Today, it's a cat, winking like it has a secret. It's adorable.

Chloe picked out clothes that are the opposite of what I need to blend in. I have on a silky cream-colored tee, and a fuchsia wool jacket over fashionably oversized brown pants – paired with fuchsia heels. It's just a few shades darker than Chloe's own signature pink. I look fantastic. The fabrics are all luxe. This is an upscale shopping district, so I don't know, maybe it is what I need to fit in after all.

Logan doesn't want to risk bringing Emi back in here, so he emailed me the file that was on Emi's phone. Does that make me a target now, if I don't manage to hand the file over? Hudson has my borrowed phone right now, transferring the file out of my email and onto a thumb drive. He should be back soon.

I'm anxious for every minute Logan is away. Arlo is outside, but he's injured. He did subdue Tanaka, but not before being kicked in the shin and punched in the jaw. Tanaka is going to face more serious repercussions, though I doubt he was the only one involved in trying to find Emi.

Across from me, Connie takes a sip of her hot tea. She has squeezed lemon into it. She asks, "How long do you suppose we will have to wait? I cannot stand inaction."

Somehow, she seems more British with a cup of tea.

Not wanting to waste the opportunity to get information, I say, "Maybe we should play a little shogi to pass the time."

Connie looks like I've suggested we eat bugs. "First off, I don't read Japanese well, and I suspect I know a lot more than you, so the two of us couldn't play even if we wanted to. Second, I hate board games."

Okay. Connie doesn't play shogi – but so many of the people around her do. If she'd been the one to empty out Noel's cache of stolen goods, it would have been easy for her to pick up a piece from someone's set. Although, we're back to how she could have done that and managed to re-join her co-workers on their way back from lunch. Maybe she had left the table, and Kudo had covered for her. I know it's implausible, but so are my other theories.

Carefully, I say, "I heard about your diffuser company and the lawsuit. And that totally stinks."

Connie takes another sip of tea. "Are you suggesting it might have been relevant to Noel's death? I doubt that has anything to do with the nasty notes my husband received. If they blamed anyone for the wrongful death suit, it would have been me. And that would be hard to justify, seeing as the whole lot happened before I even inherited the company."

"True," I need to segue into my real question. "But I heard that the lawsuit caused your financial troubles. How could a corporate issue touch your personal finances?"

"Who exactly have you been talking to?" Connie asks. "They seem to know all my business." Realizing I'm not going to tell her, she waves her own question away. "We didn't want to lose the company, so we invested our own money to cover some of the business' expenses, and to pay for the defense. The lawyers said it would be a simple case to settle, and that the recall would take care of future liability. But it was not simple, and we put in more and more money to keep it afloat. If I lose it now, everything is gone. I'll have to go through with the heist plan. Only – without Noel, there's no way I could pull that off either."

I'm already being invasive, so I ask, "Did it have something to do with the papers you tore up on set?"

She arches an eyebrow at me. "That's a bit personal. But if you must know, it was a letter from a distant cousin, disputing my claim on the company. Apparently, there was an oral promise that he would inherit."

"Maybe you should let him, if he reimburses you for the cash you invested."

Connie laughs. "I wish it was that easy." She looks down at the surface of her tea. "I wish anything was that easy. Maybe if I knew what happened to Noel. I mean the why behind it all."

"I have another random question. Was Noel allergic to almonds?"

Connie looks surprised. "How did you know that? He was deathly allergic, and was rushed to the emergency room several times as a child. He always used to complain that he could never eat granola or any other health foods, because they'd all been processed with tree nuts."

"Was this common knowledge?"

Connie shakes her head. "Noel didn't like to make a fuss or be 'that guy.' If there was a potential problem, he would usually just say he wasn't hungry."

So theoretically, if Noel had been exposed to a massive amount of diffused almond oil, it would have hit his system even faster than eating it. Perhaps fast enough that he wouldn't have time to even try to get his epi pen out of his pocket. And only someone observant enough to have seen through his refusals to eat certain foods as a sign of an allergy would have had the means to use nuts to kill him. Which makes Connie an even stronger suspect.

But – if it was her, why would she be talking so openly to me about this?

Hudson enters the coffee shop and slides into the booth next to me. He discreetly hands me a thumb drive, under the pretense of kissing me on the cheek. So I guess he's my cover-story boyfriend now.

We wait, and eventually a guy slides into a table by himself, looking nervous. He's an Asian guy in his early twenties, wearing a black turtleneck, with dark hair flopped into his eyes.

I get up and walk over to him. "Nichijo?" I ask.

He starts to get up, but I hold out an imploring hand.

"Please. I just want to talk."

"Where's Emi?" he asks.

"She's hiding. But I have something for you, if you really are trying to help her out."

Nichijo – or whatever his name actually is – says, "I can get her information to the right people to make sure those who trash the environment go to jail. Earth is the most important thing to me. I'll help Emi, because she feels the same way."

I sit down and put the thumb drive on the table. "This isn't the only copy. If you're not who I think you are – getting rid of me – or Emi – won't stop the information."

He grins. "I like you." He swoops the thumb drive off the table. "Check the news in a week or so, and there should be mentions of indictments."

"A week," I squeak, but he's already turning and walking back toward the door.

I understand it can take time to get warrants, but if it is going to take a week, that means Emi is still not safe.

Moments later Detective Yamada walks into the café. He sits down in the seat Nichijo just vacated. He leans back and asks, "So you want to tell me what this is all about?"

I order him a coffee, because this is going to take a while.

Chapter Twenty
Wednesday

Back up at my booth, it's a somber tone, as my friends cope in different ways with having come face to face with danger.

Hudson keeps saying, "I froze. I should have helped stop that guy."

I tell him, "You helped at the café. Isn't that more important?"

Dawn is just upset that she missed everything. She says, "Here Fisher and I are, off chasing leads about shogi players, and you were in real danger. Not to mention my brother has disappeared, for who knows how long."

"Well?" I ask. "Did you find out anything?"

Fisher leans over the counter from where he's manning the booth. He says, "Your nemesis plays."

For a second, I have no idea what he means. Then I point up the aisle. "Meryl? Plays shogi?"

Fisher says, "Why not?"

I shrug. "She just doesn't seem the type. Cool logical thinking seems to be required."

Fisher says, "Sometimes circumstances bring out different sides in people. She belongs to a club that meets at a café."

I guess that makes sense. She has been living in Japan for a number of years, and she may have needed an activity to reach out and make friends. But could that connect to the case? Is she secretly a master criminal?

Something tells me no.

I pull up Meryl's Instagram page and show it to Dawn. I say, "Outside this festival, Meryl's a nice person. She just doesn't like me, for circumstances I can't control." I scroll through, so Dawn can see some of what I've seen – including Meryl's pain and loss. But I go a bit farther back than before, and one of the pictures startles me. I gasp, and Dawn gives me a questioning look. I point at the picture. It's a family picnic, before Meryl's husband passed. They've gone cherry blossom viewing with a couple of friends. There's Meryl and her husband, her son and daughter-in-law, all the dogs, plus three girls her daughter-in-law's age. And there, at the edge of the photo, is Ms. Kondo – the woman who happens to be in charge of logging in the entries and distributing samples to the judges.

I say, "The woman in charge of samples for the contest is friends with Meryl's daughter-in-law. If she and Meryl wanted to switch my samples, it wouldn't have been that hard.

Dawn says, "There's something I wanted to show you, too. Logan gave me access to your sales records, and only one exhibitor here has bought your chocolate bars. Meryl made an online order over a month ago. It must have been to examine the mold shape and get copies of your wrappers. How hard would it have been to make a similar mold?"

I sigh, actually deflated now that I have proof of the sabotage. "You can 3D print a mold for almost anything. But you have to know how to use the software."

The bar Meryl had made was a near duplicate, at least visually. She had put in an amazing amount of work to be so petty. But with an exhibition fee of five thousand dollars and change – the motive is clear.

I tell Dawn, "The festival is willing to let it go, and chalk it up to sabotage from an unknown source. And after the disaster at my class today, they probably think someone seriously has it in for me. I know we have the evidence and the right to turn her in. But is that necessary?"

Dawn gawks at me. "Felicity, she's treated you horribly. Don't you want to see her get her comeuppance?"

I look down at my phone. I say, "I'm only at this festival because Savannah got me an invite. For Meryl, this is her home festival, and teaching that class obviously meant a lot to her. I don't want to take that away – and get Ms. Kondo in trouble, when she was probably only trying to help a friend." I think back to the discussion I had with Taniguchi, about *Murder on the Orient Express*. I'd said that Poirot had taken too much authority on himself by not turning in the killers in that book, just because he believed the murder victim was horrible. And I still believe that. But this is different. I don't have to turn in Meryl, if I don't want to. I'm the only injured party, so if I decide to overlook it, there's no real harm. I tell Dawn, "Maybe it's because I had a similar loss in my own life, even if it's been years, I can understand her acting out of grief. Maybe I can just talk to her about it, instead of going to the festival officials."

Dawn says, "Well, you're about to get your chance."

Meryl is indeed walking this way. She approaches the booth and says, "I couldn't figure out if you were pointing at me or trying to get my attention. But I thought I should come by and at least offer condolences for how poorly your class went. I knew you probably have a lot to learn about chocolate making, but actually setting the classroom on fire – I just wish I had been there to see it."

Dawn gives me a look like, *See? She hates you. Turn her in.*

But I say, "I was pointing at you. I apologize. That was rude. It's just that we were so surprised to discover that Ms. Kondo is your daughter-in-law's friend."

I turn my phone, showing her the picture.

Meryl goes pale. She shoots a glance at the booth next door, but Henri seems busy helping a customer choose truffles, and no one else is particularly in hearing distance. She clears her throat and says, "She's actually my daughter-in-law's best friend's sister."

I say, "I assume Ms. Kondo was the one who first recommended you for the festival. You were grieving and needed an emotional boost, as well as a financial one."

Meryl doesn't deny it.

Dawn turns her own phone towards Meryl, allowing her to see the receipt for the purchase from Greetings and Felicitations. She says, "This record stands out, because they don't ship much to Japan."

Meryl asks, "What do you want? Is this blackmail?"

I turn off my phone screen. "I just want you to withdraw your complaint about Chloe and stop trying to get us kicked out. I'm sorry for having unknowingly taken your teaching spot. We don't have to be best friends. But I think we can co-exist."

Meryl doesn't say anything in response. Complicated emotions cross her face, then without a word, she turns and walks back to her booth.

Dawn asks, "Do you think she'll withdraw the complaint?"

"Who knows." I close my eyes, drained by this confrontation even more than I had been when dealing with a guy with a gun.

Someone pokes me in the shoulder. It's Ash, returned from his talk show appearance. He's wearing a black headband with the characters that make up *Japan* written on it in white. He notices me staring at it and says, "Isn't it cool? The host of the show gave it to me, and then we made rolled omelets. Mine didn't look great – but I got to cook on television."

Imogen says, "I told him to take the headband off when we got in the taxi, but the taxi driver convinced him to wear it."

Dawn says, "You know you look like a tourist."

Ash says, "That's fine, because I am a tourist. Just being a tourist isn't bad. As long as you're not a jerk."

My phone buzzes in my hand with a call from Autumn. I pick it up as a video. She's sitting in her car.

I say, "I guess you finally got done filming all the episodes."

"I'm done," she says, "And we've officially wrapped, but Carmen and Annabelle are still chatting about marketing and swapping recipe ideas. They started talking about doing a baby shower episode for me, and I bailed."

I say, "You won't believe what I saw in Annabelle's room. There were all these posters of stunt men, and Annabelle admitted she's a huge fan."

Autumn leans her head back against the headrest and says, "Trust her to be a fan of the stunt guys when everyone else is into the actors."

She looks exhausted, but happy.

I say, "You don't think that makes her suspicious? She had a poster of Noel, the guy who was murdered. And she says they flirted on set."

Autumn says, "That all makes it sound like she's less likely to have killed him."

From over my shoulder, Ash says, "Besides, she couldn't have done it. She wasn't even there the day Noel died."

Over the camera, Autumn asks, "How could you know that?"

"Because," Ash says, "That's the day she was on the same talk show I just did. They made dorayaki. They're little pancakes that get sandwiched together, with red bean past in the middle." He seems to realize he's digressing. He shakes his hands, like shaking away thoughts to get himself back on track. "She was the one who recommended me for the show. Imogen and I had to get up super early to get over to the studio, and we just got back. It's a lot later than it was on Monday when you say you initially found the body."

I ask, "Why didn't Annabelle just tell us all that?"

Ash says, "I didn't even know you suspected her. Did you outright ask her for an alibi?"

I think back about our interactions. "Well, no."

Dawn says, "Maybe you shouldn't be discussing a case in public like this, if you're worried about your reputation with the festival."

"Gotcha," Ash says. "I have news. I've gotten permission from Emma's parents for the true crime docudrama. Emma's the girl who worked for Emma, briefly, before her untimely death at Greetings and Felicitations' grand opening."

Dawn says, "Not exactly the tack I wanted you to take."

Autumn says, "I'm going to let you go. It's in the middle of the night here, and I already get tired easy."

After we say our goodbyes and I hang up, I tell Ash, "I have something. Not news exactly. More of a coincidence." I show him a picture I took of the blue wave knife from the store. "We were looking into who all bought this knife, because it's the same as the murder weapon."

"I know," Ash says. "When the cops interviewed me, that was the first thing I told them. I got a good close-up look at the knife when we zipped Noel out of the kaiju suit. And they wanted a look at mine – I think to make sure I still have it."

I say, "When something like that happens, it doesn't occur to you to tell me? I thought you were helping me investigate."

Ash manages to look chagrined, though I can tell it is forced. He says, "There's been a lot going on. I got distracted."

A girl approaches our booth carrying a hardcover book. "Konnichiwa," she says, holding it out to me.

"Thanks," I say, taking the book. As I do, an envelope slips against the front cover. It's almost the same size as the book. "What's this?" I ask.

She shakes her head, not understanding. Then she nods and walks away.

Ash takes the book.

I examine the envelope. It doesn't look dangerous. I open it, and there is an invitation printed in ornate script. I read aloud, "Ms. Nao

Suzuki requests the presence of Mrs. Felicity Koerber for a formal kaiseki meal at her favorite restaurant. You may bring a plus 1 or even plus 2."

There's the name of the restaurant and the directions, and a request to meet at 9 o'clock in the evening.

Ash is looking over my shoulder. He says, "You know. Imogen loves sushi. And that restaurant is impossible to get into."

I tell him, "It could be dangerous."

Ash says, "Arlo's supposed to rest his ankle. And Logan is . . . elsewhere. You need somebody you can trust."

I gesture at Dawn. "Then I should take the cop." And then at Hudson. "Or the guy who didn't duck behind me when things got out of control today."

"But I didn't do anything either," Hudson protests.

Dawn says, "If you think she might be a criminal, taking a cop is a little too obvious. I could wait outside in the car if you want. Reverse how we were wired up last time."

Ash says, "See? Imogen and I are the obvious choice. And she's pretty scrappy in a fight."

"That was one time," Imogen says. "And I didn't start it."

There has to be a story there, but now is not the time to ask it.

Ash puts his hands together in a pleading motion and gives me puppy dog eyes through his rectangular glasses.

"Fine," I say. "But I'm sitting next to Imogen."

Once things have calmed down, Henri gestures me over to his booth. He hands me a lemon pot de crème decorated with raspberries and a single chocolate curl. It has a tiny gold-tinted plastic spoon.

I tell him, "You keep spoiling me."

He says, "I've never had a fellow exhibitor make a festival so lively. You handled the situation with Meryl with class. If you ever make your way to Paris, you should visit my shop. I would love to cook together with you."

That's staggering. One of the most famous men in chocolate wants to cook with me. But Logan and I have already spent so much on this trip, and we're planning a wedding – which isn't going to be on a cheap budget. A trip to Paris might not be doable just at the moment, but I'm not going to say no. I say, "I'd love that."

Obviously, I'm not telling Chloe that Henri extended an international invitation – otherwise I'll wind up kidnapped in her suitcase, so she can stream on the Champs-Élysées and eat way too many crepes.

I see Ash eyeing my pot du crème. I ask Henri, "Can I buy two more of these? I have a friend who adores food."

Henri laughs and gestures Ash over. He says, "Would you like to try some of the best desserts in France? My treat."

I think Ash is going to faint.

The rest of the afternoon flies by, especially because Imogen insists on taking me to shop for a dress to wear to the restaurant. She talks me into a black velvet dress with a sparkling rhinestone neckline. And then she does my hair, giving it volume and curling the ends under. I've never gotten this dressed up for dinner in my life.

Ash even springs for a taxi to bring us to the place. Their anticipation is contagious.

When we get inside, everything is blonde wood and neutral colors. The restaurant is tiny and the seats are all one long row up against a bar, with a serving area and the kitchen on the other side.

Nao is already there, and she's brought some people with her. Now I get her plus 1 or plus 2 references in the invite. There are only three open chairs, for me and my two guests.

Nao is also wearing a black velvet dress, though hers has a sweetheart neckline. I worry that she is going to think I am copying her, but she just says, "Nice dress," in a playful tone. "Great minds think alike."

"Actually, Imogen picked it out," I say, taking the opportunity to introduce Ash and Imogen.

Nao introduces the folks in the three chairs to the left of hers. They are all students, from the group who had visited my booth – but, notably, not the two who had told us about the rumors.

One guy asks where we are from. I say, "Texas." And before anyone can ask, I add, "Hours away from where JFK was shot."

They all laugh, and though I didn't think it was *that* funny, it breaks the ice.

The guy says, "Texas must be big."

We sit down. Not much is said before our first course arrives. We each receive a small plate with slices of seared beef, a dollop of a crab and sea urchin mixture and a thin slice of something fried that Nao explains as katsu cheese – in this case imported halloumi, since Japan isn't known for cheese, and this is actually a riff on both a European and a Korean dish. This makes the dish something of a bold risk on the part of the chef.

I take a bite, and the crisp outer coating is a perfect foil for the gooey cheese inside. It's like the best cheese stick I've ever had.

Imogen samples her sea urchin and claps her hands in happiness. Ash looks equally giddy.

I turn to Nao, who is seated to my left. "This is amazing. But why are we here?"

Nao says, "I need to know your intentions."

I blink at her, the rest of my katsu halloumi still gripped in my chopsticks. "My intentions about what?"

She holds out her hand. "I need everyone's phones. And any other recording device."

I hand my phone over, glad we didn't try to wire Dawn in on the conversation after all. The same guy who had asked about Texas leaves his seat to sweep over us with an electronic device. I presume he's checking for bugs, though that's never happened to me before, so I don't have a reference for what that looks like.

Nao says, "I know you're looking for The Cat. I have an alert set up that lets me know when people are searching for my name with any variation of cat and burglar and thief. Honestly, Felicity, you really should use a more secure browser. Or at least do anonymous searches."

I say, "I've never had anyone track my searches back before. That's not something most people would be able to do."

Nao gestures at the girl sitting to her left. "I have no idea how to even approach such a thing. But Izumi does. Specialized skills are so important."

"So all the rumors were right, then. You really are the Cat with a Thousand Names."

"No," Nao says. She leans back in her chair and makes a sweeping gesture to her left. "*We* are the Cat with a Thousand Names."

The students to her left are all beaming back at me, in a row, waving and nodding their heads.

Nao straightens up. "Since you suspect that – but can't prove it – I want to know what you are hoping to do with that information. Blackmail? Turn us in to the police?"

I don't know what would happen if I did claim one of those intentions. Would this excellent dinner turn violent? What good would voicing the rumor be to the police? If there's a Reddit thread, the police have probably heard a version of it already.

I say, "I was just trying to find out your real relationship with Noel."

"Really?" Nao draws out the word, looking nonplussed. "Why would you care that much? He was like a pawn in a shogi game."

"Interesting choice of analogy," I say. Could mentioning shogi be an attempt to get me to tip my hand? Maybe she's trying to find out if I saw the piece at the crime scene. The idea that I may well be having dinner with a murderer sends a chill down my spine. "Who's pawn was he?"

She waves a hand. "The world's. He was stealing phones and passports. He couldn't parlay that into anything else. I thought he had potential, so I tried to help him out, but he had no sense of taste. And he kept getting caught on cameras. Do you have any idea how much footage Izumi had to erase?"

I ask, "Is that what you were fighting about on the roof garden?"

"Yes," Nao says. "I told him he was on his own, that I was deleting his number from my phone. He tried to stop me. I was worried about him, but I couldn't have him calling me. I'm too sentimental to deal with that."

She doesn't strike me as the sentimental type, but I let it go. Who knows? Maybe she's more caring than she wants to let on. I say, "So you weren't angry at him? Angry enough to introduce something to his body that would kill him."

"Poison?" Nao says, intrigued. "Is that what happened?"

I don't correct her. But the fact that she made the assumption of poison over allergen makes her somewhat less plausible as a suspect.

Nao says, "I want to set the record straight. The Cat with A Thousand Names is a thief with a cause. As a former orphan, I want to look out for kids who are falling through the cracks – including some of my students. Each of us four keeps a percentage of what we take – we're no Robin Hood – but we manufacture scholarships and find other ways to get money into poor students' hands. And we only steal beautiful things with no practical use. Gems, paintings, artifacts – the loss of these doesn't do the owner real harm, or lead to that person falling into poverty."

Izumi says, "You have no idea of the thrill, or of the game in what we do."

Ash says, "I do! I love a good heist movie."

Izumi says, "It is not the same as what is on screen."

Imogen says, "Collectively, you're Kaito Kid from the Detective Conan series."

Nao frowns at the comparison, but the guy who asked about Texas, says, "Hai, hai. Sou, Sou." Which translates as *yes, it is*. So obviously, he's a fan, but Nao is not.

Nao says, "I still need to know what your plan is."

I set my chopsticks down on the little rest at the side of my plate and turn to look her full on. I say, "My plan is to figure out who killed Noel before it's time for us to go home and I have to tell Chloe's mom that she got arrested on my watch while I was chaperoning her daughter in a foreign country. So if you didn't have anything to do with that – and like you said, I have no proof of anything else – I don't plan to interfere."

After that, we enjoy the rest of the dinner. Turns out Nao is a real foodie and has something to say about where the food was sourced, similar dishes she's had before, and why certain dishes are special to Japan. I had no idea that a kaiseki meal, in addition to being orchestrated by the chef, was supposed to have a course reflecting the seasons – just like haiku poetry has a seasonal reference.

I forget that I suspect Nao of murder and we all have a fun evening. I'm pretty sure Imogen and Izuki exchange contact information.

In the taxi, I text Logan a few vague details about the evening – considering what Nao had said about my phone's security, I don't want to say anything about the Cat in writing. I can't wait to see him again, in person, to share everything that has happened. And to have him safe.

I try to be quiet going into my room at the hotel, but Chloe and Patsy are awake, playing cards. I sit down on my bed, still in the fancy black dress, and watch. After a few minutes, Patsy goes to the restroom.

Chloe takes a sip out of a bottle of green tea.

I say, "I'm shocked that you didn't try to sneak off to go meet those Youtubers."

Chloe says, "I realized I might need somebody looking out for me this time. With everything the police seem to think – I'm probably in over my head." She taps her hand of cards. "Besides, Ms. Nash can actually be pretty cool, if you give her the chance."

I fake gasp. "Am I to believe that you are actually growing up? That maybe you've learned something from this experience?"

Chloe says, "Maybe I have."

Good. At least someone is getting something out of this.

Chapter Twenty-One
Thursday

The next morning, Connie texts me that the police have released the crime scene, and that the cast and crew are going in to discuss what happens moving forward. It is supposed to be a chance for everyone to talk about what that means, without Noel. Connie isn't even sure she wants to stay on the project. Who knows? If others feel the same way, the movie might not even happen.

I head over to the building, determined to find proof that Kudo committed the crime. Or Connie. Or the two of them working together. Because if it couldn't be Annabelle, and it likely wasn't Nao, then it has to be one of them. If I can find the shogi set with the missing piece, that would at least be enough to take to the police – assuming I can convince them that I didn't just take a piece out of someone's set. Or if I can somehow find the piece that matches the one in Chloe's video, it would be even better. But I have no way to definitively identify it. Especially because chess sets come with multiple pawns.

Everything about this case keeps shifting in ways that have thrown me off. Because of Annabelle, I had assumed that the incident in the conference room had been about a girl upset that Noel hadn't wanted to pursue a relationship. But couldn't he have been fighting with Kudo? All Noel's talk of integrity and wanting to stay close to his wife – it would also make sense if Kudo had been telling him to get lost. Maybe Kudo – or whoever killed Noel – hadn't realized that Noel had already bought a ticket to Belize and would be gone soon anyway.

Maybe someone had even threatened Noel, making him feel he had to leave. It could have been related to the *You know what you did* notes. It's plausible that he could have played them off to Connie as no big deal, while laying the groundwork to leave. He might have even been trying to protect her.

Of course, Connie could have found out that he was leaving, maybe found the record for the plane ticket. She could still be the one who killed him, because of a complete misunderstanding.

I still have to investigate to make sense of it. Ash, Hudson and Dawn insist on going with me, leaving Imogen and Fisher to man the chocolate booth. Arlo's ankle still isn't better, so Patsy and Chloe are keeping him company as he hobbles around the hotel.

Keiko lets us through the movie studio's front doors, gesturing that we should head toward the set. Presumably, that is where everyone is huddled for the team meeting.

We walk down the hall. As we approach Kudo's office, I whisper, "You guys go on. I'm going to take a look around."

I try the handle, but Kudo's office door is locked. I reach in my pocket and use the edge of my hotel room key card to pop it. It only takes seconds, and I am inside.

The office looks the same as it had on Monday, with the movie posters on the walls, and the row of awards. There's a bookcase in the corner that I hadn't had time to examine when I was here before, along with a supply cabinet. I move over and scan the titles of the books, using Google Lens to translate them. Many of them are manuals for screenwriting or technical aspects of movie production. But there are also books on bicycles as a sport, and the history of the tour de France, as well as a number of coffee table style travel books, focused on Europe. It's too bad Kudo's probably a killer, because I can see him being a good match for Connie – should she acknowledge his feelings for her.

I slip on gloves and open the door to the supply cabinet. There are two shelves of office supplies, but the bottom half has been converted into a closet. Kudo has a spare suit, several shirts, and two pairs of dress shoes arranged neatly. I start to think he might be living in this space, but then I realize – with the hours he keeps, he practically does.

I'm not tall enough to see what is on the top shelf. I nose around the supply shelves, hoping for something interesting, and there in a jar with spare paper clips and rubber bands, I find a lone shogi piece. I pick it up by it's small edges, so I won't smudge any fingerprints on the face. The police probably wouldn't have known the significance of the tile, so they probably haven't printed it already. It's a pawn.

I knew Kudo had to be the killer. But finding the proof leaves me stunned.

I hear Dawn's voice in the hall, and then the door opens. I freeze and flinch back, but there's no place to hide.

Kudo looks surprised to see me. He spots the piece in my hand, but instead of looking nervous because the jig is indeed up, he grins and asks, "Do you play?"

"I'm just starting," I say, though it's a lie. Fisher is the one learning to play. I've only seen a board made out of chocolate.

Kudo says, "I could teach you some strategy, if you like. I was on the club team at my university." He steps past me and reaches for the top shelf of the cabinet, where he pulls out an ornate shogi board with a drawer built into the side for holding the pieces. He moves over to his desk and places it on the surface, next to a heavy glass cloche.

I jump as something twines between my feet, brushing my calves. Somehow, Honda is in the room, though she wasn't here a minute ago. And she's touching me with her tail.

Kudo says, "That's a happy tail, in cat body language. She likes you."

"And I like her," I say. I hold up the shogi piece. "Why isn't this piece in the drawer with the others?"

Kudo says, "Because I'm lazy. The piece must have fallen on the floor, the last time I had a match with Taniguchi. I had already put the set in the cabinet by the time I realized it, so I just tossed it in with the office supplies, to fix it next time I played. That was several weeks ago, and I rarely use physical office supplies, so I forgot all about it." He holds out a hand to take the piece.

Instead of giving it to him, I ask Dawn, "You don't happen to have an evidence bag, do you?"

Dawn rummages in her purse and takes out a clear plastic bag. "Never leave home without it." She sounds bantery, but she looks alarmed.

Kudo tilts his head. "Why is this so important?"

I say, "It has to do with the crime scene," I say, though I know it's not definitive proof. "I also know you bought a knife at the department store downstairs. And that that knife wound up sticking out of Noel's chest."

"That's preposterous," Kudo splutters. "That knife is right here, in my collection." He yanks at one of his desk drawers, and Dawn pushes me behind her as she grabs a big book from the bookcase, presumably to use as a shield. But Kudo is just staring down into the drawer. "It was here, I know it."

Dawn says, "Felicity, go out in the hall and call the police."

I'm not sure what she expects to do. She's unarmed, and Kudo still has the rest of his knife collection. I don't want to leave her alone in here.

But instead of attacking us, or trying to flee, he sinks down in his office chair. Honda jumps up on his lap, and he idly pets the cat. He asks, "Are you saying I killed Noel?"

"Didn't you?" I ask.

"It's sure going to look to the police like I did," Kudo says. "I get the knife, but tell me. What am I supposed to have done with the shogi piece?"

Dawn says, "He didn't do it."

"What?" I protest. "All the evidence points at him."

"What is he supposed to have done with the shogi piece?"

I say, "It appeared on the set after Noel's body was taken away. It's in the video Chloe took. But it wasn't there when the actors were performing again."

Dawn says, "Do you think he would have left a clue like that out for someone to find, when it would have been so simple to put the piece back in the drawer? It would have taken three seconds."

Now, Kudo looks alarmed. "Is someone trying to frame me?"

"See," Dawn says, gesturing at Kudo and the now loudly purring cat. "I'm trained at reading body language. He didn't do it."

Kudo says, "I could just be a very good actor, you know."

"Not helping," Dawn says.

Honda jumps on the desk and taps at the cloche. She must really want whatever is inside.

"What is that?" I ask, stepping closer to look at the tan lump inside.

Kudo says, "Do you have any idea how hard it is to get everyone back in the mood for shooting a campy movie, in the same building where somebody died? I brought Honda in, and we're going to celebrate resuming the production by giving her a cake made out of tuna. I thought about bringing a real cake for the cast and crew, but somehow that felt a bit tacky."

"Good call," Dawn says. "But how did Honda get in here? Wasn't she already in the studio set with you."

Kudo nods towards the door. "She is stealthy. This isn't the first time she's snuck into a room without me noticing. Sometimes I look up, and she's just there."

I say, "There has to be something more to it than that. I watched you come in, and she wasn't there." I'd first seen her up on the desk. I start looking around the base of the desk, but nothing seems out of the ordinary.

"What exactly are you doing?" Kudo asks.

I get down all fours to examine the wall behind the desk. "Looking for a cat-sized secret passage. And I think this might be it."

There's a metal circle on the wall, painted white, so that it isn't noticeable. I pull on it, and it slides open to the side.

Honda sees me doing it and meows plaintively, then starts batting it open herself. She tries to climb inside, but I pull her back out. The noise she makes shows it's clear she's insulted. This is her white circle, and I'm interfering.

"What is that?" Dawn asks.

Kudo says, "I assumed it was part of the heating system." He goes out in the hall and comes back with Keiko.

They converse, and there's some pointing at the space, then the hall.

Kudo turns to us and says, "She says this building was once a bank, and they used pneumatic mail tubes to transfer documents and funds. It looks like my cat has been using the tube system to get around the building."

"Would she really fit?" She's a small cat, and she'd been able to crawl into the opening, but it had seemed like a squeeze.

Dawn says, "She sure thinks she fits."

I ask, "Where's the hub for the system?"

Kudo asks Keiko, who points upstairs. Is that what she's been trying to keep everyone away from?

Honda squirms in my arms and tries again to make it into the tube. Kudo moves a plant stand to block the opening. Honda meows unhappily.

I wonder. Could the noise Keiko have heard upstairs the day Noel died have had something to do with the pneumatic tubes? If we're looking for a diffuser, could it have something to do with this air?

Kudo picks up Honda and gestures at the cloche. "One of you take the tuna cake. We're going to get the mood for this production back on track. The writers might actually use their writing room if they realize the noises they've been hearing are just air."

Dawn picks up the cloche, and we head towards the set.

I whisper to her, "We need to get a look at what's upstairs."

She says, "You betcha. Just as soon as we can sneak away from the meeting."

When we walk onto the set, Imogen is standing in a corner with Ash. Which means Fisher is alone manning the Greetings and Felicitations booth. Today is supposed to be one of the busiest days of the festival, so I hope he's okay with that. There are fewer people here today than before, so maybe not everyone got the message that the studio is back open. Or maybe some have decided to bail. Franco isn't here. Neither is Taniguchi.

I'm surprised Ash isn't already in the special effects lab, rummaging around.

Ash makes eye contact and gestures with his chin towards the door leading into the hall. It looks like he and Imogen are heading for the special effects lab, now that all eyes are on Kudo. He must have called his fiancé as soon as he realized Taniguchi wasn't here to stop them from snooping.

There's a table near the equipment, where there's a stack of binders with pages explaining incentives for the crew if they stay on and finish the movie, and a card to sign for Connie. Kudo directs Dawn to put the cloche down in the center of the table. He places Honda down next to it, petting her to keep her from running away. He opens the cloche, but Honda takes a few bites of tuna, then she turns and jumps onto the dinosaur head, which is still dangling from the crane. The head swings from the cat's weight.

Kudo rushes over and scolds Honda in Japanese. He clicks and she turns, starting to jump down into his arms. But she freezes when there's a popping noise. I swear I see sparks come from the crane as the bolts holding it to the floor give way, and the whole contraption falls on Kudo. Honda leaps clear of the twisting equipment, then disappears into a hole left by the crane when it fell.

Kudo gives a strangled scream before he disappears from sight. A second later, that scream, or a shocked gasp, is echoed by several folks.

I stare silently at the wreckage, unable to move. Could that have really just happened? Why had there been sparks?

Connie and Dawn both sprint for the dino head, pulling it out of the way to reveal Kudo. Juan the camera guy and a couple of the actors start trying to move the crane. I might be of help once they extract Kudo – if he's still alive – but right now I would be in the way. In the meantime, though, I'm the only one worried about the cat. I rush over to the hole in the floor and see Honda wriggling into a broken-open gap in another pneumatic tube – this time one that is running underneath and parallel to the floor. There's a deep space down here, probably for maintenance. It's only about four feet deep, so I carefully climb into it. I move over to the pipe and try to lure the cat back out with coos and imitated cat noises, but Honda couldn't turn around even if she wanted to.

I climb back out and follow the almost imperceptible noises of her moving in the tube as she crosses underneath the floor. She comes out at the wall by the snack table. I pick her up and cradle her in my arms. "You're okay, little bit."

She meows, like she already knows. Only – the little toe beans on her paws are cold, like she's been walking on ice, and her fur is cold, too. It's weird. But maybe the tubes under the floor have natural refrigeration. I remember being cold when I knelt on this floor trying to help Noel.

I turn back to the wreck of the crane. They have Kudo out from under the twist of metal, and somebody put a squishy kaiju hand under his head as a pillow. He must be alive. Dawn has taken charge of the scene, and she's putting a temporary splint on Kudo's right leg.

When I get closer, Kudo makes eye contact with me. He's trying not to move but he makes a small gesture for me to come closer to him. When I lean down, Honda climbs out of my arms and onto Kudo's chest. She lies down, loud purring with worry. No one tries to move the little calico.

Kudo whispers to me, "That was no accident. If someone's trying to frame me, it works better if I'm dead."

"You're going to be fine," I assure him. And I'm pretty sure I'm telling the truth.

He's right though. And this isn't something he would have done to himself, even if he was desperate to try to create the illusion of being targeted as the killer. There's too much damage to his body. In addition to the broken leg, he may well have damage to his internal organs. I suppose it could have been an accident, by some incredible coincidence. But those sparks hadn't seemed normal. I believe someone had been trying to kill him. And that it is the same person who had murdered Noel.

Kudo reaches out and takes Connie's hand. I move out of the way so she can scoot closer to him.

He tells her, "In case there isn't time." He stops, unable to cope with this thought, his face showing his fear. He starts again. "In case I don't make it. I want to formally confess my feelings to you. I have loved you since you showed up on my set, so quirky and full of life. It wasn't appropriate then, and now, I may not have much time. I'm sorry that our timing is off."

There are tears in Connie's eyes. She says, "I just lost the love of my life. I'm not ready to even think about this. You had better not die, because you owe me the time to heal, after what you just said."

Kudo smiles. Then he closes his eyes, and for a moment I think he's stopped breathing. But then he sighs. So I guess despite everything, he's happy.

Connie is my only other suspect. I really hope she's not lying, considering how comforting a simple word from her is to Kudo. If Connie is the killer, it's odd that she was the first one to run to his aid. Unless, of course, she had been intending to finish him off. But that would have been brazen, in a room with this many people, even for her.

What other suspects might be in the room? Juan is here, and there's that tenuous connection of him being from Belize, and Noel having had a ticket to Ambergris Caye, but that feels like a stretch. Could the crane have been set off remotely? It's a possibility. Which means it could even be Meryl, after all. There's no proof that the shogi piece in Kudo's office had been the same one that had been in Chloe's video. The assumption that that piece, from the set that had been in the supply cabinet, was the one used to frame Kudo may have blinded me to other possibilities.

Ash sends me a picture he's taken from the special effects lab, of Imogen wearing a mermaid tail. You can see the whole lab, and they're in the space alone. Which means Taniguchi really isn't here.

I text Ash back, *Stop playing around and find out if there's anyone else in the building. There's been another incident.*

He texts back, *Okay.* And then a few minutes later, *Not that we've seen. But we can check upstairs.*

And yet – how would someone know that the way to get Kudo was to rig the crane? Or are there booby traps all over the set? Assuming the killer had set off the sparks on seeing Kudo enter the area under the crane – could they have known in advance where Kudo was going to put the table? The only person who would have known that, but not been in the room, is Keiko. The one who has been trying to keep everyone from going upstairs. Which suddenly seems very suspicious. It's time to talk to her.

I get a text from Taniguchi saying, *I have gone to bring new flowers to my sister's grave. I just got the message that the set is open today. Please make my excuses for me.*

I don't have time to worry about the polite niceties in Japanese society. I grab Hudson and bring him up to Keiko's desk. It's a slow and awkward interview, given the layer of translation, but the upshot is that Keiko had no idea there had been an accident, due to the soundproofing of the sound stage, and she denies having anything to do with it. She says she just wants to go check on Kudo, make sure he has everything he needs while he waits for the ambulance. She also claims to know nothing about what's upstairs.

I say, "I think it's time to find out."

Keiko tries to protest and to keep me from climbing up, but I dart around her. Though I climb so slowly, she could probably stop me if she tried. Only, that clanking sound she had described happens again, and she skitters back down the stairs.

Hudson says something to her, and Keiko shakes her head. He tells me, "I asked her if that was the same noise you described to me, and she says no, this sound is new."

Hudson follows me up the stairs. When we reach the landing, there's a hallway, leading to rooms on one side. But on the other, there's a huge open space, supported every so often by pillars. And it's crammed full of movie memorabilia. At the back of that space, there's a vault, probably leftover from when this space was a bank. And taking a jackhammer to the wall next to the vault door is Nao. She has created a small hole in the material.

She looks disappointed to see me. She rests the jackhammer on the floor and says, "I thought you weren't going to interfere."

I say, "I have no idea what you're even doing." I gesture at the vault. "Besides the obvious."

She says, "Noel told us that the vault is full of movie and TV artifacts. Tsuburaya's original fedora. Arnold Schwarzenegger's gold and black outfit from one of his Japanese energy drink commercials. Two of the swords used in *The Seven Samurai*."

I say, "I thought you said Noel had terrible taste."

Nao says, "I'm taking his word that that's even what's in the vault. And that any of these objects are real. Do you know how hard those kinds of things are to authenticate?"

Hudson says, "The people likely to bid on them won't dare check the authentication, if it's stolen."

Nao says, "That's the thing. Everything up here belonged to the previous studio owner, who passed away unexpectedly. The new guy doesn't care. The vault was locked, so he never even bothered to check if it was empty. I can just 'discover' whatever is in there and sell it openly."

Hudson lets out a low whistle.

I ask Nao, "Are you aware that there are a ton of people downstairs, going back to work, since the police released the crime scene."

"I was not aware of that," Nao says. "Thanks for the heads up."

One of the doors in the hallway closes, and I whirl to face it. There's Logan, his hand still on the doorknob. "Fee? Is that you?"

He moves out into the open and we rush to embrace each other. He nods at Hudson, then gives a wary look at Nao. "Oh. You're not alone."

"It's okay," I tell him. "She's not interested in your other operation."

I don't think Nao even knows who Emi is.

The sheer relief at seeing Logan safe relaxes some of the tension in my body, and I rub at my own shoulder, which clearly has a knot. Logan hadn't been able to tell me his location, for fear my phone would be compromised. It's hard to believe that he and Emi have been here, right across the street from the festival, the whole time.

Emi comes out of the room. I can see through the open door that they've been in a room full of moving equipment. They've each used tarps to make bedding on opposite ends of the floor. It must have been uncomfortable. She says, "I haven't heard anything else from Nichijo. I'm sorry I've been such an inconvenience."

Another door opens, across the hall from the one Emi just came out of. Nao's three students file out, nodding greetings at Logan and Emi.

Izumi says, "It seems that we are taking a break."

I look inside the room that the students were in, and it's set up as a media room, with a huge L-shaped sofa and a table with six rolling chairs. There's a vending machine and a small refrigerator. It's probably the unused writer's room.

I ask Logan, "What made you choose that room over this one." I point from the moving supply room to the writer's room.

Logan says, "There was a much lower possibility of someone wandering into that one."

"But how would they have known from the outside?" I answer my own question. "They wouldn't."

It was kind of like the wrappers Meryl had used to swap my chocolates. The rooms look just alike from the outside, but what is inside is very different. The killer had wanted to show that Noel's belongings had seemingly disappeared. A stunt man using part of a movie set as a hiding place for contraband was such a weird thing to do, if the building proved empty, my claim otherwise made me sound like I was mentally unstable – or best-case scenario, in shock from the fall. I'd thought emptying the dollhouse-like structure had been about discrediting me, a last-ditch change of plan, because no one was supposed to be there to discover the body. But the shogi piece that had been used to prop the box's door open well before the trap was set. It's crazy – but what if there were two building-shaped boxes, and one had been empty all along? The empty one had somehow replaced the one I'd taken the phone out of. It would have had to be something that could be done remotely – maybe even automatically.

And the only way I can imagine that happening is if the whole floor panel moved.

When the collapsing crane had pulled up part of the floor, it had pulled up one rectangular sheet of plywood.

I pull up the video Chloe sent me with the overview of the set. I focus in on the floor. The oversized plywood pieces form a grid, and looking at the video, the whole mess, including Noel's body and the blood from his elbow, would have easily fit inside one panel of the grid.

My developing theory sounds like something out of a science fiction movie. Because for the killer to have later faked Noel having been stabbed, the body would have had to be preserved at or near the moment of death. I remember how the cat's paws and fur had come back cold, when she'd been lost on the set. Which could mean there had been a refrigerated chamber under the floor. The killer might have planned to freeze Noel's body and leave him there, what, indefinitely? Or until the movie was wrapping, and the killer himself was breaking down the set? Or until the circumstance was right to ditch the body somewhere. There are at least two construction sites nearby. Maybe the killer was planning to wait until a thick foundation was poured.

Given the plane ticket, if Noel disappeared into a layer of cement, the assumption would be that he had left Connie and all of her financial problems and was living the good life in Belize. It could have worked, because Noel had indeed intended to go to Belize, and he had already bought a ticket. There would have been a record of the purchase.

Noel had been sprayed in the face with atomized almond oil, and it had disabled him before he could get his epi pen out. Not that it would have helped, since it was already broken. It was a simple plan that didn't even require the murderer to be present. But since I had observed Noel's collapse and confirmed that he was dead, the idea of his disappearing off to Ambergris Caye was no longer plausible. The killer had still tried to spread that rumor, and if we hadn't found that ticket still in Noel's jacket, I would have sounded even more paranoid, because him having used the ticket would have actually been the simplest explanation for his disappearance. Since that wasn't an option, the killer had had to frame someone, and impulsive Chloe had put herself in the perfect condition to be the scapegoat. But the complicated machinery had to be disguised, because there is no way for Chloe to have set it up. Hence, Noel being retroactively stabbed with a knife, when everyone had seen Chloe handling prop knives on the set.

In this scenario, the stabbing would have been the improvisation, and trying to make it plausible would have hinged on delaying the discovery of the body, so it would be more difficult for forensics to determine for sure in what order things had happened.

I think about what Nao had said about *The Honjin Murders*, how sleight of hand and mechanical trickery are so often part of these fictional plots. I've seen actual murderers get inspired by these same complicatedly clever ideas. Melting ice and fishing line. If it can throw off an investigation, somebody's probably tried it.

If a would-be killer is a fan of the mystery genre, like the character Kendaichi is facing off against in the book, it's possible that person would go for something even more complicated. Like a way to keep blood moving after death, so it would look like Noel had been stabbed while he was alive.

And there's only one suspect here that could have had the means and opportunity to commit this murder. He's even been in Kudo's office, and would have known where Kudo had left the shogi piece. And probably that Kudo had a knife collection. He'd been acting suspicious all along, and I feel stupid that I didn't see it. But what could possibly be his motive?

Chapter Twenty-Two
Thursday

Ash sends me a message. *We went through and checked all the rooms on the first floor, in case someone might be hiding. They're empty. But there could be someone on one of the other floors.*

I presume some of those rooms were locked. Who knew Ash had lockpicking skills?

I tell him, *We're currently on the second floor.*

Of course, that doesn't mean there's no one up on the third.

Nao has returned to her project. She's abandoned the jackhammer – presumably due to sound concerns – and has taken out a stethoscope. It doesn't look like something she has done before.

"Allow me," Hudson says, taking the stethoscope from her. "I was up for a role in a movie once where I was a safecracker. I really got into my acting. It was a passion."

Nao asks, "Then why did you stop?"

Hudson looks at her like he doesn't believe she is seriously asking. But then his expression softens. "For one, I didn't get the role. And two." He gestures towards his scarred face. "Not exactly heartthrob material."

"I'd go see you," Nao says.

Hudson smiles as he turns towards the vault. It takes him a few minutes of playing with the tumblers, but eventually he gets it open.

Meanwhile, I start Googling my suspect. His name plus scandal, then plus murder, then plus death. There has to be a motive somewhere.

The three students congratulate Hudson. One moves into the vault, photographing the carefully stored and labeled artifacts of a movie era gone by.

Nao runs her hand across a label that says, *Tampopo – Ken Watanabe, 1985*. She says, "Tampopo means Dandelion. It was the breakout movie that made Watanabe a star." She studies the wooden ladle and stack of ramen bowls in the glass case behind it. "Noel found something worthwhile, after all."

"I think I found something too." I look up from my phone screen. It's such a small line from such a small article. Just a two-paragraph obituary. After detailing the short life of a young nurse, it says that *Taniguchi Ai was survived, among others, by her brother Wataru.*

I use this information to search for her name and occupation. I find some pics of her from college, and some old social media accounts. There's not much about how she died. An alumni magazine said it was a tragic bee sting.

But what connection could that have to Noel? There is one similarity. Both Noel and Ai had died from anaphylactic shock. Noel hadn't even managed to get his epi pen out of his pocket. Not that it would have helped him, being broken.

It seems unlikely that Ai could have grown to adulthood without ever encountering a bee. So why hadn't Taniguchi's sister had an epi pen? Had she even called 119 for help?

And the truth becomes blindingly obvious. She couldn't have called for help if her phone had been stolen. And if she carried an epi pen, she wouldn't have had it on her if her bag had been stolen. Ai had died six months ago, right when the movie was getting started. What if Noel had arrived in Japan, and one of the first things he had done was steal Ai's bag and phone while she was out hiking, so that when she was subsequently stung by a bee, she had no way to get help?

Of course, that's all speculation. For all I know, Ai could have died near a hospital, or outside a crowded shopping mall. Maybe her phone had nothing to do with the situation. I hand my tablet to Izumi. "How hard would it be to get the police report on this?"

She reads the obituary, then quirks an eyebrow at me. "What exactly do you want to know?"

I say, "I want to know if she had a purse or backpack on her. And what happened to her phone."

"On it," Izumi says. She goes back to the writer's room and sits down at her laptop.

I stand, still in shock, trying to absorb the idea of Taniguchi as a murderer. He seems like such a nice guy, friendly and accommodating. He's the opposite of Kudo, who has the quick temper and imposing demeanor. But sometimes people aren't what they seem.

Nao's tech genius types for what feels like only a few minutes. Then she waves me over and shares the info on Taniguchi's sister. Taniguchi Ai had been found on a remote hiking trail, with no phone or other possessions. No thief was ever found, but her phone and wallet were never recovered, even though her car and home were searched. Therefore, a theft must have occurred. There's a page or two more in the file, but none of the rest of it matters. Taniguchi found the thief – and had enacted revenge.

I know the who and why of the crime, but can't prove it. Taniguchi had to have been the one to set off the crane, injuring Kudo. He's a special effects guy, so he could have done it remotely. There's a slim possibility he could have been telling the truth about bringing flowers for his sister. Only – I don't think he'd want to be that far away from the movie studio building, in case he had to tweak his plan. Maybe he'd set up several options for sabotage, but he couldn't be sure Kudo would go near any of them.

We've checked most of the building. Is Taniguchi on the third floor? I'm sure he has to be.

I take my phone over to the vault, where I present my theory to Logan, Hudson and Nao. I say, "If I send him a message implying I know why Noel was killed, I think he will try to come find me."

Logan says, "I don't like the idea of you putting yourself at risk."

I say, "I won't be – if y'all are waiting for him at the bottom of the stairs. I'll get him talking, try to get a confession. Then you guys can hold him until the police get here."

Hudson says, "He could take the fire escape and flee. You should have someone down there waiting, just in case."

Nao's electronics guy says, "I'll come with you."

Nao looks at Logan, "And I'll go with you. After all, I have a stun gun."

I call Ash and ask if he wants to help me capture the evidence when I confront Taniguchi.

Ash says, "Heck yeah, I'm in. Do you know how long I've been wanting to do something like this? I'm going to get to interview myself for the podcast."

The plan comes together, and I make the call to Taniguchi, telling him that I know what he did, and I'll go to the police if he doesn't come to the studio and give me money. I hang up before he has time to respond.

A second later, there are ominous footsteps on the stairs. It seems too fast for Taniguchi to have processed the threat and decided to respond. And the footsteps are coming up the stairs, not down. A vaguely familiar voice says, "I knew if I followed you long enough, you would lead me straight to the girl."

It's Jack, the guy with the box who I had bumped into at the mall. And – my brain finally kicks into place – the guy who had sat down next to us at the coffee shop when we had been talking to Annabelle. This guy is wearing a gray coat, similar to the one Wataru Tanaka had been wearing when he'd been arrested. Could he be the guy we had seen at the airport, and who had followed us through the city? I'm pretty sure he was.

Only now, instead of holding a box, he's got a gun.

"Jack," I say, trying to sound flustered and disappointed, even as I turn on the dictation function on my phone, leaving it in my pocket. "You're not a chocolatier, are you?"

"Afraid not," Jack says. "I'm not even from Tampa."

I don't have time to deal with this. We've already sent the message to Taniguchi. Jack is about to mess up everything. Jack grabs my arm and twirls me close to him.

"In the vault," he says, gesturing with the gun. "Everybody except Emi. Or the chocolate maker gets it."

Logan moves in front of Emi, trying to keep his promise to protect her from danger. But I can see him wavering. He looks at me, and I can tell, he's going to do something stupid to try and protect us both.

But Emi steps out from behind him. "It's okay," she tells Logan, bringing a comforting hand up to his cheek. "This is not your fault."

I see pain in his eyes. The two big mistakes in his life had involved people dying when it *was* his fault. If any of us gets hurt here today, after Logan agreed to my half-conched plan, he's going to convince himself it *is* his fault, just like before. Even if it isn't the same.

Reluctantly, Logan follows the others into the vault. I don't even want to think about what this is going to do to him emotionally if Emi dies despite him trying to protect her. I can't let that happen.

"Close it," Jack says, gesturing at Emi with the gun.

The moment the gun isn't trained on me, I stomp hard on Jack's foot. He lets me go. I push Emi into the vault and close the door myself. It's a cavernous space. They should have enough air to last until the cops get here.

I attach the audio to a text, sending the audio of what's just happened to Detective Yamada. And then I sprint for the fire escape. Hudson is supposed to be at the bottom of it, but when I yank open the door and step out onto the platform, I don't see him.

Jack exits right behind me. Somehow, he gets around me, blocking the way down. Which means the only way to go is up. Jack grabs at me again, and I duck away, climbing upward. Why doesn't he just shoot me? Not that I'm complaining, but it would certainly make more sense if he's here to shut us up.

I make it up onto the roof. I shout back at Jack, "It's too late. I've already turned over the file."

Jack says, "Maybe so. I wasn't able to get a close look at what happened yesterday at the coffee shop. But in case you are lying, I'm going to need your phone."

"And then what? You let me go?"

Jack gives me a disappointed look, as though I should know better.

I say, "Right. I don't see the advantage here in giving you anything. You already killed Noel." And the implication is that as soon as he gets what he wants, he's going to kill me.

Jack gestures with the gun. "It's alright. I'll just get your phone off you after. I'm supposed to find out how much you know and who you might have told." He takes a step forward.

As Jack advances, I back across the roof. I say, "I already called the cops. I told one of their detectives everything. They're actually on their way already."

"Yeah, right," Jack says.

I'm not bluffing – but I'm not sure I would have believed me either.

I back up another step and hit something solid – the crane for the roof stunt. It's a lot bigger than the one that collapsed inside the studio. I put a hand on the cold metal, trying to figure out a way to use it to help me here. There's no way I'm going to get into the operator's seat to swing the crane arm without Jack grabbing me first.

But there is still an air mat set up below. I'd seen it when I'd approached the building this morning.

This is crazy. Am I really considering jumping off a building? Intentionally? By myself?

I climb up on the crane arm.

"Get down from there," Jack says. "Or I will shoot you."

"You're going to do that anyway," I protest.

"But not until I've interviewed you."

I flatten myself against the crane arm and start inching out onto it. Jack is climbing up behind me. There's a black button on the arm, clearly wired as part of the special effects. I don't know what it does. For all I know, it could drop the crane off the building. But if I don't change this situation now, I'm as good as dead.

Not knowing if this will save or doom me, I press the button. A kaiju prop swings out of nowhere. It hits Jack, and he goes sprawling. Then something pops and there's a shower of glitter.

Jack gets back up, gun still drawn, and takes a shot at me. I crawl the last few inches to the end of the crane and drop down onto the hook dangling from it. I can see the air mat, thankfully still inflated.

"Where do you think you're going to go?" Jack asks. "You're really going to jump off a building?"

He takes another shot at me, and I pretend he's hit me. Clutching at my shoulder, I make a show of losing my balance. I force myself to let go and plummet to the mat below. This fall is half the distance of the one I'd taken on Monday, and I struggle to get into the hips-first position Connie had showed me. I land with an oof.

I get off the mat and run for the wooden city façade. If I can get through the door to one of the fake buildings, maybe I can get somewhere that Jack can't find me. I take my phone out and text to all my friends that I'm outside. Please, please let someone have enough phone signal to receive it. And the ability to get here in time.

I reach the safety of the fake city and wrench open the door to a supposed coffee shop. Only, when I get through the doorway, I get hit in the face by a sticky gel.

Taniguchi is standing there, holding a water gun. He says, "Come with me, or Chloe never leaves the set."

It's only been a few seconds, but I already feel a little groggy. I wipe as much of the goop off my face as I can onto the sleeves of my shirt. Have I been poisoned? Is it too late? Faking confidence, I say, "Since your plan to frame Kudo failed, you're back to trying to frame a little girl?"

Taniguchi says, "They would never convict her. I just wanted to create confusion around the case. Since you ruined my plan for a perfect murder, what else could I do? Still, I don't have to kill her if your suspicions of me die with you."

I surreptitiously turn the dictation function back on my phone. It sounds like Taniguchi is in the mood to confess, and even if he tries to kill me, I'm betting I can hit send before he does.

He puts the water gun in one pocket and draws a knife from the other. I know he's willing to use a blade, but that must not be the death he has planned for me, or he'd just kill me here. I could try to run, and probably escape a fatal stabbing. But then what happens to Chloe? I follow Taniguchi back towards the building. He opens the back door onto the set. "Everyone went to the hospital with Director Kudo. So I assure you, we are quite alone."

"Except for the maniac shooting at me on the roof," I point out.

"Somehow, I don't think he will be a problem," Taniguchi says. "My camera on the crane shows he's bleeding from several significant cuts from the baby kaiju prop. He'll need to head for medical attention."

It's sad when I'm disappointed that the first person who was trying to kill me today isn't going to show up now.

Taniguchi must not have cameras everywhere, though, or he would have realized Ash and Imogen are still running around in the building. I hold out a ray of hope for one of them rushing in to help salvage the situation.

"Where's Chloe?" I ask.

Taniguchi gestures over to the craft services table, where instead of sandwiches, Chloe is laid out, unconscious. She lets out a soft snore, and my shoulders relax. She's still breathing. But there's a heavy weight suspended over her, and I get the feeling that if I try anything, Taniguchi has a quick way to drop it.

"Don't worry," he says. "She drank a bottle of tea with a couple of muscle relaxers dissolved in it. It was kind of you to leave them in your room." I gasp. He really hadn't been in the building. He'd been in the hotel. What about Patsy? And Arlo? "Don't worry," Taniguchi continues, "None of your friends saw me. And Chloe was already unconscious when I brought her here. She doesn't have to die."

I need to get Taniguchi talking, get his confession before the police get here and he realizes he either has to kill me or let me go. He's implied a threat to me, but he hasn't acted on it. If I can stall for time, maybe he won't. But I'm feeling a bit out of it, from whatever was in the goo.

He throws me a zip-tie and gestures for me to secure myself to a nearby prop. It's a ten-foot-tall bottle of green goo with a partly formed kaiju in it. I couldn't move it if I tried. It's like one of those huge fish tanks you see at an aquarium.

Taniguchi says, "The police already consider you a suspect in Noel's murder, and you were here when Kudo got hurt. You're actually a better scapegoat than Kudo was. So when I tell them that you attacked me after I accused you of Noel's murder, it really is going to look like self-defense."

I put the zip-tie on loose, but I can tell I'm not going to be able to undo it. There's a sharp edge on the bottom of the metal loop I'd threaded the zip-tie through. I may be able to saw through the plastic and if there's a chance to change the situation, I'll be in a position to take it. Yet another reason to keep him talking.

I ask, "What was the sound Keiko heard upstairs on Monday, before you all left for lunch? It had something to do with the pneumatic system, didn't it? Maybe a test of the mechanism that killed Noel?"

Taniguchi tuts. "Throw me your phone, and we can talk."

I use my unbound hand to reach in my pocket and send as much of the audio as I already have. Then I toss him my phone.

Taniguchi sucks at his teeth. "You know it is a simple matter to unsend a text these days." He does just that, then he puts my phone in his pocket.

Frustration is building inside of me, only aided by the throbbing in my side from falling onto the air mat, and a buzzing in my head from the gel. "Fine," I say. "Let's talk."

Taniguchi says, "I wasn't testing the mechanism, I was priming it. I had no idea when Noel would return and open that box. It was my luck that he brought in his contraband less than an hour after I set my trap."

I say, "I've put together most of it. How one whole panel of plywood recesses into the floor and slides to one side, to be replaced by an identically built panel. So when the police were searching for Noel's body, he was actually underneath the floor, being near frozen to confuse the time of death. It's genius, really, to give yourself an alibi."

Taniguchi says, "That's the part of it that the logical side of me enjoyed. I wasn't sure *when* Noel would die, only that he would be alone, because he wouldn't access the spot where he had hidden the stolen goods if anyone was in the building. My sister died alone. So it was only fitting."

He is fiddling with something that's leaning against the wall. It's a hydraulic jack. What is he planning to do with that? Whatever it is, it makes me feel queasy inside.

I try to sound confident when I say, "The murder would be automated, but getting rid of Noel's body couldn't be. So what was the plan? I know there's a lot of construction going on."

Taniguchi looks surprised. He says, "Great minds really do think alike. It's actually sad that yours won't be functioning shortly." He starts moving the dolly over toward me. "Yes, I intended to take the body and dispose of it when I was taking junk from the FX process to the dump. One little side stop, and Noel would have been part of the foundation for that new shopping center."

"But then I showed up, and that changed. But Noel was already dead. You must have moved him into the kaiju suit before we found the plane ticket in the pocket of his jacket. So why change the story about him leaving town?"

"Was it?" Taniguchi asks. "Men don't leave the country without their passports, and surely Connie would have that. I didn't have the time I thought I would to make it discreetly disappear, looking like Noel had come home to pack his things, only to leave again while she was still on set."

I hadn't even thought about travel documents, but I wave a dismissive hand. "Either way, you needed to shift suspicion away from you."

Taniguchi says, "It was almost too easy to blame the girl who had actually been alone in the building when Noel came in. It was Chloe's fault, really, for forcing her way on set and making herself such an easy target. I transferred her fingerprints onto Kudo's knife. If there were two plausible suspects, how would the police choose between the two? It would give them a lot to consider, and keep them from looking for other suspects."

"But even that got messed up," I point out. "Those suits weren't supposed to be used for filming for several days, which would have further muddied the time of death, and the order in which the attacks had killed him. You couldn't have counted on Ash's impulsive nature. Or on everyone carrying around cameras to analyze the set."

Taniguchi goes around to the far side of the giant prop I'm attached to and wedges the jack under the edge of the tube.

Clearly, he's planning to crush me under the weight of this thing. I point out, "This isn't going to look like self-defense."

"It's plausible something heavy got knocked over as we were fighting for the knife. Something that can make you dead or unconscious. It will be a lot easier both physically and psychologically for me to stab you when you aren't looking at me like that." He starts pumping the handle to lift the jack.

"I do have one more question," I say quickly. "How did you know Noel was the thief who took your sister's epi pen? The police couldn't figure it out. You must have gone through a whole master plan worth of deduction."

"Not really," Taniguchi says. "I found my sister's phone when I found the stash of stolen things Noel had put on the set. I'd seen him messing around with a particular building and I got curious. It didn't take much from there to figure out what had happened. I waited for him to realize that he had taken Ai's phone, leaving her unable to call for help, to die alone and helpless. When he didn't, I sent him hints, showing the time and place where his crime happened. Then I sent accusatory notes, so he couldn't deny the crime. Nothing. He didn't turn himself in, didn't so much as apologize. I had no choice but to punish him myself."

He starts angrily pumping the jack, and I feel the prop shift. I saw faster at the plastic band on my wrist.

"What did I do to deserve this?" I ask.

"You weren't supposed to be here," Taniguchi says accusatorily. "No one was supposed to get hurt – except Bell San. He was so bad to so many people – even before he killed my sister. Why did you have to get into the middle of this? And why wouldn't you leave it alone? I'm having a hard time doing this to you. I'm no murderer."

"Then don't kill me," I protest. "Crushing me isn't any less violent than stabbing me."

I hear a small noise, and I realize the door leading into the hall is open a bit. And there's a phone sticking through it, attached to a hand that most likely belongs to Ash.

"What else am I going to do at this point?" Taniguchi says. "Sometimes you have to sacrifice a piece to win the game."

"That's a shogi reference, isn't it?" I say, trying to draw out the conversation.

If Ash has a plan, he's sure taking his sweet time. But I've sawed almost completely through the zip tie.

Ash bursts through the door. He says "Sometimes the sacrifice is too great to justify, just to win the game. You got your revenge on me, let these innocent girls go."

"And go to jail?" Taniguchi starts pumping the jack again. Almost to himself he adds, "And now you have to die too."

"What was that?" Ash asks.

Taniguchi says, "This is going to fall on Felicity any second if you don't hand over that phone."

Ash says, "You're going to jail for something either way. I've been livestreaming this whole time." He walks over to Taniguchi and shoves his phone in the guy's face to prove it. "I don't usually livestream, but I'm using a friend's account."

Taniguchi grabs Ash's phone and stomps on it. Despite the knife, Ash steps between me and Taniguchi. He says, "Fee, go to Imogen. She's waiting at the door. With another camera."

Taniguchi hesitates, not sure how to handle being caught on camera. He glares at Ash. Then with a mighty shout, Taniguchi pushes the prop with all his strength, and it topples towards me. I yank my hand back, and the zip tie breaks. I'm able to scramble out of the way and start backing towards Imogen.

With a frustrated growl, Taniguchi pushes Ash to the floor, then throws his knife at me. It hits me in the arm. But I act like it hit me in the chest. To be convincing I'm going to have to do that backward fall. I can't. Even as pumped up as I am with adrenaline and pain, I can't let go and just fall backwards. But if I don't do it this second, it won't be convincing. I force myself to balance backwards, tip past the point where I could catch myself and try to look like I'm not able to try.

I bite back noise as I hit the floor and the knife, which hadn't gone deep, dislodges from my arm. I pull it back up to my armpit, trying to move as little as possible. I'm supposed to be playing dead.

Taniguchi advances on me, to get his knife back and try to attack my friends.

Before he gets close enough to try, Ash jumps on his back and tries to bring his arms down. Taniguchi bucks him off and turns on Ash, but he no longer has a weapon.

Before he can find one, there's a squeak from the doorway, and Imogen walks in, her hands up, no longer holding her phone. Jack, walking behind her, has it. He also still has his gun. He's obviously injured. Taniguchi hadn't been bluffing about that, and Jack looks angry. He stalks over to me and holds out a hand. "Phone?"

I guess I'm not very convincing. I say, "He has it," and point to Taniguchi. Ash lets the man go and backs away. He jumps for cover into the hole left by the collapsed crane.

Jack growls, shoots Taniguchi in the leg, and proceeds to pull the phone out of Taniguchi's pocket before he can get it out himself. I let out a squeak of shock. Taniguchi sits down heavily on the floor, cradling his leg, whining.

Jack turns back toward me, and I think this is it, my life is over, but then his eyes go wide as the door burst open and all of my friends who had been locked in the vault – plus our actor locksmith Hudson – come rushing into the room.

Logan sees me in danger and barrels towards Jack – who decides that taking my phone is good enough and rushes out the door to the hallway. Only, he rushes right back in, because the police are heading this way. He climbs onto one of the other props, a giant version of the dragon-butterfly kaiju, but the police surround him, and he ditches the gun, waving his open hands at them in a way that reminds me of King Kong in the old movies.

Logan ignores this spectacle and turns to kneel on the floor next to me. "Fee, how bad is it."

I show him my arm. "It's just a flesh wound."

Connie walks through the door, carrying a deflated duffle bag. Obviously, she'd come to get Kudo some things for his stay in the hospital. This room is full of scripts and binders, and he has clothes in his office. But she hasn't picked up anything yet. As she takes in the chaos, she frowns. "Right. What's all this then?"

Jack winds up in handcuffs. I get my phone back. And Taniguchi winds up on a stretcher, about to be carried out by the Japanese version of EMTs. My arm only takes a couple of stitches, and Logan stays by my side the whole time I'm at the hospital.

While we're waiting, texts come in. One is from Nao, hoping things are going okay. She had melted away the minute the police showed up, as had her crew. But Hudson tells me that the hole in the wall (he doesn't mention which wall, though I know it had to be the vault) allowed the tech wizard to get enough signal to tell him where they were. It isn't surprising to me that she'd been able to easily find his phone number.

When I'm done getting my stitches, Ash is waiting outside with a big bouquet of flowers. The waiting room is filled with friends, even though my injury wasn't serious.

Logan turns to talk to Emi, and I walk down the hall with Ash. I'm a bit upset about the livestream, which apparently has been Hudson's most ever viewed stream – in the short time it was up, before he got done with the police and got a chance to take it down.

I say, "Ash, do you realize how close you came to livestreaming my death? Don't do that again. That is not how I want to be remembered."

"How do you want to be remembered?" Ash asks. "Going out in a blaze of glory? Dead at home at a hundred and two?"

"I'm not doing this with you," I say.

Ash says, "I want to be burned up in a star, a thousand years from now, after exploring the furthest reaches of the galaxy."

"So it's too uncomfortable to think about anything real?" I ask.

"Exactly," Ash agrees. "I'm already shaking from jumping out in front of you to stop Taniguchi. That's real enough for one day."

"It's the last thing I ever expected you to do," I say.

"Yeah," he says. "But you're a good friend. And in that moment, with no one else there to help you, I realized some things are worth the sacrifice."

Epilogue

We've extended our stay in Japan for an extra week, in part to sort everything with the police. In part to have time to actually enjoy Tokyo. Chloe got to do her collab, and Imogen took us to the bathing suit friendly onsen. And on our very last day, the guys at the movie studio are throwing us a going away party. Kudo's aunt showed up with a whole table worth of food, including roll-your-own sushi, and bowls of cucumber salad, daikon and carrot salad, and potato salad. The cast and crew are gathered around the table with me, Patsy, Arlo and Fisher. We all keep sampling things and telling Kudo's aunt how delicious they are.

Ash, Imogen, and Dawn are all getting lessons on camera and boom-mike operation from Jose and Franco. I'm surprised that Dawn seems to be getting into it, taking a turn at pointing the camera, while Imogen does a little song and dance in front of the green screen.

Chloe has invited all of her Youtuber friends, who are gathered up near some of the more interesting props. Both Annabelle and Hudson have joined them, and they're taking a group picture. I'm glad I brought her on this trip. I think it has changed both of our perspectives.

"Aunt Fee!" Chloe calls, gesturing me over. "A couple of these guys want to do a stream with you, before you leave. They're the ones who only stream about cats, and they want to hear all about how Honda helped you solve a crime."

"In that case." I hold up a finger and run to get a tray of chocolate samples. I return and hold it out to the Youtubers. "I thought you would be the ones who most appreciate my mike bar." I had to practice saying mē-ke, because every time I look at it, I want to say Mike.

One of the youtubers says, "Doesn't mike mean calico? This is so mixed up, just like a calico cat. What's in it?"

"You're right. It's my special bar, in honor of Honda. There's milk chocolate with black sesame, plain white chocolate, and persimmon flavored white chocolate. I thwapped spoonfuls of each chocolate somewhat randomly into the molds, so that it looks like calico pattern." I gesture at Annabelle. "I got to use the best kitchen."

Annabelle says, "It was fun. Once I get it edited, it's going to make a great episode."

One of the other Youtubers says, "I want to taste the chocolate that won your category in the chocolate festival awards."

"I can bring it when we stream," I say.

Logan waves, and I head back over to him. Emi is here – sans sunglasses and head scarf. Whistleblowing accomplished, she too is going home. Sadly, though, there has still been no sign of the girl who had sent her the file.

Emi says, "I want to thank you for helping me. It can't have been easy to risk your fiancé's life – and your own – for someone you just met."

Logan says, "I can help find someone currently doing private security, if you'd like."

Emi says, "I think I'll be okay. I'm going to tell my husband everything, and let him help me decide if we should move, or try to disappear – or just face life, dangers and all." Emi kisses Logan on the cheek. She turns to me and says, "I may not have had a crush on him back in the day, but I do now. You're lucky to have seen what I missed." Emi holds out a box.

"What's this?" I ask, opening it. It's a butterfly pin, with a lapis lazuli center.

Emi says, "It's a brooch to wear at your wedding. It seemed more appropriate than a kaiju brooch – though don't think I wasn't tempted to have one made." She flounces off, her manicure and hair still perfect, despite all she's been through.

Kudo hobbles over to us. He's got one of those scooter things that you bend a knee to ride. Connie is with him, making sure he's moving okay. He says, "Thank you both for everything. If either of you ever want to be in a movie, all you have to do is ask."

"Thanks," Logan says, "But I'll probably pass."

Connie says, "Hudson let me have a look at the video. For a first timer, you took that fall exceptionally well."

"But you have notes?" I ask.

"We can save that for later. Today is about being happy while being sad. Every morning alone hurts, but knowing I have friends helps." She glances at Kudo. It's probably right that they're just friends at this point. She needs to heal before she can be open to something new. But it's nice that Kudo and Connie are healing together – him physically, her emotionally.

Dawn comes over and shows me her phone. "Look what I did."

There's video of Imogen dancing – only the green screen has been replaced by a montage of locations – the Eiffle Tower, the Pyramids at Giza, a beach somewhere with crystal blue water.

"Nice," I say.

Dawn says, "I want to thank you, for giving me a glimpse of your world. I'm glad you're about to be my sister-in-law."

Giddy bubbles of happiness well inside me. Dawn actually does think what I do for a living is cool. It's a big step for us – as family.

She reaches for one of the chocolate samples on my tray. She asks, "How exactly do you get persimmon into chocolate?"

I start to explain, but Arlo comes in with a giant cake that has Godzilla drawn in frosting.

He says, "I tried to get one of the kaiju from the movie, but this is all they could do."

"Good enough." I step to the center of the room and say, "I want to thank you all, too. I've come halfway across the world, to a place where I don't speak the language, and I've made friends here that could last for life. If any of you ever wind up in Texas, you have to come to Greetings and Felicitations so we can spend time together."

"Maybe we'll get a layover on the way back to Belize," Franco says.

That gets a smattering of applause.

I say, "Again, Galveston is over an hour away from the Houston airport, and a lot farther from Dallas. But if you make it work that would be fantastic."

This gets me a smattering of laughter.

I say, "I want to take a selfie with everyone, to go on my Instagram, but I'm not sure how to fit everything in."

"Let me," Chloe says. She takes my camera and sets it on the kaiju head that was salvaged from the crane. It blinks a timer, and she races back into the picture, holding her hand near her face in a v-for-victory sign.

After the timer goes off, Connie claps me on the shoulder. My mostly healed arm only complains a little.

Connie says, "Well done you."

ACKNOWLEDGEMENTS

Special thanks to Jael Rattigan of French Broad Chocolates in South Carolina, who has consulted extensively on this series. And to Sander Wolf of DallasChocolate.org, who put me in touch with so many experts in the chocolate field.

I'd like to thank Sakiko Umabe for showing us her favorite spots in Tokyo in 2017, and again last year. I promise by the time we visit next time, I'll be more fluent! And to David Batista, for taking us thrift shopping in Kyoto. If you had to move half way around the world – at least now we have a place to stay when we visit. Special thanks to Miranda Cook of Starboard Speakers for booking me on the Japan Cruise, which we turned into the research trip for this book. Parts of it are purely a travelogue.

Thanks to Dusty Rainbolt for finding us the new kittens we adopted – there's a lot of Addi in Honda—and the members of the Cat Writers Association for having me out to their Southwest Regional Retreat last year as the main speaker, and hosting me again this year. I'm glad I joined, and you all helped me think about how I was adding the cat to this book.

I'd also like to thank Vanilla Beans Chocolate in Yokohama for the extensive chocolate tasting, and Green Bean to Bar Chocolate in Fukuoka for letting us film inside their store. I still think about the beauty of that mont blanc chocolate mousse.

I have to thank Jake, as usual, for reading the manuscript umpteen times, being my biggest fan and cheerleader, and doing all the formatting things to make this thing happen. He always keeps me going, even when things are stressful. And he's a good sport when traveling and I want to stop every five minutes with my camera.

And thanks to my agent, Jennie, for her input on this series, and her encouragement to keep moving forward.

And for this series especially, I'd like to thank my family for giving me a love of the ocean and a curiosity about history. The Cajun side of both mine and Jake's families comes through in Felicity's family in the books. This has given me an excuse to reach out to family members for recipes and inspiration, many of which you can find on the Bean to Bar Bonuses section of my website. Thanks y'all!

Thanks to James and Rachel Knowles for continuing to sharing their knowledge of bunny behavior, despite the loss of the ever-adorable Yuki.

I'd like to thank Stacie Jefferson for being a huge supporter and catching the nit-picky errors in the draft. I'd also like to thank Cassie, Monica and Tessa, who are my support network in general. Y'all are amazing!

Thank you all, dear readers, for spending time in Felicity's world. I hope you enjoyed getting to know her. Her ninth adventure will be available for you soon.

Did Felicity's story make you hungry?

Visit the Bean to Bar Mysteries Bonus Recipes page on Amber's website to find out how to make some of the food mentioned in the book.

Bio

Amber Royer writes the *Chocoverse* comic telenovela-style foodie-inspired space opera series, and the *Bean to Bar Mysteries*. She also teaches creative writing and is an author coach. Her workbook/textbook Story Like a Journalist and her Thoughtful Journal series allow her to connect with writers. Amber and her husband live in the DFW Area, where you can often find them at local coffee shops or taking landscape/architecture/wildlife photographs. They both love to travel, and Amber records her adventures on Instagram – along with pics of her pair of tuxedo cats. If you are very nice to Amber, she might make you cupcakes. Chocolate cupcakes, of course! Amber blogs about creative writing technique and all things chocolate at www.amberroyer.com[1].

1. http://www.amberroyer.com/

www.ingramcontent.com/pod-product-compliance
Ingram Content Group UK Ltd.
Pitfield, Milton Keynes, MK11 3LW, UK
UKHW031001240225
455493UK00011B/673